"Haven't you ever been in love?"

Ruth asked.

David paused. "I was infatuated once, but she was married at the time. Actually, she was completely unaware that I was smitten."

Ruth's pulse quickened with the outlandish intuition that he was talking about *her*. "It sounds as if you created a fantasy."

He smiled. "That's what I told myself. But I was so taken with my creation that no other woman could compare."

Ruth could barely speak. "You got over her, of course."

"I thought I had. Until recently, I hadn't consciously thought of her in years." He squeezed her hand.

"David!" Ruth tried to pull her hand free, but he tightened his clasp and continued.

"Now I find that not only is my old fantasy intact, but in reality she's just as I imagined her...."

Dear Reader,

If you're looking for an extra-special reading experience—something rich and memorable, something deeply emotional, something totally romantic—your search is over! For in your hands you hold one of Silhouette's extremely **Special Editions**.

Dedicated to the proposition that *not* all romances are created equal, Silhouette **Special Edition** aims to deliver the best and the brightest in women's fiction—six books each month by such stellar authors as Nora Roberts, Lynda Trent, Tracy Sinclair and Ginna Gray, along with some dazzling new writers destined to become tomorrow's romance stars.

Pick and choose among titles if you must—we hope you'll soon equate all Silhouette **Special Editions** with consistently gratifying romance reading.

And don't forget the two Silhouette *Classics* at your bookseller's each month—reissues of the most beloved Silhouette **Special Editions** and Silhouette *Intimate Moments* of yesteryear.

Today's bestsellers, tomorrow's *Classics*—that's Silhouette **Special Edition**. We hope you'll stay with us in the months to come, because month after month, we intend to become more special than ever.

From all the authors and editors of Silhouette **Special Edition**,
Warmest wishes,

Leslie Kazanjian
Senior Editor

CAROLE HALSTON
Intensive Care

Silhouette Special Edition

Published by Silhouette Books New York

America's Publisher of Contemporary Romance

Special thanks to Charlotte and Aaron Elkins,
fellow writers who welcomed me to their home
in Sequim on the Olympic Peninsula.

SILHOUETTE BOOKS
300 East 42nd St., New York, N.Y. 10017

ISBN: 0-373-09461-2

First Silhouette Books printing June 1988

Printed in the U.S.A.

Books by Carole Halston

Silhouette Romance

Stand-In Bride #62
Love Legacy #83
Undercover Girl #152
Sunset in Paradise #208

Silhouette Special Edition

Keys to Daniel's House #8
Collision Course #41
The Marriage Bonus #86
Summer Course in Love #115
A Hard Bargain #139
Something Lost, Something Gained #163
A Common Heritage #211
The Black Knight #223
Almost Heaven #253
Surprise Offense #291
Matched Pair #328
Honeymoon for One #356
The Baby Trap #388
High Bid #423
Intensive Care #461

CAROLE HALSTON

is a Louisiana native, residing on the north shore of Lake Pontchartrain, near New Orleans. She enjoys traveling with her husband to research less familiar locations for settings but is always happy to return home to her own unique region, a rich source in itself for romantic stories about warm, wonderful people.

the Strait of Georgia

the Strait of Juan de Fuca

Port Angeles

Lake Crescent

Sequim

Olympic National Park

Kalaloch

Lake Quinault

Seattle

Olympia

THE OLYMPIC PENINSULA

Chapter One

David Bradford strolled along the Seattle waterfront in the direction of Ivar's Acre of Clams, enjoying a sense of anonymity. The overcast sky didn't dampen his spirits. It was good to get away from the hospital for a couple of hours and be plain David Bradford, not Dr. Bradford, young medical genius. He was glad to shed his premature dignity and air of authority along with his starched white physician's coat and take a healthy pleasure in looking at pretty women passing by.

On a June day like today when he was out alone, a stranger moving among strangers, David could set free the romantic dreamer in him. He could fantasize about a chance meeting with someone warm and delightful who would like him on sight and want to know him simply because he appealed to her as strongly as she appealed to him. There would be mutual personal interest as well as physical attraction.

David didn't just want a sexual fling, an exciting affair, nor would he be ready for a serious relationship for at least several years. He yearned for a special girlfriend, just as average guys have in high school, someone who was fun and companionable, someone with whom he could share his thoughts and feelings. David hadn't ever "gone steady." He'd missed the normal life of a teenager. The social and emotional side of him had suffered because of his accelerated schooling.

He knew his wistful longings would come as a surprise to the female nurses and interns and medical students who smiled at him invitingly and addressed him with a flirtatious awe. They managed to make "Dr. Bradford" sound like the title of a minor godhead with his choice of vestal virgins. Without being conceited, David was reasonably certain he could date a number of the very attractive young women he saw daily.

What bothered him, though, was knowing that they were intrigued by the distinguished young doctor and not by the rather shy individual behind the degrees and the early prestige. Would they be interested in him if they met him and talked to him without knowing his background or his profession? he wondered.

Putting aside that deep-seated element of doubt, he'd learned the drawbacks of mixing his private and professional lives. When he went out on a date, he didn't want his conversation reported through the hospital grapevine or his good-night kiss rated at the nurses' station. Perhaps if he had a stronger male ego, he wouldn't mind about the latter, but for all his specialized knowledge and skill in his branch of medicine, he didn't have a lot of experience with lovemaking.

It would be better, David thought, to find a woman completely apart from his working world, someone who would relate to him just as a man. Then he wouldn't have to measure up to an image. He could let down his guard without worrying about potential embarrassment from hospital gossip.

What he wanted from a female companion was to be *liked*, not admired, to be treated casually, not catered to because of his staff position. He wanted to be desirable as a date because he was amusing, considerate and fun, not just because his earning power made him a good catch.

David's problem was getting out on his own and meeting women who weren't associated in any way with medicine or hospitals. His schedule was demanding, and he was reserved and shy. Approaching a member of the opposite sex didn't come easy to him, but on a day like today he was sure that he could, with the least encouragement.

In this optimistic frame of mind, David reached Ivar's, where he intended to have lunch. Bypassing the entrance to the restaurant, he stood in one of several lines at the streetside counter and ordered a clam chowder and fish and chips. After a short wait, he picked up his food and carried the cardboard tray to the adjacent outdoor dining area, which was roofed and glass-enclosed for year-round use.

From the entrance he noticed a pretty young woman sitting alone at a table. She had shoulder-length tawny hair and appeared to be in her early twenties. From the way she was glancing out at Elliott Bay with such vivid interest, David guessed she was probably an out-of-state visitor to the Puget Sound area. He'd ask her if he could share her table with her, he decided, and felt his adrenaline pick up with his unaccustomed boldness as he headed in her direction.

But he was too late, he saw with disappointment. She was preparing to leave. From his more complete view of her attire, he had apparently identified her wrongly. She was probably a downtown employee on her lunch break, not a visitor. Her simple skirt-and-blouse combination and low-heeled shoes impressed him as a working outfit, and while she didn't seem hurried, she gave the impression of having a time commitment.

David felt a surge of envy for her co-workers as she passed him, including him in a friendly smiling glance that seemed to approve of the world in general. His brief eye contact with her and closeup view of her face gave him a little jolt of pleasure. She had lovely blue-gray eyes, nice features and a fresh complexion, but what made her noticeably attractive was a glow of well-being. A love of life shone in her expression and put energy into her movements. David would bet that her lighthearted state wasn't rare, either. She didn't seem the tiresome, moody sort, exhilarated and then down in the dumps.

If only he'd been thirty minutes earlier, he thought regretfully, standing beside the table where she had sat and looking after her. Perhaps he might have eaten lunch with her, talked to her, gotten to know her.

He could follow her, introduce himself. David was startled to realize how seriously he was considering the idea. Asking a young woman if he could sit with her at her table was one thing; rushing after her in hot pursuit was something entirely different.

Yet Fate seemed to be tempting him with the opportunity to act on uncharacteristic impulse. Before she left, the young woman took a few moments to go over to the pier outside and fling the remnants of her lunch to a flock of greedy seagulls and then she walked away with a swinging stride, taking her smiling cheer away with her.

Someone with her looks and vivaciousness couldn't possibly be unattached, David reasoned, standing rooted to the spot and clutching his tray after she was gone from sight. Sure, there was still time to put his lunch down and catch up with her, but common sense advised against it. She'd turn out to have a steady boyfriend. Just as bad, she could be available and tell him point-blank that he wasn't her type, make him feel two inches tall. She might not be his type, in reality. Her magnetic appeal could well be just an illusion that would shatter at the sound of her voice.

The chances were ninety-nine to one that David would have ended up feeling like an utter fool, pursuing a captivating stranger down the street from Ivar's. Yet as he found himself another table, sat down and ate his lunch, he was aware that the day had gone flat because he hadn't taken the risk.

After he had eaten, David walked to a downtown store that specialized in quality outdoor clothing and fishing and camping gear. He could use a lightweight waterproof jacket for his camping trip on the Olympic Peninsula the coming weekend.

Entering, he found himself in the men's clothing department, where he seemed to be the only customer. Nor did there appear to be a clerk available to assist him, David noted as he threaded his way through racks of shirts and slacks in search of the jackets. The shoe section, located to his right and on a slightly lower level, was crowded, and he could see customers at the far end of the store in the women's department—

David stopped abruptly, all thought of his shopping mission forgotten as he spotted a feminine head with shoulder-length tawny hair. *Was that her?* he asked himself incredulously, staring. The best way to find out, obviously, was to go nearer for a closer look. If it was the same young woman he'd seen at Ivar's, he'd say hello this time, he promised himself.

It was her. David made the sure identification from the shoe department, his heart beating much faster than its normal rate. She was a salesclerk, wearing an official name tag and waiting on a customer. The certainty that he would soon know her name was absurdly pleasing to him.

He had guessed right, then, that she was a downtown employee on her lunch break. What an incredible coincidence that he should see her at Ivar's when he had plans to shop afterward at her place of employment. With all his advanced learning, David wasn't a superstitious man, but this smacked of Fate.

Trying not to be too blatant, he watched, waiting for his opportunity to approach her between customers. When it came, he headed straight for her, intending to introduce himself and make the overture he hadn't had the nerve to make earlier. But she made the natural assumption that he was there to shop and took away his initiative in her line of duty.

"Hello," she greeted him with a friendly smile. "Can I help you find something today?"

"Well, actually—" Her name was Ruth, and she spoke with a slight Southern drawl. Her voice added a new dimension to her charm for him. It went perfectly with her smile and her warm, vivid presence. Being at such close range to her and the full object of her attention seemed to reduce David's IQ by at least half. "What I mean to say—"

"I'll bet you're looking for a present and don't know exactly what you want," Ruth predicted cheerfully. "We have a nice selection of merchandise, something to please almost any woman." She paused to glance smilingly over at a customer who'd stopped nearby and was searching through a rack of blouses. "Someone will be with you in a minute, ma'am," she promised, and then transferred her attention back to David. "How about a sweater? We just got in a shipment of Shaker-style cotton sweaters that are very popular. They come in gorgeous colors. Would you like to look at them?"

"I seem to have picked a very busy time," David began apologetically, meaning to explain that his mission was entirely personal.

"Don't let that bother you," Ruth urged him kindly. "Just take your time and find something you really like. I'll show you those sweaters I mentioned and then, if you'd prefer to look around on your own, I'll leave you to browse. Right over this way, please."

Feeling helpless, David followed her. He needed to clear up her mistake immediately and ask to see her away from work, not take up more of her time under false pretenses.

"I love all these colors," Ruth confided as she came to a standstill beside a table of folded sweaters arranged into stacks by color. "I'd like to have one of each, but this blue-gray is my favorite." She smoothed her left hand lovingly over the top sweater on a stack, giving David a clear view of a narrow diamond circlet on her ring finger. Then she picked up the sweater and shook it out for him to examine. Looking at him and noting the sick disappointment he couldn't hide, she made a crestfallen face. "You don't like it. I can tell. But don't feel bad. I'm not offended. We all have our different tastes."

"No—no, I like the sweater," he assured her in a hollow voice. "The color is very nice." The blue-gray matched her eyes perfectly. She'd look lovely in the sweater but never wear it or any other garment for him. She was married.

"We have a number of other styles, cardigans as well as pullovers, in different weaves and colors. I'd be happy to show them to you," Ruth offered as she refolded the sweater with practiced efficiency, plainly assuming that he was merely being polite in saying that he liked it. "Or maybe you're thinking of something else besides a sweater. I might be able to steer you in the right direction if I knew the age category of the person you're buying for and also whether she's a feminine or a tailored type."

"Actually, I really do like that sweater you showed me," David insisted bleakly. "I think I'll take it." Making a purchase seemed the only way to extricate himself from the situation. He was too deflated to make a light explanation of his true purpose for being in her department and pass his error off as a joke, nor would he feel right just walking away like an unsatisfied customer when she'd conscientiously done her job and tried to help him.

"What size?" Ruth asked, her hint of uncertainty betraying that her salesperson's instincts weren't satisfied by his decision to purchase the sweater. "They come in small, medium and large," she added, interpreting David's blank response as an indication that he wasn't familiar with the sizing of women's sweaters. "I usually take a medium myself, if that'll help you make a comparison."

"A medium should do, then." As would a small or a large, for his purposes. David didn't have the vaguest idea what he'd do with the sweater; maybe drop it into a charity bin.

"She can always bring it back and get a different size, if it doesn't fit," Ruth reassured him on the way to the cash register. "Or make an exchange, if the color or the style doesn't suit her."

Her genuine concern that his purchase would work out well for him made David feel ten times as sorry that she belonged to another man. He'd half fallen in love with her on sight, and every minute in her company made her more attractive to him. Damn, why did she have to be married, when she seemed exactly the kind of woman he was looking for?—warm, full of life, fun.

The sweater was close to fifty dollars, including tax. David produced a credit card to pay for it, not flinching at the price. He didn't care about the money. At the moment his buying power didn't seem to be of much real value.

Ruth glanced at the card as she took it and then gave it a closer, interested look. "We have the same last name," she remarked. "My married name is Bradford." Her confiding smile with a hint of shyness was cruelly disarming. "I'm not very used to it yet, though. My husband and I have only been married a few weeks. Twenty-five days, to be exact."

"I'm sure it will take a while," David managed to say politely, trying to adjust to what seemed a cruel joke on him from start to finish. She was newly married and happy, still shining with a bride's radiance. It had been her joy in being married to another man named Bradford that had caused David to notice her and be drawn to her.

"Sign here, please." Ruth had been proceeding with the transaction efficiently, without any further conversation. David knew that she'd inferred from his manner that he wasn't interested in her personal life. There was no good reason, but he wanted to erase the impression before he left.

"Is your husband from Seattle?" he asked as he wrote his name on the line she'd indicated. "I would guess from your accent that you're not."

"Tom and I are both from Texas." The little diamonds in Ruth's wedding band caught the light and twinkled as she tore off the perforated edge holding the layers of the charge form together. "We moved here for him to take a job with Boeing. He's an engineer."

Her note of warm pride made David question his own choice of career for just a second. "As far as I know, there isn't a Texas branch in my family tree," he mused. "It's not likely that we're related."

Ruth was slipping the sweater along with his copy of the charge slip into a bag. Her quick smiling glance told him the possibility wouldn't have occurred to her. Apparently, she didn't view him as anyone who could be distant kin to her husband, David concluded glumly. She'd probably married a virile, muscular guy, the kind with a five-o'clock shadow by noon.

"I guess Bradford isn't an unusual name," Ruth reflected, handing David the bag. "I do hope you'll come back and shop with us again. You can have that gift wrapped up at Customer Service on the second floor, if you have time."

"Thank you, but I guess I am in something of a hurry."

David left the store and returned to the hospital without doing the shopping he'd come for. It was silly, but he felt incredibly let down over the chance meeting with Ruth Bradford. An hour ago he hadn't known she existed, and now the world seemed an emptier place because she already belonged to someone else.

On her way to wait on another customer, Ruth glanced back to see David leaving and shook her head in puzzlement. Anyone could tell from the slight sag in his shoulders and the way he walked that he wasn't in good spirits. Whatever his reasons for buying the sweater, he wasn't happy with it. Ruth liked her customers to go away happy.

Maybe he'd broken up with his girlfriend and was buying her a gift with little real hope of getting back in her good graces. That would explain his defeated air. But then you'd think he'd try to choose something special. Ruth didn't have time for more than a moment's thought, and then she forgot about David and didn't think of him again during the busy afternoon. He came to mind briefly when she was describing her day to Tom later at home, but she didn't mention him, since Tom was in no mood to be entertained with stories about her customers.

"I sure wish I liked my job half as much as you like yours," he grumbled, slumped beside her on the sofa. "I'm beginning to wonder if engineering is all it's cracked up to be. And this damned dreary Seattle weather doesn't help. How can people stand to go days on end without seeing the sun?"

"My job's just a lot easier than yours," Ruth consoled, hugging him around the middle. "Plus, I worked in Austin for three years as a salesgirl. The change was easy for me. Hang in there for another couple of weeks, honey, and they'll be promoting you to head engineer. Take my word for it." She slipped her hand up around his neck and drew his head down for her kiss. "The sun did peep out a couple of times today," she murmured breathlessly a few minutes later. "You must have missed it."

"You like it here, don't you?" Tom accused huskily, unbuttoning her blouse.

Ruth helped him take it off and undid the clasp of her bra and shed it for him, too. "I love it here," she confessed, and gasped with pleasure as he bent his head to her bared breast. "I love that, too," she breathed happily. "I love you. I love our apartment. I love life. Be happy with me, Tom, please!"

It was two months later when David made another shopping trip to the store where Ruth Bradford worked. He wanted a new canteen and one or two other camping items, and this particular store was the best place in Seattle to buy them. The memory of his last shopping expedition there made him cringe with embarrassment, but he could see the humor now. Still, he didn't plan to go near the women's department.

Taking an elevator, he went directly to the second floor, where the camping gear was located. With his mind on his immediate purpose, he strode briskly into the appropriate section and couldn't believe his eyes for a moment. Ruth was finishing up a sales transaction at the cash register, handing a customer a large bulky parcel. Probably a sleeping bag, David guessed irrelevantly.

It hadn't occurred to him that she might be working in some other department. Why this one, today? David's problem was that he wasn't at all certain that his luck was incredibly bad. For all his chagrin, he'd felt a leap of gladness at the sight of her that he couldn't deny.

His response was a perfectly normal one, he reasoned as he located the canteens on his own. Ruth was an attractive woman with a warm, outgoing manner. Just because she was married didn't mean another man besides her husband couldn't admire her looks, appreciate her smile and charm.

"Can I help you?" Ruth offered pleasantly as she approached him down the aisle, and at the sound of her voice David's logic melted. He'd forgotten the effect it had on him before, infusing him with her sincerity and enthusiasm for life. For a moment, he didn't dare look at her.

"Thanks, but I think I can find what I need," he replied, and glanced at her with a polite smile before he returned his attention to the canteen he was examining.

"If you can't find something you're looking for, please ask." With that, Ruth left him.

David couldn't tell whether she'd remembered him. Probably she didn't. It was some consolation for his not having made an impression on her to know that he didn't stand out in her memory as one of her more idiotic customers. Surely his credit card would jog her memory. David summoned all his poise and dignity to hide his suspense as he took the canteen he'd chosen and the several other items to the cash register.

But Ruth didn't even glance at his card or seem to take any notice of his signature. "Camping seems like it would be fun," she reflected wistfully as she put his purchases in a bag. "One of these days I'd like to try it."

"Is that why you switched to this department?" David amazed himself by asking. "The last time you waited on me, you were in the women's clothing department," he added when she looked at him in faint surprise. "That was a couple of months ago. I'm sure you don't remember me."

"But I do," Ruth said promptly. "I recognized you right away. Your last name is Bradford, like mine, and I sold you a sweater you didn't seem to like very much." She smiled with appealing candor. "The way you reacted to me a few minutes ago, I thought you might remember me, too, as a pushy salesperson."

"No, not at all," David denied. "You were very helpful that day. And the sweater worked out fine." He smiled, remembering how delighted his young patient had been with her going-home gift. "The young lady I gave it to was very appreciative."

"I'm so glad," Ruth declared, genuinely pleased. "Sometimes I guess I come across as too enthusiastic about merchandise that I like a lot myself." She placed his bag on the counter within convenient reach. "To answer your question, I haven't switched departments. I'm just helping out up here today because this floor's shorthanded."

David leaned against the counter as he glanced around. "Are you handling this department alone?" She still hadn't handed him his bag; it wasn't an open invitation to stay and chat, but it gave him the option to linger, since she wasn't busy.

"The other person's out to lunch. Normally there're four salespeople up here, but it's been slow most of the day, and the majority of the customers have been like you." Ruth smiled at him. "They know what they want and don't need any help, which is fortunate, since I really can't recommend one product over another. I've never been camping in my life."

"Don't people camp in Texas?"

"Oh, sure. I just never have. Actually I never had much interest in it before I moved to Seattle, mainly because I thought of camping as staying in crowded state parks with electrical hookups." She made a wry face that David thought was adorable. "I've gotten a different point of view here, where so many people I meet are into camping and hiking and enjoying nature. It really sounds nice to get away to a quiet, pretty place, take walks in the woods or on the seashore, sleep in a tent, cook on a campfire..." She sighed.

"It is nice, very nice. I think you would like it." David was trying desperately not to imagine how wonderful it would be to do all of those things with her. She was married and would do them with her husband, not David. "There are any number of great camping places over on the Olympic Peninsula, as I'm sure you've heard. You can camp in your own tent or rent a cabin. Some of the wilderness areas have shelters, but you probably don't want to try anything too rugged at first."

Ruth shook her head ruefully. "I doubt I'll be able to talk Tom into camping on the peninsula. We drove around it one Saturday, and he didn't like it at all."

David hoped his face didn't show his reaction. How could anyone *not like* the Olympic Peninsula? "Did you go up to Hurricane Ridge and look at the glaciers, drive in to the rangers' stations at the Hoh River or the Queets and walk in the rain forest, see the stacks at Ruby Beach?"

Ruth was smiling regretfully, shaking her head. "It was drizzling rain most of the day, unfortunately. I couldn't get Tom to stop the car, except for lunch when we got down to Aberdeen. He broke the speed limit most of the way. I'll have my work cut out for me just to get him back there for a day, but I would like to see all that."

"You just circled the peninsula on Highway 101?"

Ruth nodded. "Like I said, it was misting rain. He thought the evergreen forests were terribly gloomy. Tom likes sunshiny weather with the temperature in the seventies. He hates the climate here. Actually I don't think he'd be keen on camping even if the weather were better, though. He likes to be comfortable. His idea of a perfect weekend is to get in some tennis and golf and barbecue steaks with friends."

"What about you? Is that what you like to do, too?" David had no reason to ask, no right to know. He just couldn't help himself.

Ruth reached up with her left hand to tuck her hair behind her ear, giving him a glimpse of her wedding ring. "I'm strictly a spectator when it comes to tennis and golf. Tom's offered to teach me, but I'd never be good enough to play with him, and that would be my only reason for trying. Batting a ball back and forth across a net or from one little hole in the ground to another seems pretty silly to me." She shrugged. "I guess it's my background. The little town I grew up in didn't have a single tennis court, much less a golf course, whereas Tom's folks live in a Houston suburb and belong to a country club. He has trophies he's won in tournaments."

David picked up his bag and tucked it under his arm, sick at heart at the picture he saw. This lovely, vibrant young woman had married a typical country club jock, a selfish macho type who would always want to do what he wanted to do on weekends and holidays and expect her to accommodate him. Eventually he'd probably put a large diamond on her finger next to the diamond circlet, buy her a house in a country club subdivision, take her on expensive, fashionable vacations, but she deserved so much more of a chance to sample the richness and variety of life.

"It was nice talking to you, but I have to go." David managed a strained smile. "Goodbye now."

"Have a nice camping trip," Ruth called after him.

"Thanks. I will," David tossed back over his shoulder. Privately he had his doubts. He was going alone, and it would be hard, he knew, not to let thoughts of her and this conversation intrude and spoil his pleasure.

What an odd but nice young man, Ruth thought, watching him leave. He had such an air of distinction for someone his age, and yet beneath his dignified manner, he seemed rather shy. Her guess was that he was probably connected with the university, perhaps a very youthful professor. He looked intelligent and struck her as someone highly educated, perhaps because of the way he spoke with crisp, perfect pronunciation.

Actually he didn't seem like the outdoors type. His height was about average, maybe five ten or eleven, but he was slender, with a kind of sensitive good looks, sandy-colored hair, gray eyes and a nice, boyish smile. Ruth suspected that once you got to know him and he unbent a little, he would be a lot of fun. Remembering his expression when he'd told her his girlfriend had liked the sweater, she was glad to know he had someone special. It was odd, she guessed, to feel concern for a total stranger, but somehow she hated to think of David Bradford being alone.

She herself was so happy with Tom. Ruth smiled, visualizing her husband, and then sighed. If only he were happier with his job and could learn to like Seattle, everything would be perfect. Well, almost everything. She wasn't looking forward to his parents' visit. He'd been awfully critical of the apartment and her housekeeping ever since they'd called and said they were coming. Ruth was holding her tongue. The visit wouldn't last forever. Her in-laws would leave and things would be back to normal.

A customer came in, breaking Ruth's train of thought and signaling an end to the shopping lull.

David didn't go back to the store again until January. On several occasions during the five months, he'd ordered items from mail-order houses, including the store's own catalog. With his leisure time at a minimum, he didn't especially want to use it shopping. Picking up the phone and dialing a toll-free number was quick and easy. UPS delivered the order within days. Most important, he steered clear of running into a pretty married salesclerk from Texas who for some reason appealed to him in a way no other woman did.

Perhaps it was just the lure of the forbidden. He tried to analyze the attraction and dismiss it. Even if she weren't married, she wouldn't exactly be the perfect match for David. Evidently she had little or no formal education beyond high school. He gathered she was from a middle-class family with no social pretensions, and her parents were probably not well educated.

David wasn't a snob, but his background was considerably different. Both his parents were doctors noted in their separate fields, his mother a pediatrician and his father a heart specialist. Both were from old New York money and were well-traveled, cultured, informed people. They weren't snobs either, but they would naturally look askance at any serious involvement between David and a salesgirl in a department store. On David's part, an involvement with Ruth Bradford would be serious, no matter how imprudent. He knew that.

But it was never to be. There was simply no point in nurturing an infatuation of so little substance. David judged himself cured by the time the store held its annual after-Christmas sale. According to the full-page ad in the newspaper, every item of merchandise was discounted. It was too good to pass up. Even if he did encounter Ruth, she'd be much too busy to chat with him.

There was no guarantee that she still worked there, for that matter. She could have changed jobs, moved back to Texas, quit to have a baby. David thought about never seeing Ruth Bradford again and felt a sense of loss and emptiness that made him question going to the sale after all.

But he went despite his qualms. From the men's department he glimpsed her at the opposite end and was relieved and glad. She still worked there, still lived in Seattle. After he'd done his shopping, he would pass through the women's department and take the side exit, say hello to her. What would be the harm in that?

As on that day in June when he'd first seen her at Ivar's on the waterfront, David almost missed her. As a matter of principle, he forced himself to take advantage of the good buys and made several purchases before he headed over to her department. On his way through the shoe department, he saw her leaving the store through the same exit he intended to take. She was wearing an all-weather coat, presumably going on a break.

Unlike the day at Ivar's, David didn't hesitate to act on his impulse to follow her. With no thought to the curious looks in his direction, he broke into a walking run. Emerging below street level in an underground mall with shops and restaurants, he paused a split second before he called out her name, struck by her posture and the way she was walking with her gaze downward. If it weren't for her hair, he would have thought he was a victim of mistaken identity.

"Ruth!"

She stopped and turned around. After a moment's surprise, she mustered a smile as he came up to her.

"I came by to say hello and saw you leaving," he explained, his voice faltering as he stared at her face. It was plainly an effort for her to keep the strained smile in place, and her eyes were shadowed and unhappy. "What's wrong?" he asked with genuine alarm.

"Oh, just some post-holiday blues, combined with a hectic day." She noted his store shopping bags. "I see you found yourself some bargains."

"I'm feeling a little guilty about them, seeing how tired you look. How about letting me buy you a cup of coffee or whatever you'd like to drink?"

Ruth made another attempt at a smile to soften the refusal on her face. "Thanks for the offer, but I'm afraid I wouldn't be very good company."

"You don't have to be 'good company' with me," David persisted gently. "For all we know, I may even be a distant relative. My last name's Bradford, remember."

"That's not a big fact in your favor at the moment," Ruth said bitterly, and then immediately looked appalled.

"I'm sorry. I didn't mean to make a pest of myself."

"You didn't. You were just being nice, and I appreciate it. Really. I didn't mean to take my bad mood out on you." The kind regret in Ruth's expression tightened David's chest. As rotten as she felt, she could still be considerate of a virtual stranger.

"I don't mind, if it helps. I'd still like to buy you that cup of coffee."

Ruth shook her head. "No offense, but I really don't feel like company." She smiled wanly. "I know how bored I used to get hearing married people talk about their problems, especially in-law problems. It just never made any sense to me that a couple's not liking each other's parents was an issue. After all, you marry a person, not his family. He marries you, not your—" Ruth broke off, blinking hard and swallowing. "It was nice to see you again," she said huskily. "The next time you come to shop, hopefully I'll be in a more cheerful frame of mind. Now, if you'll excuse me, I have an errand to run."

David's skilled surgeon's hands tightened their hold on the paper bags he carried until his knuckles ached with the pain. It was all he could do to keep from going after her, but what could he do to heal her hurt? What could he say to turn her world bright and beautiful again?

Her husband was the man with the power to make her unhappy or glad, not David. What an insensitive man he must be if he could look at her the way she was today and not despise himself, knowing that he was responsible for killing her wonderful spirit, extinguishing the glow of her personality. Why had she married a man who wouldn't put her before his family, before everything and everybody else?

The way David would....

The fierce, jealous reflection sobered and frightened him. There wouldn't be any "next time" he came to the store. He couldn't trust himself to see Ruth Bradford again. His strong attraction to her had deepened into something dangerously close to caring.

Chapter Two

Ruth put down the Sunday paper, deciding she'd finish reading it later, and went for a walk in her new neighborhood, undeterred by the gentle misting rain. When she'd lived in Seattle before, with Tom, she'd always enjoyed walking in the rain, especially this time of year, with the trees a vibrant spring green and no bite in the June air. For her there was some appeal in the cool, soft gloom of Seattle that Tom could never fathom.

It had baffled and annoyed him from the first that she had adapted so quickly to a climate entirely alien to both of them, as they were used to a searing Texas sun. Later he'd given his own resentful interpretation when she opposed leaving Seattle to move back to Texas. "You just like being as far away as possible from that backwoods place you grew up in and that trashy family of yours," he'd accused angrily.

"That's not true!" she'd denied, hurt and insulted. "But even if it was, at least I can make it on my own, away from where I grew up, and you can't. You want to quit engineering and run home to take a job selling cars for your father. I'm wondering if there's really something wrong with your job at Boeing or whether you just don't have a lot on the ball!"

Her scornful remarks had been unfair, she knew, as had his. After three years in Seattle, Tom had been desperate for a change. He hated the climate, hated his work as an engineer, disliked their lifestyle. Going back to Houston and living a carbon copy of his parents' way of life had been right for him. It just hadn't been right for her. Their marriage was doomed when she started packing, but then it had been doomed from their exchange of wedding vows. They should never have married and shouldn't have stayed together when it was clear they were wrong for each other. Like too many couples, neither one of them would admit failure until they'd killed everything good between them. That had taken another two years.

Ruth had stayed on in Houston another year after the separation, then moved to Austin again, thinking she might be satisfied in the same surroundings where she'd spent three carefree years between leaving home after high school and marrying Tom. But she hadn't been content in Austin, either. She'd thought longingly of Seattle. It had seemed like a misty, remote haven.

Tom had been right in a way, she finally admitted to herself. She had a need to live far away from her home state, far away from her family and the attitudes and values she had grown up with. It wasn't that she was ashamed of her parents or contemptuous of their way of life. That way of life just wasn't hers. She needed the miles of distance in order to breathe freely. She needed to be far enough away not to have to resist the constant tugging of family ties on every holiday, birthday or red-letter calendar event.

Her return to Seattle had a feeling of homecoming. There was naturally some nostalgia and sadness as she recalled the honeymoon days of her marriage, but it was good to be coming back without Tom, a relief to know she didn't have to pet and pamper and cajole someone else into taking a more positive attitude. It was better to have no companion at all, she knew from experience, than one who'd be a wet blanket.

She would make friends within a short time and in the meanwhile enjoy whatever she did alone. There was comfort in knowing she didn't need a husband to support her. She'd been working in retail sales since she was eighteen and was good at it. She could move anywhere in the country, get a job and do it well. After arriving in Seattle two weeks ago, she'd made only one application, at the same downtown store where she'd worked before, and been hired on the spot. The personnel manager still remembered her after four years.

Ruth had explained frankly her ambition to move beyond a floor job into management. She was twenty-eight now and on her own, intending to make a career of working in a department store like this one. He'd assured her that there was room for advancement and agreed that she could be assigned to the several departments over a period of time so that she'd be familiar with each of them. When a department head position came open, she would be considered.

Ruth took the job, pleased with her prospects. She'd liked working at the store before. Those among her former coworkers who were still employees welcomed her back. In the process of getting reacquainted with them, she was reminded of people and incidents she'd forgotten, including customers who stood out for one reason or another. It surprised her that she could recall so much in detail, once her memory was triggered.

Today, as she returned from her walk, settled down with a fresh cup of coffee and resumed reading the paper, the moment her gaze touched on the picture of a distinguished, nice-looking man in his early thirties, it was like flipping a switch. She'd waited on him in the store when she first moved to Seattle after being married. His last name was also Bradford. His first name eluded her until she checked the caption: *Dr. David Bradford.*

He was a doctor, then. Ruth hadn't known his profession. She scanned the accompanying article, getting the gist of the information. The university hospital was delighted to welcome Dr. David Bradford, one of the top neurosurgeons in the country, back to its surgical staff. He was returning from Chicago, where he'd been the past five years.

Only thirty-four years old, he was young to have attained his reputation, but he had been enrolled in college at sixteen and was graduated from Johns Hopkins Medical School at twenty-two. In his family it was the rule rather than the exception to be brilliant. His grandfather on his mother's side was a Nobel Prize winner for his work in developing a special surgical technique. His paternal grandfather was a noted scientist. Both his parents were physicians, his mother a pediatrician and his father a cardiologist, the latter affiliated with a famous eastern clinic.

Impressed, Ruth studied the photograph, letting her mind go back. It was amazing, but she could recall two separate occasions when she had waited on David Bradford. The first time had been in the women's department. She'd sold him an article of clothing, a gift for a girlfriend. A sweater, perhaps?

If he had paid cash, surely he wouldn't stand out this clearly in her memory, but he'd used a credit card, and she remembered that she'd commented on his name and revealed what it had been almost impossible for her to keep to herself those days: that she was just married. They'd chatted.

Some period of time afterward, she'd waited on him upstairs in the department with camping gear. Perhaps that instance stood out in her mind because she'd worked in that department only one day during her four years at the store, and she'd been rather nervous, since she knew so little about the merchandise. She and David Bradford had talked about camping on the Olympic Peninsula, she remembered.

After that, had she waited on him again? Ruth thought hard, but nothing surfaced, and it wasn't important anyway. There was just a certain novelty in knowing she'd had a genius as a customer and treated him like any ordinary person. Now, knowing what she did about him, she'd be far more respectful if he walked into her department in the store.

The added years had given a more definite cast to his features, made them not quite so boyish, but there was still no trace of hauteur or arrogance in his expression. He looked assured, with no trace of the diffidence she'd sensed beneath his reserve, but she'd bet that he would still be a very pleasant customer. Now, though, she doubted that he would take the time to chat as he had when he was younger.

Was there any chance that he'd remember her if he did come into the store and she waited on him? Ruth discounted the possibility as she glanced at the other articles on the page. A man of his importance wouldn't remember a salesgirl he'd seen a couple of times that many years ago.

Later as she was leaving her apartment to take a bus to the waterfront, the sun peeped out and then shone brightly, as though nature were endorsing her plans for the afternoon. She'd eat lunch and then she'd take the Washington State ferry over to Bainbridge Island, a thirty-minute ride across Elliott Bay. After a leisurely walk around the little village near the landing, she'd make the return trip on the same pedestrian fare. The sunshine would make her excursion pleasant, but she'd have enjoyed it in the rain, too.

Now that she was back in Seattle on her own, she was going to explore her environs to her heart's content. She even hoped eventually to try camping on the Olympic Peninsula, though not alone. In Seattle the odds were good that she'd make friends with some camping enthusiasts and be invited.

Was Dr. David Bradford still an avid camper? The thought flashed idly into her mind and she recalled that the newspaper article hadn't mentioned a wife. He must not have married, or maybe he was among the divorce statistics, like her.

On Monday, David had a couple of free hours before his lunch date with two medical colleagues. He left the hospital, relieved to have some time to himself, and drove downtown. After a week back in Seattle, he hadn't had a chance to get down to the waterfront and walk around.

It would be good to mingle with the crowds, take a breather from being Dr. David Bradford. He'd be glad when he'd settled in and become a familiar face at the hospital. All the attention was flattering, but wearing. He wasn't cut from celebrity cloth.

The public market at Pike Place was as colorful and busy as he remembered. He strolled through, glancing at the wares displayed by enterprising vendors: handmade items ranging from the useful to the bizarre, T-shirts, imported trinkets. The seafood markets were thronged with local shoppers as well as tourists, the latter either noting the huge variety and the reasonable prices with envy or gawking with curiosity and distaste at unfamiliar sea life like the huge, awkward geoduck clam, whose siphon grew too large to be fully retracted.

"Those things are gross," David heard a young woman comment to the man with her. "Can you imagine eating something that ugly?"

"They pronounce that name 'gooey-duck,'" the man informed her, sounding equally repulsed.

Remembering his own similar reaction years earlier, David smiled to himself as he left the market and strolled along the waterfront. He could feel himself unwinding and had the sensation, really for the first time, that he was back in Seattle, where he'd chosen to come for personal as well as professional reasons.

The Pacific Northwest appealed to David. He was ready to put down roots, take a civic interest, make his home here. Since he'd become a doctor he'd dedicated himself to his work, at the expense of his private life. It was difficult, he'd learned, to keep a balance in a career where one's expertise and skill are crucial to those who require it, but he intended to start taking a reasonable amount of time off.

He was looking forward with the keenest enthusiasm to doing some camping on the Olympic Peninsula. First he'd have to buy new camping paraphernalia, since he'd given all of his away five years ago when he'd left Seattle. It had been just as well. He wouldn't have used it.

Why not buy some new camping gear today? he asked himself, and liked the idea immediately. The store that would have everything he needed was in easy walking distance. He'd noticed an ad in yesterday's newspaper confirming that it was still in business and at the same location.

There wouldn't be any necessity to take his purchases with him. Instead, he could arrange to have them delivered.

It was difficult for David to believe he'd declared the store off-limits for himself years earlier because he'd had such a powerful crush on a married salesgirl who worked there. The newspaper ad had jogged his memory, bringing her face and her name easily to mind. Ruth Bradford. She was probably back in Texas by now, maybe even with a different last name. The Bradford guy hadn't sounded like a prize. If she had divorced him, it wasn't likely that with her looks and personality she'd stayed single long.

Even though he didn't expect to find Ruth Bradford still working at the store, David knew he'd have to make a complete tour of all the departments to satisfy himself that she wasn't there. He felt a certain curious interest at the thought of seeing her again. It didn't seem possible that she could ever have been as fresh, warm and spontaneous as he remembered her. He more than suspected that he'd conjured her out of a fantasy.

Aside from some redecorating, the store seemed much the same, David noted as he made his way to the elevators, intending to do his major shopping first. The shoe department was still centrally located and flanked by the men's and the women's clothing departments. He glanced to right and left but didn't catch a glimpse of a female salesclerk who resembled Ruth Bradford.

On the second floor he found the camping equipment in the same place and felt a thrill of anticipation as he picked out a tent, butane camp stove, lantern, a camper's cook set for two people, two sleeping bags and two waffle-foam mattresses. When he wanted to invite a feminine companion camping with him, he'd be prepared, but it would have to be someone compatible. Otherwise, he'd go alone.

Gone were the days when he would feel down on himself because he didn't have a date for a holiday or weekend excursion. No company at all was far preferable to the wrong company, he'd discovered. As for his romantic notion that there was some special woman out there in the world for him, he'd lost faith in that. To find someone compatible was more a realistic possibility.

"Oh, and I'll need a canteen and a light backpack for hiking," he told the salesclerk waiting on him, a young man in his late twenties. David remembered buying a canteen the day Ruth Bradford waited on him in this department.

At the cash register, he produced his credit card to charge his purchases and experienced an odd and totally unexpected sense of déjà vu when the salesclerk, whose name pin identified him as Larry, glanced at the card and then looked questioningly at David. David's first thought was, Don't tell me this fellow's last name is Bradford!

"Say, didn't I read an article about you in yesterday's paper?" Larry asked in a respectful voice. "Aren't you a new doctor in town?"

David smiled and nodded in cheerful acknowledgment. "It's good to be back in Seattle. I'll be a regular customer. I'm hoping to get in a lot of camping on the peninsula."

Larry, looking pleased with himself, wasn't to be sidetracked from his accurate identification. "I thought you looked familiar. No offense, but I hope I'll never be a patient. You're a—" He faltered.

"Neurosurgeon," David supplied. "I was one of those kids who took his mother's advice when she said, 'Son, grow up and be a brain surgeon.'" He was used to the nonmedical person's horrified fascination with his profession and found that outside of the hospital, dealing with it lightly was best.

Larry smiled, but his curious, admiring expression didn't change. "Seriously, it's good to know you superqualified specialists are here when we get some complicated illness and need you," he commented soberly as he presented the charge slip for David to sign.

"They teach us to write like this in medical school," David quipped as he scrawled his illegible signature, aware that the man was giving close attention to his hands, no doubt visualizing them in surgical gloves and holding a scalpel. "I'll print my address so that your delivery man will be able to read it."

Without being rude, he wanted to conclude his business and be on his way. If Larry hadn't recognized him, David might have enjoyed chatting with him a minute or two, as one man to another. But as soon as David's identity was made known to a stranger, along with the facts about his background that so impressed people, he was someone set apart. Idle conversation wasn't possible.

Feeling vaguely resentful of the well-intentioned publicity the Seattle newspaper had given his arrival in the city, David took the elevator down, sharing it with several other customers and two store employees. He was sensitive to the glances in his direction and assumed a serious, distracted expression that he'd long ago perfected to discourage curious overtures.

As he emerged from the elevator, David's thoughts were on leaving the store and walking a few minutes more before he headed back to his car. Gone now was any interest in verifying that Ruth Bradford wasn't among the sales personnel. He felt certain that she wasn't, but, either way, what did it matter?

There was neither expectation nor curiosity in his glance down toward the women's department. The slightest twinge of either emotion would have kept him from being so utterly unprepared for seeing her. Not believing his eyes, he stopped and stared, mumbling an apology to another customer who bumped into him.

Ruth Bradford stood in full view as she sorted through a rack of garments, pulling out some and relocating them. David couldn't spare any of his powers of observation for what she was doing. He could see from that distance that her figure hadn't changed. She was still too shapely for fashion-slim standards. Her hair was the same honey-blond color, but it was shorter. The ends curved under about the middle of her neck instead of falling to shoulder length, but she wore it parted off center, as before, and still tucked the tress at either side of her face behind her ears. When she raised a hand, her left hand, to check for an escaped strand, David found the gesture incredibly familiar. He was too far away to see her wedding ring, but he well remembered the hard twinkle of the diamond circlet.

Shaking off his surprise, he deliberated for barely an instant before he decided that he would go closer for a better look and speak to her. There was no reason not to satisfy his curiosity. He was no longer an impressionable romantic in his twenties, capable of being ensnared by a pretty salesgirl's smile.

A sense of mild suspense made David's heart beat faster as he made his way toward Ruth Bradford, wondering whether she'd have any recollection of him. He had his answer when she glanced up and saw him before he was even close enough for her to offer him assistance. Her face showed an instant, startled recognition, and she immediately stopped what she was doing and seemed to collect herself, almost self-consciously. David was taken aback for a split second until comprehension struck him.

The newspaper article with his picture in yesterday's paper. He guessed she'd seen it, too.

"Could I help you find something today, sir?" Ruth blurted as David Bradford came up to her. She found it totally unexpected, after just reading about him and wondering if she would ever see him in the store, to look up and see him headed straight for her.

"How about a nice sweater in blue-gray, size medium?" David replied, and was pleased to see blank astonishment wipe the deference from her face.

"You remember that, too, after all these years!" Ruth exclaimed. "When I saw your picture yesterday and read the article about you in the paper, I wondered—" She broke off, flustered at what she was about to say, but his attention seemed fixed on her hand as she reached up nervously to smooth her hair behind her ear. His gaze followed her hand all the way down until she dangled it at her side. "I guess you must have an awfully good memory, being so intelligent," she suggested lamely.

"Some things are hard to forget," David mused with a little self-deprecating smile. "Like buying a sweater when you don't have any idea what you'll do with it." Ruth Bradford could probably sell him several sweaters today, he was amazed to discover, especially as the ring finger on her left hand was bare. She was as pretty as he remembered, with that refreshingly natural quality that was a composite of looks, voice and personality.

"But didn't you buy the sweater *for* someone?" Ruth asked, disconcerted that her heartbeat had quickened with a feminine response to the wry undertone in his voice and the expression in his clear gray eyes.

David gave his head a quick, definite shake. "I ended up giving it to a teenage patient when she was discharged."

"Why did you buy it, then? Why—" Ruth broke off, flustered by her sudden intuitive solution to the mystery, which couldn't possibly be true. But then she couldn't quite believe the whole conversation, which he'd deliberately instigated.

"Why was I shopping in your department when I wasn't looking for a gift for a female friend?" David finished her question for her with a rueful little half smile and then supplied the answer she'd already guessed, speaking with the pleasant succinctness Ruth admired. "I saw you from the men's department and came down, intending to introduce myself and talk to you. When I discovered you were wearing a wedding ring, the least embarrassing and painful option seemed making a purchase."

Ruth stared at him with wide-eyed incredulity. "You bought an expensive sweater when all you had to do was make an excuse and walk away? But I guess the money didn't matter," she reflected reasonably, supplying her own insight into his inexplicable behavior. "You were already a full-fledged doctor." And he would have been earning a large income for someone his age, she continued in her thoughts. Now he must be very highly paid, with his reputation and importance.

David followed her train of thought, regretting that the reminder of who he was made her turn polite and self-conscious again. "No, the money didn't matter, since I didn't have any dependents. And still don't," he added, noting her conscientious glance toward three women shoppers entering the department together in conversation. "If I'm going to take up your time, I suppose you'd better sell me something today," he suggested as she looked apologetically back at him.

Ruth gazed at him uncertainly. "You're here to shop, then?"

"No, but I'm sure I'll be able to find a grateful recipient for anything I buy," David replied lightly. He didn't have to glance at his watch to know that he should be walking back to his car soon if he was going to make his lunch date. That was going to depend on Ruth, he decided, coming to a quick decision. "It would make a lot more sense if we just had lunch together. That is, if you haven't already taken your lunch break and are free."

Ruth's mouth parted with her astonishment. "Why, yes, I am—I mean, I haven't—but, really, I couldn't . . ." She stammered to a halt, unable to find the words to protest the sheer unlikeliness of the two of them having lunch together.

"We're old acquaintances, after all," David pointed out persuasively, despite the fact that he shared her qualms about his impulsive invitation. "I'd appreciate the company."

"But I just can't imagine that we would find much to talk about," Ruth demurred. "You have all kinds of degrees, and I haven't been to college a day in my life. We have absolutely nothing in common."

It pleased David inordinately that despite her reservations, she seemed to want to accept. "Not even the same last name?" he asked lightly. "I hope I'm not touching on a painful subject, but I couldn't help noticing that you aren't wearing a wedding ring."

Ruth glanced down at her hand with a startled expression and then smiled with a guilty candor that David found both charming and intriguing. "I'm divorced, but my last name is still Bradford. It's so much nicer than my maiden name that I kept it." She made a disdainful face when David raised his eyebrows in discreet questioning. "My maiden name is Cook."

"Ruth Cook." He tried the unfamiliar combination.

"Ruth Ellen Cook for the first eighteen years of my life," Ruth corrected him feelingly. "In the south it's common to be called by your first and middle names. I dropped the Ellen when I moved away from home on my own after high school. But I really shouldn't be talking to you, when I have customers.'' She glanced around, self-conscious as well as concerned that she was being remiss. He couldn't possibly be interested in her personal history, which was so ordinary compared to his. ''It was very nice to see you again,'' she told him with sincere regret, sorry not just that she had to dismiss him but for being so obviously unsuitable as a lunch companion for him. ''Good luck in your new life here in Seattle.''

''I'm sure I'll be glad I came back once I've made a few friends and don't have to eat lunch alone,'' David cajoled with blatant dishonesty. ''I just arrived a week ago Saturday.''

Ruth wavered, surprised and complimented that he wasn't taking the out she'd provided him. ''I've just been here two weeks myself,'' she said uncertainly.

''Then you haven't lived in Seattle all along. I assume you went back to Texas—but here I go, keeping you from doing your job.'' He broke off, apologetic. ''Why don't you have lunch with me and fill me in then? I have to make a phone call and buy more parking time. That'll take me fifteen or twenty minutes.''

''I can take off in about twenty minutes....'' Ruth was still uncertain, but not reluctant.

''That works out perfectly. Why don't we meet somewhere?'' David hesitated and then couldn't resist. ''Say Ivar's down on the waterfront?'' It was hard for him to keep his voice clear of any ironic reminiscence. Later he'd probably confess to her the whimsical nature of his choice of a meeting place.

Ruth nodded in quick agreement, relieved that he hadn't picked a formal, indoor restaurant. She agreed to meet him in half an hour and then stood there for several seconds, trying to dispel her sense of disbelief while she watched him leave her, walking with a light, purposeful stride. Just yesterday she'd read about him in the newspaper, been awed to think she'd waited on him as a customer, and now she was having lunch with him.

Such things didn't happen, did they?

With a little shake of her head, Ruth went to wait on a customer, but her mind wasn't on her job. She glanced surreptitiously at her watch, nervously keeping track of the time.

David Bradford's world was so removed from hers that they might as well live on two separate planets, but he was also an attractive, personable man. She wouldn't mind in the least keeping him company over lunch, if she didn't feel so inadequate as a conversationalist. There was nothing about her life or occupation that could possibly interest him, and she didn't have intellectual tastes in books, music or entertainment that she could discuss with someone highly educated.

Her only hope, as far as conversational subject matter was concerned, was to talk about him, an idea that appealed to her. She was curious about him and wouldn't have any lack of questions, including one that she wasn't likely to ask, since it was so personal: Why didn't he have any "dependents," namely a wife?

Chapter Three

David figured his best excuse for canceling a lunch appointment with two male colleagues was a generalized version of the truth. He'd gone downtown, happened to run into an attractive woman he'd known formerly, couldn't resist inviting her to lunch to renew their acquaintance, and she had accepted.

"I hope you'll excuse my rudeness," he concluded apologetically after he'd made his explanation to Lane Carruthers, who was also a surgeon, but in his mid-forties and married. His wife was from a prominent Seattle family and a noted hostess and fund-raiser.

"Don't worry about it," Carruthers advised him heartily. "If I were your age and single, I'd do the same." He chuckled. "You sure in the devil didn't waste any time getting in circulation. I'll see you later this afternoon back here at the hospital. Oh, and Bradford, if you want to bring a date to the shindig at our place Friday night, feel free. After all, you're the guest of honor. I'll warn you, though, there'll be a couple of dozen disappointed females.''

"What man in his right mind would bring a date with numbers like that?'' David evaded jokingly.

Hanging up the telephone, he reflected somewhat uncomfortably about his instant rejection of the idea of bringing Ruth Bradford to the Carrutherses' party, a black-tie affair that would be reported in the society pages. It was no insult to her for him to assume that she'd feel ill at ease among a crowd of top medical people, university dignitaries and business leaders in the city. Look at the way she'd reacted to having lunch with him.

And, truthfully, David would have qualms himself about her feelings, particularly with so much attention being paid to him. Any woman he brought to the party would come in for close inspection, and he wasn't sure Ruth could handle it. There would be a stir of speculation over his interest in a pretty salesclerk from a local department store, and David was a private person.

But he didn't know why he was analyzing the matter other than to soothe a vague sense of guilt. He had no intention of asking Ruth Bradford to go out with him, period. His having lunch with her today was nothing more than a spur-of-the-moment impulse, but one he didn't regret as he returned to his leased car to feed the parking meter and then headed to Ivar's.

Ruth came into sight about five minutes after David had been waiting for her. Watching her approach before she spotted him, he puzzled over his reckless sense of gladness that the day had taken this unexpected turn. What was there about Ruth Bradford that gave her a special appeal? Dressed simply, and not expensively, in a white skirt and a red blouse, she was pretty, but he'd dated women just as attractive, a few even who were beautiful.

There was as much anxiety as eagerness in her searching glances ahead of her. Why did he feel this absurd sense of pleasure to know that she was looking for *him*? David didn't have a chance to figure it out before Ruth saw him and smiled tentatively. As he smiled back and went quickly to greet her, he couldn't remember when he'd felt so lucky to be singled out as her date by a woman in a public place.

"Hi. I'm glad you didn't back out," he told her lightly, but with utter sincerity.

Ruth struggled not to look as flustered as she felt. She'd been struck with disbelief all over again, seeing him as he stood to one side waiting for her, watching her with an intent, abstracted expression. In a navy blazer, pale blue shirt and striped tie, he could have been any professional man, except for the unconscious air of distinction that set him apart. What was he thinking as he watched her approach? she asked herself with a touch of panic. Was he regretting having asked her to lunch?

"I hope you haven't been waiting long," she told him apologetically, even though she wasn't late. She couldn't think of anything else to say.

"I've only been here a couple of minutes," David assured her. "The food aroma has given me an appetite, though." He inhaled the scent of deep-fried seafood being dispensed at the streetside counter several steps beyond them. "Would you like to eat here?" He gestured toward the entrance of the restaurant. "Or maybe Elliot's? For that matter, there's no problem getting a taxi. We could go somewhere else, if you'd prefer," he offered, trying to read her expression, which looked more dismayed with every suggestion.

"I have only an hour," Ruth demurred. "I was under the impression that you meant to have lunch outside here...."
But he probably didn't eat take-out food in crowded, noisy

places, as she was quite accustomed to doing on her lunch hour.

"That would suit me fine," David said heartily, comprehending her response now. "I would have suggested it, but I didn't want to seem like a cheapskate." Or that he would hesitate to take her to a nice restaurant. "This used to be my favorite place to have a quick lunch when I could get away and come downtown."

Ruth was privately skeptical but relieved nonetheless. "Then why don't we eat outside here, if you really don't mind?"

"Mind? You played right into my hands," he declared, and guided her with a light touch over to the congested area in front of the take-out counter, where several lines were formed. "Why don't I stand in line and get our food while you grab us a table?" He pretended to study the posted menu, which he'd glanced at on arrival and could recite for her. "What would you like?"

Ruth hesitated. "The fish and chips will be fine."

"Are you sure?" David didn't want to make an issue of her choice, but he suspected she'd made her selection on the basis of price. "Why not the salmon? And how about an order of chowder? I'm trying my best to be a big spender and buy you an expensive lunch," he added facetiously when she looked uncomfortable.

Ruth smiled sheepishly, which made him think he'd guessed right in thinking she hadn't picked her real preference. "I like the plain fish, which is usually cod," she said, surprising him. "Even in restaurants I'll order cod rather than salmon, if it's on the menu. I just happen to like the taste and texture of it better, unlike most people."

"I like cod, too. One reason I order it in restaurants is that it's usually prepared simply and the taste isn't lost in fancy sauces."

"That's very true," Ruth agreed, knowing that he was only being polite in pretending to share her unrefined taste.

"I'm glad you didn't let me pressure you into changing your order." David grinned at her. "You might have been annoyed when I showed up at the table with my own order of fish and chips."

Ruth managed to smile back at him, despite her skepticism and dismay. She wished he wouldn't order the same thing she did simply to put her at ease.

"I would have been put out," she said, swallowing her protest, which would only embroil them in more awkwardness. So far everything was going even worse than she'd feared. She'd never felt so socially inadequate, and it didn't help that he was so sensitive to her feelings and so nice.

"Two orders of fish and chips, then. What about a cup of clam chowder? I'm having one myself." David found himself faced again with the delicate problem of reading her reaction. She was torn between a yes and no answer, but why?

"No, thank you," Ruth replied reluctantly.

"Lots of people don't like seafood in soup." David didn't dare give in to his curiosity about her decision process.

"It's not that I don't like it," Ruth corrected him honestly. "I love it."

"Why not have some, then?"

Ruth sighed. "I guess maybe I will."

David couldn't help being baffled by her air of faint resignation. He raised his eyebrows questioningly.

"Today's Monday," she explained with a sheepish smile. "Every Monday I go on a diet. The fish and chips are high enough in calories without the chowder."

"But why should you diet?" David scoffed. "You don't need to lose weight. You look good the size you are." Somehow he managed to keep his eyes from dropping and reconfirming his honest opinion that her proportions were very pleasing at her present weight. She already looked embarrassed, apparently regretting her frankness.

"Thanks, but I really wasn't hunting for compliments." Ruth lifted her shoulders in a philosophic shrug. "The truth is that I can always afford to lose five to ten pounds, but I just have no will power where food's concerned. Now, you—" She inspected David's slender build, making him wish as he hadn't in years that he had a broader set of shoulders and a deeper chest. "I'll bet you're one of those people who can eat and never gain a pound."

"I can always afford to put on the five or ten pounds you think you need to lose," he replied ruefully. "But then it would probably settle around the middle, not turn to muscle."

"I didn't mean—" Ruth was appalled that her remarks could be construed critically. "You look fine the way you are. You're not a big-boned, brawny type...." Her voice drifted off, and she met his gaze with mortified eyes. "I think you're very nice-looking."

"And I think you're very pretty." David gently squeezed her shoulder and then dropped his hand, against all his inclinations. He wanted to keep it there, keep touching her. "I'm not offended, so don't be embarrassed." He smiled wryly. "Actually I'm used to encountering resentment from you weight-watcher types. Sometimes I look up in restaurants and see a round-cheeked lady or gentleman glaring at me when I've put down a big meal and then have a fattening dessert. So no more talk of dieting today or I'll get paranoid. Agreed?"

"Agreed." Ruth wanted to tell him that not only was he a nice-*looking* man, he was *nice*, period. But she didn't have the nerve. Instead she left him to find a table inside the glass-protected eating enclosure, hoping to be more poised by the time he joined her.

From his place at the end of a line, David took appreciative notice of Ruth's figure from the back view and didn't change his opinion that she didn't need to lose weight. Her skirt wasn't tight, but its tailored style showed the curve of her hips, the firm, rounded shape of her buttocks. She might meet with criticism from the fashion-enslaved female eye, but he had no complaints with her figure. The slight lushness was sexy, and it was her. He wouldn't have her pared down to model slimness any more than he'd want her to take speech lessons and rid herself of her Texas accent with the slight drawl and broad pronunciation. Even nervous, she was charmingly expressive, her pretty blue-gray eyes and face broadcasting her emotions.

David hoped she would relax over lunch and be herself, stop being so impressed by who he was. He smiled to himself and yet winced a little at the same time, remembering how she'd gotten herself bogged down in awkwardness commenting on his physique. "I think you're very nice-looking," she'd said in desperation, but sounded sincere. But did being "nice-looking" mean that he appealed to her as a man? He was oddly optimistic that it did, considering that he had no plans for asking her out.

She was sitting facing him when he took their food inside. David wasn't absolutely certain, but he thought it might be the same table where she'd sat the day seven years ago when he'd seen her for the first time.

"That looks very good," Ruth commented with more than politeness as he rested the cardboard tray on the table and served her and then himself a Styrofoam cup of creamy chowder, an order of crispy fish chunks with fried potatoes and a soft drink. It surprised her that the sight and smell of the food stirred her hunger in his presence, but then she was ravenous, having eaten nothing so far that day.

"I forgot to ask what you wanted to drink," David remarked as he sat across from her. "I hope a soft drink's okay."

"Thank you. It's fine."

"A regular drink, not diet," he added with threatening emphasis.

Ruth was dipping her spoon into her chowder and looked up with a guiltily confiding smile. "Good. I hate diet drinks, even though I drink them part of the time."

"On Mondays?" he asked blandly, and joined her in sampling the chowder, making a sound of approval that matched the appreciative expression on her face.

"Monday's always a diet-drink day," Ruth admitted. "Tuesday usually is, too. But Wednesday is iffy, and Thursday—well, by Thursday my willpower is shot." She took another couple of spoonfuls of the rich, creamy chowder, savoring the taste. "This is delicious. I'd never tasted clam chowder before I moved to Seattle."

David lowered his gaze and dipped his spoon just in time as she glanced over at him. It was such a temptation to watch her instead of eat. "I guess chili's more of a popular dish in Texas," he mused.

"Very popular, and every restaurant claims its chili is better than anybody else's. The ingredients are all basically the same, but there must be a thousand different recipes," Ruth answered, conscious that he was encouraging her to talk about something familiar out of consideration for her, not interest. He couldn't possibly care what foods were popular in Texas. "Have you ever been to Texas?" she asked, purely to relinquish the role of talking. She doubted that he had been to her home state.

David's eyebrows quirked upward in response more to her politely skeptical tone than to the quick transition. "How can you tell that I haven't?" he asked, genuinely curious. "Does it show?" Immediately he regretted not having given a straightforward reply when he saw how he'd disconcerted her. Apparently her intuition wasn't flattering for him, and she was embarrassed at having shared it. "No, I haven't made it down to Texas yet," he went on lightly. "Actually I've only known a couple of Texans, besides you. There was one guy in medical school who was from Austin." Mention of the Texas capital city elicited her immediate relieved attention, he noted. "He was going back there to practice. He claimed he wouldn't live anywhere else in the world, and from what he said, it sounded like a great place. Have you been there?"

"I lived in Austin for four years," Ruth replied with inward discouragement. If she backtracked and tried to explain why she couldn't transport him to Texas in her mind, she'd only make a fool of herself again, as she had earlier with the weight business. For the first time in her life she wished she were more articulate, more practiced in the subtleties of verbal expression. "Austin is a great place," she went on doggedly. "It's a clean city with a friendly atmosphere, good restaurants and lots of entertainment. Country and western music fans come from all over the country for the stage shows and concerts. If you ever get to Texas and have the time, I'd recommend Austin."

"I'll get to Texas eventually." David was rather surprised to discover his own certainty. Before now, he'd never thought one way or another about going there, never felt in any way deficient because he hadn't. "I'll be sure to remember your advice if I have the chance to visit Austin." A promise he more than suspected he would keep, however much time elapsed. "When did you live in Austin? Was it before you married and moved here to Seattle?"

"Actually before and after." Ruth explained briefly while she finished up her chowder. "I had been living there three years when Tom and I got married. Then a year ago I moved back. By myself, of course, since I was divorced." She put aside her empty cup, noting with an embarrassed glance that his was still half full. "I skipped breakfast this morning," she confessed. "This food tastes even better than usual on an empty stomach."

"I have the advantage on you, then, since I ate breakfast." David speeded up his eating, not just to catch up with her but as a convenient cover for his thoughts. If Austin was such a great place to live, why had she come back to Seattle? The most obvious possibility was that her return related somehow to her ex-husband. With more than idle curiosity and something akin to displeasure, he set about finding out.

"Did your ex-husband stay with Boeing in spite of his dislike of the Seattle climate?" he asked casually, feeling extremely transparent.

Ruth regarded him with open amazement. "You do have a fantastic memory," she marveled. "But then I suppose you would, having such a high IQ. No, Tom's not with Boeing anymore. He isn't even in engineering now. He works for his father in Houston. His father has a Cadillac dealership."

So she hadn't come back to Seattle because her ex-husband was here. Somehow David would have felt better about establishing that fact if she'd spoken with a tinge of animosity or contempt about the man with whom she'd been so glowingly in love. Did she still care for him?

"I don't seem to detect any bitterness," he observed in a carefully neutral tone.

Ruth shrugged. "It's been two years since Tom and I split up, and I've tried to put the whole thing behind me. There's not much point in being bitter. We just have to learn from our mistakes."

"You certainly have a reasonable attitude," David praised. "Most of the divorced people I've known tend to blame their ex-spouses for the breakup." Why didn't she? He wouldn't be averse to some of the same bias on her part.

Ruth made a guilty face. "I went through that stage myself, but I can't honestly blame Tom any more than I blame myself. Our big mistake was getting married in the first place, since we came from such totally different backgrounds." She paused for a bite of fish, and David took a bite himself while he waited for her to continue, remembering that he was supposed to be eating, too.

"The marriage experts are right when they say opposites attract but aren't likely to stay married," Ruth went on thoughtfully. "Two people need to have a lot in common and want the same things out of life if they're going to stay together over the long term. But I'm sure you don't need me to give you the benefit of my experience." She was suddenly self-consciously aware that he was listening with keen attention. "With your intelligence and education, you can analyze situations in advance, not have to learn the hard way, like I did."

David shrugged aside the self-disparaging concession to his superior intellect. "Psychology isn't my field. I'm no expert in any kind of human relations, believe me. When you consider the divorce statistics, marriage seems a tough proposition these days no matter how people pair up. It certainly makes sense that a man and a woman would have to be highly compatible and agree on a lifestyle, but as to their backgrounds having to be similar, I'm not sure. My gut reaction is that it sounds rather dull to marry someone who's lived a similar existence. Don't you agree?"

"I don't suppose you'd find a lot of women with a background like yours," Ruth speculated candidly, regarding him with open, admiring interest. "Not many people go to college at sixteen, have a grandfather who's a Nobel Prize winner and a father and a mother with doctors' degrees."

"Fortunately, I'm not really looking for a female clone," he retorted mildly, mentally cursing the timing of the damned newspaper article. "You know, you have me at an unfair advantage. Thanks to the local press, you know my whole life history, while I know next to nothing about you."

"There's nothing interesting about me to know," Ruth protested with as much disappointment as reluctance. She had been just about to gather her nerve and ask him why he hadn't married. "I can tell you my life story in about two minutes."

David smiled at her faintly disgruntled tone. "It didn't take you that long to read yesterday's newspaper blurb about me, did it?"

She smiled back, capitulating with good grace. "Don't say I didn't warn you that you'd be bored. I'm from Baker, Texas, which you won't find on the map. It's not even a town, actually, just a little hick community with as many house trailers as regular houses. The majority of the people have no more than a high school education, and a lot of them, including my parents, don't have that. There are a few really poor families on welfare and one or two that are fairly well-off, but it's mostly just a hard-working laborer class."

Ruth paused to take a sip of her drink, thinking of how totally out of place David Bradford would be in Baker, Texas, even more than Tom had been.

"My father's an automobile mechanic," she went on, glancing at David's hands, which she'd already admired.

They were supple and nicely shaped, cleaner than she'd ever seen her father's big-knuckled hands, which even after a thorough scrubbing had grease embedded in the folds and rimming the broad nails. "He works at the local gas station. My mother's a housewife and mother. They own their own home, which started out as a house trailer, but it has added-on rooms that were badly needed, since they had eight children." Ruth smiled at the flicker of expression in David's face over the number of children. He'd managed so far to show no response to the mundane facts of her life, which was so different from his. "The newspaper article didn't mention whether you had brothers or sisters. Are you an only child?" She resumed eating, encouraging him to give more than a yes or no answer.

"That's a strictly rhetorical question, I can tell," David accused, and took her quick smile as a sign that it was safe to continue in the same bantering vein. "Are you always such a good judge of character, or am I wearing a sign that says 'Limited travel and no siblings'?" He looked down at himself with pretended bafflement.

"I figured if you did have a brother or sister, they'd be somebody important, too, and would have been mentioned in the article," Ruth replied reasonably. "And I assume you have traveled, probably outside of the United States. Somehow I just doubt you've had much time or reason to see the southern states."

"Your instinct is right on the mark. I've been to Atlanta and Miami, but only in the airports. And I am an only child. Are you the oldest of the eight children in your family?" He turned the conversation neatly back to her, unable to hide a smile as she sighed and nodded resignedly.

"I'm twenty-eight, and the youngest, my little brother Brian, is ten."

"That's quite an age difference. He must have been born when you were a senior in high school." She apparently had no children. Had she burned out on babysitting, having grown up in a large family?

"The night of my graduation, actually. My mother started to go into labor during the ceremony." Ruth felt a little twinge of guilt, remembering.

"I suppose that must have really messed up your graduation-night celebration," David mused, responding with sympathy to her expression.

"Not at all. It was the best graduation present my mother could possibly have given me."

David knew he looked as curious and intrigued as he was. "You were looking forward to another brother or sister?"

"Not really," Ruth admitted. "For purely selfish reasons I wanted my mother to hurry up and have her baby. As soon as she got back on her feet, I was going to follow through with my plans to go to Austin and get a job. I wouldn't have felt right leaving with the baby due."

"Why Austin? Did you have relatives there to live with, or friends of the family?"

Ruth shook her head. "No, I didn't know a soul there. It just sounded like a fun place to live, with a lot going on. I wanted to go somewhere far enough from Baker to be entirely on my own," she added frankly. "To begin with, three of us were going, but both of my girlfriends ended up deciding to get married. So I went by myself. I'd gotten money for graduation presents and had some saved. It was enough for a bus ticket and living expenses for a week or two while I looked for a job. I was lucky enough to get one right away, working in a boutique, and had no trouble finding some apartment mates when I asked around. A couple of years later I met Tom, when he came to town for a weekend with some college buddies. We got married after he finished up his engineering degree, and moved immediately here to Seattle. So now you know my whole, boring life story," she declared, finishing up breezily. "I warned you it wasn't interesting, like yours."

"I wish I had something half as adventurous to tell," David replied with the utmost sincerity. "I would never have had the confidence to go off on my own at eighteen."

"You went away to college when you were only sixteen," Ruth pointed out. "That sounds adventurous to me."

"It was a tremendous adjustment," he conceded, "but all my living arrangements were made in advance, by my parents. I stayed in the home of a faculty member who was an old friend of the family." His parents had driven him when he moved, and provided him with ample pocket money. There was no comparison between his leaving home to enter college and her boarding a bus for an unfamiliar city with limited funds and blind faith in her ability to support herself with the benefit of a high school education. Hadn't her parents objected? he wanted to ask, along with a lot more questions. Had she found her home environment so intolerable that she was desperate to escape it? She hadn't seemed either ashamed or bitter in speaking about her family and background. There had just been that faint suggestion of guilt.

"It must not have been easy for you, being two years younger than the other college freshmen," Ruth speculated thoughtfully, on a different wavelength from his entirely. "Two years can be a big gap in the teens. I'm trying to imagine myself as a sophomore in high school, going to classes with seniors."

"I'll bet the senior boys wouldn't have minded." It was easy for David to conjure a picture of a cute, bouncy sixteen-year-old Ruth. His vision made him regret that he hadn't known her in high school. "You're right. I did find it difficult socially being out of my age group," he reflected in a more sober vein, seeing that she looked slightly rebuffed that he hadn't made a serious reply. "I made friends, but I was always like a kid brother, to the girls as well as the guys." He smiled ruefully. "Believe me, there were lots of times when I'd gladly have traded being an oddball, precocious kid for a C average and a football scholarship."

"The worst thing in the world for any teenager is not to be like everybody else," Ruth mused, thinking that the adolescent dissatisfactions he'd confided were far in the past for David Bradford. He wasn't the assertively male type, wearing his ego on his sleeve. His was a quieter, more reserved kind of assurance, but it told her that he'd had relationships with the opposite sex that weren't sisterly. An attractive, highly successful man like him would suffer no shortage of feminine attention.

"My guess is that you were popular with the boys and had lots of friends in high school," David speculated, forcing Ruth to make what was becoming a familiar adjustment in her train of thought from him back to herself. His wistful note disconcerted her.

"I was more interested in having fun than in making good grades," she admitted. "C's were perfectly acceptable in my book. I know it's hard for you to imagine, but I never had any intentions of going to college."

"I find it difficult imagining having the option," David replied honestly. "There was never an 'if' and not much of a choice of 'where.' My parents had the majority vote."

"My parents were proud as punch that I got a high school diploma." Ruth shook her head, her expression cheerfully reflective. "The two of us might have grown up on different planets. It's been fun, though, and interesting, talking to you."

David noted the past tense, the assumption that today was a rare, one-time occasion. Well, wasn't it? "The pleasure's entirely mutual," he told her, evading his own question. "This is the first time I can truly say I've enjoyed myself since I arrived in Seattle. It's been hectic. But then, you've just moved back yourself. How long had you been away?"

"Four years altogether. Three in Houston and then the year in Austin before I came back here." Relaxed now, Ruth answered in a natural manner, no longer self-conscious or apologetic about supplying the information about herself that he seemed genuinely interested in piecing together. There was a lot she wanted to ask him in the short amount of time remaining of her lunch hour.

"You were gone four years and walked right back into your job. I'm not surprised. You're very good at your work."

Ruth warmed with embarrassed pleasure at the compliment she couldn't honestly deny. "Fortunately, it wasn't something I had to learn from a book. I just fell into it accidentally and liked it. Having contact with a lot of different people suits my personality."

"I'd starve if I had to depend on my selling ability to earn an income."

Ruth tried to picture him approaching a customer and failed. "You don't really strike me as a salesperson type," she admitted. "Though actually I never think in terms of 'selling' anybody anything. The merchandise has to sell itself. My job is guiding customers in the right direction, figuring out what they're looking for or what's likely to please them, if they don't have something definite in mind—I didn't pressure you into buying that sweater," she broke off laughingly when David grinned with amused recollection.

"No, you didn't," he agreed. "But it was obviously fated that I should buy something from you." The time had come, he thought, for a humorous confession.

"Fated?" Ruth was puzzled and fascinated by his tone and expression.

"I haven't told you the whole story about that day." David glanced around them, taking in the lunch bustle that he hadn't been noticing at all, any more than he'd paid attention to the view of Elliott Bay or the busy traffic out on the street. He didn't think she'd been conscious of her surroundings either, which pleased him. "The reason you caught my eye in the store that day was that I'd seen you less than an hour earlier here, on your lunch hour."

"You had?"

David smiled, easily reading her train of thought. "No, I didn't follow you. Although I thought about it. You got up and left just as I was heading for your table, working up my nerve to ask if I could join you. After I'd eaten, I went to the one store where I had some shopping to do. When I caught sight of you, it seemed like an omen that I was destined to meet you. I didn't realize until I got closer that you were an employee, not a customer." He shrugged. "You know the rest. It didn't take long for me to discover that Cupid was up to cruel tricks, piercing me with his arrow. You were not only married but married to a man named Bradford."

"That was quite a coincidence," Ruth remarked, feeling both awkward and highly complimented. It seemed a tribute to her that she had sparked his romantic interest when he was a younger man, to the extent that he'd been disappointed that she wasn't available, even though she worked in a department store, while he had advanced degrees and was a doctor. "I could have passed Robert Redford and not noticed him those first few months in Seattle," she said contritely. "I didn't have eyes for any man but Tom."

A tunnel vision that eventually had revealed more to dislike than to love, Ruth might have added. Her adoration of Tom, like David Bradford's fleeting attraction to her, was obviously in the past. Though certainly not of the same magnitude, both emotions had led to disappointment of varying degrees.

But she didn't need to draw the parallel for the man sitting across from her. He was far her mental superior and didn't need her to enlighten him. Looking at him today, she found it difficult to believe she'd walked past him once and not seen him or felt the currents of his admiration and interest.

But it was just as well. They were still unwise emotions.

Chapter Four

Yesterday when I saw your picture in the paper, I remembered right away you'd been a customer in the store," Ruth told him, glad that she hadn't thrown away the paper. She was going to clip out the picture and the article. "I was interested to find out who you were and what you did. Those times I waited on you, you impressed me as being very intelligent. I assumed that your field, whatever it was, required a lot of education and that you were on the way to being someone important in it." Not because he was aggressive or ambitious, she thought, but exceptional, unlike Tom, who, though college-educated, was just an ordinary kind of guy who'd be mediocre in any career, left to his own merits. Tom was no smarter than she herself.

"There must have been some telepathic messages between your brain and mine yesterday," David mused, wondering about the other impressions she was thinking about but wasn't sharing. "What time of day did you read the paper?"

"Telepathic messages?" Ruth repeated doubtfully, responding to the literal notion of communication between their brains.

"It was about noon when I glanced through the paper, spotted your store's ad and wondered if you still worked there."

Ruth gazed at him, wide-eyed. "That's about the same time I got back from my walk and read the section with the article about you. Do you know I even stopped to ask myself whether you'd remember me if you came into the store and I waited on you again? Of course, I didn't expect you to. Or dream I'd have the chance to find out so soon." He hadn't come to the store today for the sole purpose of determining whether she still worked there, had he? "You don't seriously believe in telepathy and ESP and—and things of that nature, do you?" she asked, pretending a sudden renewed interest in eating her lunch. She hoped he couldn't read minds, or he'd guess the silly thought that had just passed through hers.

"I'm normally a skeptic about anything that seems to defy a rational explanation," David replied. "But like most people I get goosebumps when I hear a story about someone having a flat tire and getting to the airport a couple of minutes too late to catch a plane that crashes." He smiled. "Today I had the odd feeling that I'd stepped into the twilight zone when I paid for some camping equipment at your store with my credit card, and the fellow waiting on me took an immediate interest in it. I half expected him to say, 'Bradford's my name, too.'"

"What did he say?" Ruth asked too brightly to hide her sense of letdown. Of course he'd had a legitimate reason for coming to the store today. He hadn't come looking for her.

Fortunately, David didn't seem to notice her forced note. He recounted the incident with her co-worker Larry, and she forgot herself in the enjoyment of hearing him talk and watching the play of expression on his face. His clear pronunciation fell pleasantly on her ears, the humorous tone dry and good-natured but not sarcastic. He didn't make fun of Larry.

She admired the way he never faltered for a word and yet didn't make a show of his vocabulary. If he was lowering his speech level slightly for her benefit, it was a considerateness that came naturally to him and wasn't an insult to her. David Bradford was just a very nice man, in addition to being extremely intelligent and attractive.

Ruth was glad he'd overridden her objections about having lunch with him and she'd had this opportunity, even though it aroused a strange and unfamiliar regret that she was who she was and he was so far outside of her league.

She was aware of the need to make the most of her limited time, which meant keeping the conversation centered on him, but he traded question for question, and she found herself doing her fair share of talking as her lunch hour fled far too quickly.

"I have to get back to the store," she announced reluctantly, consulting her watch. Back to her working world, so different from his, back to normal life, which didn't include a personal relationship with a man like him.

"And I need to be getting back to the hospital."

His tone, with its faint regret and resignation, so matched what Ruth was feeling that her own emotions seemed to sharpen and become more complicated. Suddenly she wanted to get the parting over very quickly, for both their sakes.

"Thank you for lunch," she said, striving to give a cheerful, hurried impression as she slipped the strap of her handbag over her shoulder and prepared to get up. "I've enjoyed it thoroughly. I wish you the best of luck and hope you'll come by and say hello when you're in the store to shop. I'd appreciate it if you'd feed the seagulls our left-overs, since I have to run." Ruth asked the favor as she rose, giving him a handy excuse to remain behind while she made her exit.

David was on his feet with her, certain of nothing except that he didn't want her to rush away and leave him like this.

"It won't take long to feed those hungry scavengers," he pointed out, dumping the remains of their two lunches to-gether and handing the plate to her to hold while he cleared the table with a few swift movements. "Then I'll walk back to the store with you."

"But I don't expect you to do that," Ruth protested, noting his consideration in removing their lunch debris for the benefit of those who would use the table after them.

"I'd like to, if you don't mind." On the way back to the store he would come to some decision about whether to ask her out.

"Well, no, of course, I don't *mind*," Ruth replied help-lessly, and let him escort her out to the pier to toss the food remnants to the greedy gulls and then along the street, the whole time telling herself not to jump to conclusions about why he was insisting on accompanying her back to the store. His car might be parked in a nearby location so that he wasn't going out of his way. Or perhaps he'd remembered some item at the store he'd forgotten to buy.

"Did you find everything you needed up in the camping department today?" she asked conversationally.

"Yes, and I needed all the basic equipment for camp-ing—tent, cookstove, lantern and so on." David met her quick glance, hoping that he didn't look guilty. The thought of the two sleeping bags gave a disturbing, intimate dimension to her single status. Now they could conceivably go camping together, the way he'd once fantasized.

"How did you get interested in camping?" Ruth asked.

"I got my first taste of it as a small boy," David answered, glad to have his train of thought interrupted before he could take it any further and start visualizing the two of them together in some of his favorite places on the peninsula. "My parents have a cabin in upper New York State, located on a number of acres with a lake. It's very rustic. When they could get away for a weekend or a holiday, and occasionally for a whole week, we'd go up there. I had a pup tent and would sleep outside."

Ruth asked him more questions and relaxed completely in the pleasure of listening to him and enjoying the sound of his voice, with its tone of fond reminiscence. She couldn't relate at all to the glimpse he gave her into his background, but she found it fascinating, like a movie, with him a very appealing major character. She liked David Bradford more and more.

"It sounds kind of like the setting in *On Golden Pond*," she commented. "Did you fish on the lake with your father?"

"No, he wasn't a fisherman. Maybe that's why I have no interest in fishing. We had a rowboat and canoes and spent a lot of time on the lake but never put a line in the water. My father is a nature photographer and would have us up at daybreak to go for a row around the lake or a hike into the woods to take pictures. The rest of the time he'd have been happy just chopping wood for the fireplace. God knows how big a woodstack we'd have had if my mother hadn't been constantly dragging him—and me, too—off to hunt for mushrooms. She's a self-read expert on wild mushrooms."

His parents as he described them didn't fit any of Ruth's preconceived notions about a man and wife who were both professionals and evidently well-paid, earning a large income between them. She tried to imagine Tom's father wielding an ax and her perfectly groomed former mother-in-law walking in the woods. Her own parents at the bottom end of the income scale would opt for an entirely different kind of vacation if they could afford one. They'd go on a luxury cruise or a gambling spree in Vegas.

"Are your parents members of a country club?" she asked. "Do they like golf and tennis and bridge?"

Those were the leisure-time pursuits she associated with people she'd known in a higher financial bracket, like her ex-husband's parents and their friends, David reflected, comprehending her puzzlement. "No, they're more Sierra Club types." And had enough background and wealth that they could afford to be individuals and not worry about social status, he could have added, but didn't, for fear of sounding snobbish. "They like to walk and ride bicycles for exercise."

"It seems as though you've taken after them."

"I suppose I am like my parents in some ways," he admitted. "I'm not a country club person either, and when I have a chance to take off for a couple of days and relax, I don't care to go to a crowded resort. I find it very satisfying to get away to some quiet, relatively isolated spot without all the everyday conveniences. It's not an urge to test myself in survival skills. The camping I do is tame, compared to real wilderness camping, but it's still a return to a simpler, more primitive existence."

Ruth's curiosity was suddenly too personal to indulge. Did he like to get away by himself or with a woman friend? she would've liked to ask as they walked several steps in silence. What would it be like, she let herself wonder, to go camping with David Bradford, to be completely alone with him in some beautiful, remote spot, cook meals on a campstove or a campfire, sleep in a tent....

"Did you ever get to try camping?" David asked, aware that the store was only a couple of blocks away. The walk had turned out to be all too short. He had to decide soon. Was he going to ask to see her again?

"No, I never did." Ruth's cheeks burned at the faint embarrassment in her voice. His question had caught her in the middle of intimate thoughts. "Why did you have to buy new camping equipment?" she rushed on to ask. "Was yours worn-out, or did you lose it in the process of moving?"

"Neither." David knew that she was just making nervous conversation now, apparently aware as he was that they were nearing her place of employment. "I gave it away when I left Seattle and moved to Chicago. I didn't anticipate having much opportunity for camping, and, to tell the truth, I was a little burned out on it." He met her quick glance of surprise with a rueful smile. "I'd found camping didn't lend itself well to having female companionship. As it turned out, I wouldn't have had time to make use of my camping gear anyway. I seldom managed to get off several days in a row."

"You must think you'll have more free time here," Ruth ventured, not daring to comment on what really interested her: did he plan to give camping with women companions another try?

"I'm definitely going to take more time off." David looked up ahead to where the corner of the store was just coming into view. "What kind of schedule do you have?" he asked casually. "Do you have to work on Saturdays?" He had the coming Saturday off.

Ruth followed his gaze up the street and had to keep her feet from dragging. She'd like to make the walk last a little longer. "I have to work some Saturdays. We have a rotating schedule. I don't really mind working on a weekend. It's nice to have a weekday off, too."

Her tone of faint regret seemed to contradict her words. Was she working this Saturday and disappointed at the thought that she'd have to turn him down if he asked her to do something? The possibility that he might not have the option of her company erased all of David's indecision.

"What about this Saturday? Do you have to work?"

"No, I have this Saturday off—" Ruth broke off, hit by delayed comprehension, and looked at him with open surprise.

"So do I," David said casually, ignoring her reaction. "I'd given some thought to taking a drive over to the peninsula for the day. Would you be interested? There's no predicting the weather, of course," he went on before she could answer. "If it's a clear day, we can go up to Hurricane Ridge. If it's overcast or even raining lightly, there's still the rain forests and the beach. We wouldn't be stuck in the car the whole day, in any event. That is, if you don't mind getting out and walking in the rain."

"I like walking in the rain," Ruth replied uncertainly. "But I don't know...." It didn't make any sense for them to see each other, to get to know each other any better. She was a salesclerk with a high school diploma and an average IQ, from a lower-middle-class family, and he was a doctor, brilliant in his field, from an entirely different kind of background. No dating service would match the two of them in a million years.

David gazed ahead at the store where she worked, sharing fully in her reservations, which she didn't have to state. Yet he had no desire to rescind his invitation. In fact, he would be extremely disappointed if she turned him down.

"I guess it would be pretty much of a gamble to go off for a day together," he mused with pretended gravity, drawing a quick glance from her. "We'd probably run out of things to talk about, the way we have today. There'd be more of those long, awkward silences we had at lunch and on the walk here." He smiled at her and felt a lighthearted sense of relief when she smiled back and he knew he could persuade her. "I'd like to take the risk. I'd enjoy your company."

"And I'd enjoy yours," Ruth replied honestly. "I'd love to go with you on Saturday. I don't have any plans. Our situations are similar, I guess. We've both just moved back to town and haven't had time to get involved with a new set of friends." She didn't want him to think she was jumping to unreasonable conclusions where he was concerned. He just apparently hadn't had time to meet a woman he wanted to date.

"I'm sure you make friends very quickly." David had to shove aside an unpleasant sensation at the thought that it was only a matter of time before she'd meet a man she liked, someone with whom she was more comfortable than she was with him. "We can stop for breakfast on the way," he promised after they'd agreed on an early hour for him to pick her up. "I trust your willpower will be at a low ebb by the weekend, and you'll join me for breakfast."

Ruth met his teasing glance with a smile. "My willpower is so weak by the weekend that it's nonexistent," she admitted cheerfully.

They paused for a red light and then crossed the street with the change to green and walked to the store entrance.

"You need to give me your address and telephone number," David reminded her, halting with her near the glass door.

"Oh. Sure." Ruth opened her handbag and started to dig for a piece of paper and a pen.

"Maybe we'd better stand back out of the traffic," he suggested, taking her arm and drawing her to one side as a customer inside the store pushed the door open. The auburn-haired young woman making her exit looked familiar, and she obviously recognized him, since she stopped, smiling at him politely. David searched his memory in vain for her identity as she greeted him.

"Dr. Bradford. Are you doing some shopping? I can see you don't recognize me," she noted cheerfully. "I'm Christy Ames, a surgical nurse at the university hospital. We've met, but it must be impossible for you to keep all the faces and names straight at this point."

"Ms. Ames. Of course." David smiled apologetically.

"It's going to be a thrill working with you." Christy's gaze took in Ruth, who'd abandoned her search for paper and stood there, waiting awkwardly to see if she'd be recognized, too. The nurse had been a customer of hers earlier in the day.

"I came back to get that green outfit," Christy told Ruth. "I just couldn't resist it. Well, I guess I'd better try to get a hundred and one errands done," she went on breezily. Ruth noted that the woman included both of them with a forced, uncomfortable smile and seemed to be trying not to let her curiosity show.

"It's back to work tomorrow. Nice to see you, Dr. Bradford. Goodbye now." Before either of them could respond with an answering goodbye, she bustled away with both Ruth and David looking after her.

Her chance meeting with him in company with Ruth would be duly reported to her fellow nurses and co-workers at the hospital, David reflected with distaste. By now he should have been accustomed to having his personal life be a matter of curious interest, but it still seemed an invasion of privacy. Was he any more bothered today than usual? He'd have to answer that for himself later. Now he had to cope with the sudden awkwardness between himself and Ruth.

"It's always embarrassing to meet people out of context and not recognize them," he remarked.

"Especially when they recognize you and remember you by name," Ruth replied miserably. "I guess you have to deal with that all the time, in your position. About Saturday. I'd better change my mind. I have some things I should get done...."

"I wish you'd put them off," David said simply, too aware of the risks to her pride to openly question her turnabout. "I certainly haven't changed my mind." And he hadn't, despite his wish that the little scene just now hadn't transpired. Ruth looked at him searchingly, her conflict written on her face, and then sighed as she dug in her purse again.

He was obviously just too nice a man to want to back out and hurt her feelings, Ruth thought, finding a pen and paper. His considerateness and sense of delicacy kept her from being blunt and telling him she'd seen the look on his face when the nurse was walking off. Ruth wanted to discuss the matter tactfully and agree that she and David simply weren't suited for going out together, but there just wasn't time. She prided herself on being a prompt, dependable employee, and she was on the verge of being late in returning from her lunch hour.

"If something comes up between now and Saturday, just don't feel bad," she pleaded, jotting down her telephone number and address. "I'll understand. Honestly."

"It would have to be something extremely important," David replied quietly, taking the slip of paper from her. "I'll see you on Saturday."

On the way to his car, he lamented the untimely encounter with Christy Ames and wished that he'd handled it better. It had just come as a surprise. If he saw Ruth on a regular basis, he could expect to run into hospital personnel from time to time when he was with her. Not that it was at all likely that he would be seeing her on a regular basis.

But then the whole course of events today had been unlikely. On his way to the store earlier, he'd have ridiculed the very notion that he would ever end up inviting Ruth Bradford to lunch, even if she should turn out still to be an employee, which he had doubted. When he'd gone to meet her at Ivar's, after he'd canceled a lunch engagement with two of his colleagues, he hadn't foreseen any possibility of asking her out on future occasions. Now he was planning to spend a whole day with her on Saturday.

It was a prospect that filled him with anticipation as he considered options that would be influenced by the weather. If it was clear—and he hoped it would be—they'd drive up to Hurricane Ridge. He'd like to share with her the heady feeling of being on top of the world that he always got on Hurricane Ridge. He could picture her exhilaration so vividly that his pulse quickened. Her lovely eyes would light up and her lips would curve into her spontaneous smile. Her voice would have a lilt of excitement.

David would like to see again the way she'd been the first time he saw her, aglow with the sheer love of life, eager expectancy shining in her face. But that had been the radiance of a recent bride, he reminded himself, and sternly put aside further thoughts of Saturday, concentrating instead on his afternoon at the hospital, where he would resume his professional identity and proceed with the business of becoming oriented in his new position.

Ruth had a busy afternoon that didn't allow much time for mulling over the day's surprise happenings and thinking about David Bradford. Fortunately it was also a very satisfying afternoon, making her feel good about herself and her job. She had appreciative customers and an impressive number of sales by the end of her working day. Her sense of self-esteem got a much-needed boosting.

Then at quitting time her co-worker Larry Osborne, who'd waited on David Bradford in the camping department that day, invited her to go for a drink and have an early pizza supper with him. Ruth wasn't surprised, since Larry had made his interest plain, but she felt that the timing was ironic.

She would have accepted anyway, she told herself, without the prospect of shoptalk and getting Larry's version of waiting on David. Larry was rather stolid, but a pleasant, likable man, a Seattle native about Ruth's age. Being in his company would be far preferable to eating and spending the evening alone, and her diet was already shot for the day anyway.

They went to a nearby hotel in the modest price range and had a drink in the street-level bar.

"We were swamped down in the women's department this afternoon," Ruth complained cheerfully, sipping her whiskey sour.

"We were busy upstairs, too." Larry swigged his draft beer. "Seems like the whole population of Seattle and surrounding area is planning on going camping."

"My customers were buying, not just looking. I don't mind being busy when the cash register is, too." She knew for certain that he'd had at least one customer in the buying category.

"I had a couple of people come in and buy the whole kit and caboodle, from tent to flashlights. I got to feeling bad suggesting things after a while. They bought everything I mentioned." He shook his head and took another swallow of beer. "It must be nice, having that kind of money to plunk down just to try something. You figure if they don't have the first bit of gear, they have to be novices. Although I had this one customer this morning..." Ruth held her breath as his face lit up with recollection. "Say, did you read in the paper yesterday about this big-shot medical specialist? He's a brain surgeon. Bradford's his last name. Same as yours, as a matter of fact." He grinned in anticipation of his own wisecrack. "No relation, I take it."

Ruth smiled, feeling like a hypocrite. "Yes, I did read the article about him."

"Very pleasant kind of fellow. Looked familiar right off, but the whole time I was waiting on him, I couldn't place him. He knew exactly what he wanted and didn't check price tags. He must have done some camping at one time, although he doesn't seem the real outdoorsman type."

Ruth's conscience got the better of her. Obviously she wasn't cut out to be an undercover agent. It seemed unfair to either man not to admit a prior acquaintanceship with the latter.

"Dr. Bradford was a customer at the store when he lived in Seattle before. I remembered him when I saw his picture in the paper yesterday. I waited on him myself a time or two. Amazing, how some customers stick in your mind."

"Yeah, there's some you'd like to forget," Larry agreed, shooting his eyebrows up for emphasis. "For being such a big shot, this Doc Bradford was real modest-acting, though. Seemed almost embarrassed when I finally figured out who he was and mentioned reading about him in the paper. He's got a sense of humor, too." Larry grinned. "Said he was one of those kids who took his mother seriously when she told him to grow up and be a brain surgeon."

Ruth could see David's expression, hear his light tone as he made the remark. Suddenly she was ready to change the

subject. "It sure makes our job easier to have nice customers, doesn't it?" she mused brightly.

Larry hadn't finished giving his impressions of his interesting customer. "The guy has this air about him, too, that
tells you he's 'somebody.' Apparently he has the normal
male instincts, though." He wiggled his eyebrows insinuat-
ingly. "He bought two very comfy sleeping bags and a
cookset for two."

"I doubt very many people go camping alone," Ruth remarked, striving to sound casually indifferent. Larry's rev-
elation had caused a definite pang. Now she didn't have to
wonder whether David Bradford planned to have female
company when he went camping, once he'd met someone
suitable to invite. "I guess you must be a camper yourself,
Larry, since you grew up in this area."

"I've done my share." With Ruth's encouragement,
Larry told her in some detail about his camping experience
while they finished their drinks. The subject of David
Bradford and working at the store was dropped.

Over supper at a nearby Italian restaurant, they exchanged details about their personal backgrounds and got
further acquainted. Ruth kept thinking in the back of her
mind that this was the second time today she'd sketched her
past to a man over an informal meal.

Yet there was no sense of repetition. The two men were so
totally different, the two situations bearing only the most
superficial similarity. With Larry she felt thoroughly comfortable and relaxed. There was none of the unsureness or
the vibrating awareness she'd felt with David Bradford. It
wasn't quite fair to Larry to make such a comparison, she
realized with a guilty twinge. The pure novelty of being in
the company of a man like David Bradford would naturally
add a stimulating element that wouldn't be there with a man
on her social and income level.

Larry couldn't be faulted for not having a fascinating background. He was just an ordinary person like her—nice, but not at all exciting. Ruth could listen with three quarters of her attention and think her own thoughts while he replied at some length to her questions about himself. Unlike David Bradford, he was perfectly content to do the majority of the talking and let Ruth's shorter answers about herself suffice.

Afterward she marveled at the fact that she'd revealed a great deal more about herself to the man with whom she had nothing in common than to her co-worker. With David she hadn't been able to guide the conversation. She'd had to contend with his keen, perceptive interest in her. There had been a constant tension between his curiosity and hers, a tension that was totally lacking with Larry.

Getting ready for bed that night, Ruth wished she could stop going over the two impromptu social events of her day, stop contrasting the two men. With the benefit of hindsight, she thought it would have been better, in fairness to Larry and for her own sake, not to have gone out with him until a later time, when he wouldn't have suffered so in comparison with another, much more impressive man. She'd have been able to make a fairer judgment and not been left faintly depressed when she stopped to consider that Larry was probably typical of her options for eligible men. Like her, he didn't have a college degree. He was from a working-class family and had four brothers and sisters. He seemed a decent, solid type, good husband material, but . . . boring.

David Bradford had differed with her today when she'd stated her position on choosing a marriage partner. It sounded dull to him to marry someone from the same background, he'd said thoughtfully. Maybe he was right. Maybe she'd be bored with all the men who would be a sensible choice for a husband for her. Ruth guessed that if that turned out to be the case, she'd just have to settle for a dull, comfortable relationship eventually. She wouldn't want to stay single the rest of her life. She'd want someone again, when she had enough courage to take the risk of giving herself.

But it would have to be a match with everything going for it. Ruth didn't ever want to go through another breakup of a marriage. She'd rather be lonely and safe than subject herself to that hurt and misery.

Feeling bleak and dispirited, Ruth decided she'd read awhile before she went to bed. In her mood, she couldn't possibly hope for good dreams. But the search for her magazine beneath several items of discarded clothing and scattered newspapers brought back memories of Tom's complaints about her disorganized housekeeping. They'd been teasing remarks early on in their marriage and then more and more harshly critical. Eventually he had tied that shortcoming, like all her others, to her background, making cutting remarks about her lack of opportunity to learn the graces of a homemaker. After all, he'd jeered, she'd grown up in a house trailer and had a poor example to follow with her mother's housekeeping.

Sighing, Ruth started to gather up the newspaper to throw it away. She did tend to be untidy and wasn't a fanatic about cleanliness, but she was a better housekeeper than her mother. When she went home, she couldn't help noticing that the bathroom needed cleaning and the stove was coated with grease, but she could understand, having lived there and shared all the daily drudgery, why her mother let things slide and cleaned through the middle. The cooking and cleaning and laundry were endless with a large family.

There was no getting that across to Tom, though, whose mother had a maid. One of two children, he was completely without sympathy for poor people who had more children than they could afford, who "bred like rabbits," in his words. David Bradford would be able to relate to her home background even less, since he was an only child with a mother who was a professional and probably did no housework.

Reminded of the article about David she meant to clip out and save, Ruth dropped the stack of newspapers she'd collected, searched through it for the right section and was about to look for her scissors when the phone rang, startling her.

Who could be calling her at this hour but someone back home in Texas with bad news? she reasoned with immediate alarm and flew to answer it, clutching the section of newspaper in one hand.

"Hello." She spoke into the receiver with dread.

"Hello, Ruth. This is David Bradford. I hope this isn't too late to call you."

Ruth went weak with a combination of relief and surprise. "No, it's okay. I just couldn't imagine who could be calling me locally and got a little panicky." She drew in a breath, preparing herself. He'd called to cancel out on Saturday, naturally.

"I'm sorry. I didn't mean to frighten you. I tried to call you a couple of times earlier."

"I got the chance to blow my diet completely and couldn't resist," Ruth said lightly. "Fried food for lunch and then pizza and beer for supper. What a Monday. I'll have to fast for the rest of the week."

Pizza and beer didn't sound to David like supper with another female. "Be sure and save a calorie allotment for Saturday," he cautioned, and understood the surprised silence from her end. His tone clearly asserted a prior male claim. "It occurred to me after I'd left you today that I'd gotten your telephone number but hadn't given you mine in case you needed to reach me. Do you have a pen handy?'' That was his ostensible reason for calling, anyway, he thought.

"Just a minute, I'll find one," Ruth said, coming out of her trance. "Okay," she told him after a fruitless search of all the drawers in reach had turned up scissors but no pen. Finally she'd dumped the contents of her purse on the counter.

"This is my home number." David gave her the seven digits, and Ruth repeated them after she'd faithfully written them on the margin of the newspaper section she'd carried to the phone. "And here's a number where I can be reached at the hospital."

Ruth wrote that down, too, feeling as though she were being entrusted with privileged but unnecessary information. There didn't seem the remotest possibility that she'd use either of the numbers, especially not the one at the hospital. She couldn't imagine calling him there. When she asked to speak to the prestigious Dr. Bradford, she'd have to reveal her own identity, probably to a whole network of hospital employees.

"I'll keep these numbers handy, just in case," she said politely.

"I'll try to check the weather forecasts between now and Saturday," David promised. Now that his stated purpose for calling had been accomplished, he didn't want to hang up.

"So will I. We always have a newspaper in the employees' lounge at the store. Plus there's a TV. Maybe I can catch the noon weather report. I don't have a TV yet," Ruth added lamely, cringing at how boring she must sound.

"Two weeks without television. That must be some kind of record for an American," David commented lightly. "Don't you like to watch TV?"

y'd touched upon a range of topics, shared tastes and
ns, with open mentions of their disparate back-
ds, just generally gotten to know each other better and
e each other better, too. There was simply no point in
lishing the groundwork for a closer relationship, which
what they seemed to be on the verge of doing, surpris-
y enough.

eturning the telephone to its place on the kitchenette
nter, she spotted the newspaper section with his num-
s written in the margin and felt a little thrill that worried
. Should she call him in the next couple of days and can-
out on the all-day excursion to the peninsula? All her
stincts warned that it wouldn't be wise to spend a whole
y with him.

But she knew she wouldn't heed them....

"Sure, I like to watch some program: get a TV, but I don't miss not having one "You see, I grew up with a TV blaring all my ex-husband was a TV fanatic. I guess relief not to have one going constantly. Wha you like TV?"

"My TV viewing was restricted when I wa only allowed to watch certain programs. So developed a habit of watching TV, even tho some very good programs occasionally. I get out of my stereo than my TV set."

"I can hear your stereo in the background. music you're listening to? I like it."

"Tchaikovsky," David replied after a slight p. tle embarrassed to admit that he was listening to R *Juliet,* a highly romantic, emotional piece.

"I figured you'd probably listen to classical music said reasonably. He didn't need to feel apologetic al cultured taste.

"I listen to whatever suits my mood," David c dicted sheepishly. "Everything from old Peter, Pau Mary tunes to Dixieland to Gilbert and Sullivan. My isn't at all highbrow. What kind of music do you like?'

"I like country and western, naturally, especially Wi Nelson and Jimmy Buffett and some of the other recordi. artists associated with the Austin City sound. But I also lo songs from old musicals...."

Ruth picked up the telephone while she was talking and took it over to a chair placed nearby so she could make herself comfortable during long phone conversations. When she hung up, almost an hour later, she sat there, torn between wanting to savor the warm, wonderful glow she was feeling and wanting to dispel it.

Chapter Five

When had he ever talked that long with a woman on the telephone? David asked himself as he went over to turn off the stereo. Never. He'd missed out entirely on the adolescent stage of hours-long conversations with a steady girlfriend after being with her at school all day. It was something he knew about strictly secondhand, from movies and TV.

He could easily have stayed on the line longer, too, for the sheer pleasure of hearing Ruth's voice. It conveyed her personality and physical presence so vividly that talking to her on the phone was incredibly sensual.

Maybe he'd better put off going to bed, listen to some different kind of music to wreck his mood, David reflected. If he went to sleep with Ruth Bradford's voice in his ears, he wouldn't trust himself not to take her along with him into dreams that would be intimate, and that wasn't a good idea.

He'd made love to Ruth Bradford in his sleeping fantasies years earlier, taken sweet liberties, joining not just his body but his soul to her, romantic young fool that he'd been. Waking from those dreams to reality had been bleak and jarring, but even at the time, David realized now, there'd been a comforting element in the dismal fact that his infatuation was one-sided. He'd been safe to be a modern version of a lovesick swain, since Ruth had been married to a man she loved, safely out of David's reach as well as unsuited for him.

But now Ruth wasn't married. She was free, apparently unattached, and didn't find him unattractive. Dreaming about her now would be far more dangerous, since she'd lost none of her special appeal and becoming involved with her was a real possibility. But it wasn't a good idea . . . was it?

A serious relationship between them was out of the question, wasn't it?

David put on some light modern jazz and considered the obvious problems. There was a tremendous disparity in education and background, as he knew Ruth herself was keenly aware. As far as intelligence was concerned, she might not have a freakishly high IQ, like the one he'd been blessed or damned with, but she was obviously bright. Perceptive, too, and so openly expressive. He loved the play of thoughts across her pretty, mobile features, and her eyes were incredibly lovely no matter what her emotion—surprise, dismay, embarrassment, curiosity, concern.

It was easy for him to picture her in moods in which he hadn't actually seen her yet. Tenderly amused, convulsed with laughter, wildly exhilarated, sexually aroused. . . .

David got up abruptly and turned off the music, which wasn't doing the trick, and took a current medical journal to bed with him. He'd read awhile before he went to sleep.

* * *

By Friday afternoon Ruth had turned down two other invitations for Saturday. One was from Larry, who had invited her to an afternoon cookout and party at his apartment complex, which had a swimming pool and a cabana. It was a bring-your-own-steaks-and-beer, casual kind of get-together with neighbors, he'd explained, most of whom were single and about his and Ruth's age. When Ruth had refused him, saying she was sorry but she had plans, he'd expressed disappointment.

"That's too bad," he'd told her with a downcast expression. "Of course, I was looking forward to your company myself, but I also thought it would be a good chance for you to meet some nice people who live and work here in Seattle. Are you sure you won't change your mind?"

Ruth had shaken her head apologetically. "I've been invited to drive over to the Olympic Peninsula for the day. I couldn't possibly back out."

"Here I thought I was getting in on the ground floor with you, and you've already met some other guy," Larry had complained, more serious than joking.

Ruth had reminded him lightly that she'd lived in Seattle previously and still knew a few people from then. She knew she could have put Larry's mind at rest and told him that he had no male competition for her as yet, but she didn't want to encourage any further questions about Saturday. Aside from its being none of his business, she wouldn't consider telling him that she was spending Saturday with Dr. David Bradford, the customer who'd so impressed Larry.

It made Ruth uncomfortable imagining Larry's reaction to such a disclosure. Why, he would wonder, was a man in David's position paying attention to her? Ruth could appreciate the question. She could also sympathize with what would probably be Larry's next thought: Ruth would be better off coming to his party, where she'd meet people with whom she had something in common. What would she find to talk about for a whole day with a guy so outside of her league? he would ask himself, and maybe her.

As the week passed, Ruth had had more and more doubts herself but dealt with them by trying to put Saturday out of her mind. So far she hadn't gotten around to contacting the married couples who'd been friends of hers and Tom's and still lived in the Seattle area. Most of the men had worked at Boeing. Several had transferred in the meantime, she knew, and at least two of the couples besides her and Tom had split up. In the evenings it provided some diversion to make a call or two, do the inevitable reminiscing and catch up on news.

"Yes, we really will have to get together," Ruth would agree in response to all the friendly overtures, but now that she was divorced and in the singles category, her interests were different. Most of the women had children and, whether they worked at a job or not, were concerned primarily with home and family matters. Ruth understood, too, that the breakup of her marriage represented a threat to those who'd known her and Tom as a couple.

By Thursday evening, though, the news of her arrival had spread and plans were in the making, she had discovered when she called Jane and Bob Zimmerman. Jane had answered and taken away the conversation immediately.

"Ruth! I heard you were back in town! I'm just *dying* to see you! We'd heard about you and Tom, of course, and everybody's terribly sorry...." But not surprised, Ruth had surmised. Jane had never been one of her favorite people, maybe because Tom had pointed her out as a model homemaker more than once.

"Susan Marshall and I have decided the best thing is just to get everybody together, since none of us can wait to see you," Jane had gone on after Ruth had lied convincingly and said she and Tom had parted the best of friends. "I was just on the phone before you called, setting up a party here at my house Saturday afternoon. Do you have a car, or would you like somebody to pick you up?"

"I'm afraid I can't come to your house on Saturday," Ruth had said apologetically. "I already have plans."

"Oh." The one word had been an eloquent blend of surprise, chagrin and curious speculation. "Susan and I didn't even stop to think that you might not be free. She said you'd just been back in Seattle a couple of weeks...."

Was Ruth just a fast worker, or had she taken up with some man she'd known before when she'd been married? Jane was clearly asking herself.

"I'm terribly sorry," Ruth had said a little briskly. "I wish you'd called and spoken to me in advance. I am free on Sunday."

"No, Sunday's out." Jane had hesitated. "You could bring a date on Saturday. It would be a little strange, I admit, but you and Tom are divorced."

Ruth had tried to imagine taking David Bradford to Jane's house and introducing him to the married couples she'd known when she was Tom's wife. They would have read the article about David on Sunday and would look from David to Ruth with poorly concealed astonishment. There was a certain shock appeal to the scene, she had to admit, especially since the opinion of several members of the old group had drifted down to her in Texas. Some, including Jane, thought she'd married well in Tom and should have held on to him.

"I'll be going over to the peninsula on Saturday," she'd explained to Jane. "We'll just have to make it some other time."

"By all means, we will."

But they probably wouldn't, Ruth knew as she'd hung up with mixed feelings, knowing that it was a missed opportunity. She would have enjoyed seeing everyone, even Jane. After all, there were some good times to recollect, as well as bad, and her reason for refusing the get-together with her old married crowd seemed almost fictitious.

Ruth had trouble believing that the Saturday outing with David Bradford would materialize. When he called early on Friday evening, she prepared herself for a cancellation when she first heard his voice.

"Have you seen the weather forecast?" David inquired, aware that she hadn't reacted with a great deal of enthusiasm when he identified himself.

"Why, yes, I have," Ruth replied. Bad weather couldn't be the excuse. The forecasters predicted a beautiful, clear day tomorrow.

"It looks like we're in luck, but just to be on the safe side, be sure to bring along a rain poncho." David knew he was a shade too hearty. "And a sweater, too. It gets cool at the higher altitudes." Her brief silence was suspenseful for him. Was she about to tell him she changed her mind?

"I'll be sure to do that," Ruth promised, disconcerted by her quick rush of relief and nervous pleasure that took the stiffening right out of her knees. He *wasn't* canceling! "I've been keeping up with the weather outlook all week," she added.

"So have I. I hope eight o'clock isn't too early for you."

"No, eight o'clock's fine. I'll be going to bed at my usual time, since I don't plan to go out."

David guessed he'd been pretty obvious in fishing for that information, which he found immensely cheering. If interest in some other guy was behind her lukewarm attitude, she probably would've had a date with the guy tonight.

"I intend to turn in at a reasonable time, too," he told her. "Unfortunately, I do have to go out. One of my colleagues and his wife are giving me a welcome party. It's a fancy, black-tie affair, and I'm really not in the mood for it." He'd much rather take Ruth to dinner at some nice, quiet restaurant.

"You'll probably enjoy yourself after you get there." Ruth had a vision of him looking very handsome and distinguished in his tuxedo. There would be single women at the party, in gorgeous dresses, invited for the express purpose of meeting him. "Usually I find the atmosphere of a party gets me in the mood, even if I'm not looking forward to it."

Her hint of wistfulness made David guiltily aware that he could have invited her to the Carrutherses' party and hadn't even considered it. "I hope that works for me tonight," he said. "But somehow I'm afraid I'll be keeping track of the time." And thinking about her and driving over to the peninsula tomorrow, which he was eagerly looking forward to. "I'll pick you up at eight, then. I have your address, but perhaps you could give me some directions?"

"It might be simpler for me just to meet you," Ruth suggested. "I'm probably out of the way for you, and I wouldn't mind."

"But I wouldn't think of it. It's no trouble at all to pick you up. Just tell me the general location of your neighborhood, and I won't have any problems." David was a little offended that she assumed he wouldn't need to know where she lived for future occasions. But after all, would he ever be picking her up again?

Ruth didn't argue. She explained the most direct route to her area, which was a little shabby but respectable, with a number of large, older houses that had been converted into apartments.

"You can just park out front on the street. I'll keep an eye out for you. What color is your car?"

"Silver-gray. And it's not actually my car," David corrected. "I leased it to try it out before I bought one."

What kind of car would he drive? Ruth wondered, but she didn't inquire about the make, figuring that she'd find out soon enough without making an issue of the fact that he could afford to drive whatever prestige car appealed to him. Somehow she didn't expect anything ostentatious, like a racy sports car, but a quality import.

The next morning, stationed at a window of her apartment overlooking the street, she watched a silver-gray car pull up to the curb shortly before eight, recognized it as a new domestic car and regarded it skeptically until the driver got out. There was no mistaking David, even though she hadn't seen him before wearing comfortable, rugged outdoors clothing like that sold in the men's department of her store. She stood there, appreciating how attractive and yet *average* he looked in his khaki twill slacks and plaid shirt open at the throat. He could be any man in his thirties, eagerly setting out on an all-day outing.

His expression showed anticipation as well as curious interest as he surveyed the facade of her apartment house. Only when he'd located her in her window did Ruth stir herself to movement. She waved to him and then grabbed her purse and the sweater and rain poncho she had laid out and rushed down to meet him, feeling exhilarated.

He'd walked up the front bricked walk and waited for her at the foot of the steps as she emerged from the front door. "Did you have any problems finding the address?" she inquired breathlessly, conscious that he was surveying her admiringly. She'd decided on a cotton skirt-and-blouse outfit, rather than slacks. The skirt was a solid pink and the blouse pink and white stripes. Her soft-leather kiltie moccasins with ties were a deeper shade of pink. Naturally she'd bought the whole outfit with her employee's discount at the store.

"No. None at all. You look very pretty." David verbalized the compliment he was paying her with his eyes.

"Thank you." Ruth walked beside him to the car, her initial surprise at the sight of it returning. The manufacturer had gotten excellent press for the car's styling and performance. It wasn't priced like an economy car, but, still...a Ford? "I haven't ridden in one of these new Fords," she remarked casually.

David opened the door for her. "I'm very impressed with it so far. I've about decided that if it passes the mountain driving test today, I'll put my name on the list at the local dealer. The cars are so popular you have to wait in line to buy one. Shall I take those things for you and put them in the back seat?"

Ruth handed him her sweater and poncho and settled in the front passenger seat.

"Are you one of those patriotic car buyers who insist upon buying an American-made car?" she asked him skeptically when he got in behind the wheel. It was one of Tom's selling pitches to Cadillac customers.

David shook his head, smiling at her openly curious expression. "No, but like a lot more Americans, I've claimed all along that I'd buy an American car if our car manufacturers in this country would get off their duffs and start producing a product that was technically on a par with their foreign competition. This car, along with some of the other late models in its category, is a step in the right direction." His smile became a rueful grin. "Now suddenly there isn't any convenient excuse to drive a classy import. Of course, I could use the stock argument that there isn't a truly 'American-made' car any more. American cars usually have at least some of their parts manufactured elsewhere. But there is a certain patriotic appeal in owning a Ford, I have to admit.''

Ruth smiled back at him, intrigued with his whole purchasing rationale. She might have known there'd be an intelligent but entertaining explanation behind his driving the car. "Just wait until the car dealer finds out your occupation," she mused teasingly. "He'll come out personally and show you his super deluxe top-of-the-line car in the showcase window. Ford dealers usually sell Lincolns, don't they?''

David groaned. "I'm losing my patriotism fast. I can see the car you're talking about. Big, with lots of chrome, and gaudy somehow, no matter what the color. Lots of computerized gauges as proof that it's really state of the art and not an outdated gas guzzler under the hood." He started the car and pulled out onto the quiet street after checking for traffic. "That's right. You have an insider's view on car dealers, don't you. What do you suggest, that I keep quiet about my profession when I go in to buy a car?''

"You can try," Ruth said cheerfully, "but any good car salesman will get the information out of you. That's rule one in selling cars, to find out the customer's occupation.''

"To determine his or her buying power?''

"That and also to know what sales pitch to use. A smart salesman will approach selling the same car to a doctor and, say, an attorney entirely differently.''

David glanced over at her with a curious but wry expression.

"A doctor usually has a very demanding schedule," Ruth went on obligingly. "He's called to the hospital on emergencies and so forth and thus needs the most *dependable* transportation he can buy. But he also needs to reserve his energy for those long hours, which he can do by driving a *comfortable* car. Plus since he works so hard, he *deserves* the best." She met his amused gaze with a broad smile. "An attorney, on the other hand, has to be at the courthouse on time for big, important cases. He needs a comfortable, roomy car for giving rides to rich clients. Plus, it's an absolute must for him to come across as successful, not as a small-time ambulance-chaser."

"In short, he needs the same dependable, comfortable, luxurious auto as our hardworking, humanitarian doctor," David said dryly.

"You catch on fast."

"Apparently not. Thinking back, I'm embarrassed to admit how gullible I've been. In Chicago, for example, I dropped by a Porsche dealership just to browse and drove away as the proud, virtuous owner of the highest-priced model on the lot."

"A Porsche." Ruth visualized him behind the wheel of one of the racy, powerful sports cars and smiled inwardly at her vision. She suspected he'd have been just a touch self-conscious as he looked now, glancing questioningly over at her, wanting to know her thoughts. "Did you enjoy being a Porsche owner?" she asked.

"I enjoyed driving the car, but I never quite got over the feeling that I was impersonating a Porsche owner. You have to be a bit of a showman and like being conspicuous to pull off driving a sports car. The same way with a motorcycle," he added.

Ruth nodded, understanding what he meant. "And you don't like being conspicuous?"

"No, I'm more the conservative, inhibited type, I'm afraid. Did you drive a car up to Seattle?"

Ruth wanted to challenge the derogatory element in his analysis of himself, which implied that he was dull. He was anything but that, in her opinion, but she was shy in giving it, and answered him instead. "No, I sold my car in Austin. I thought I'd try using public transportation, and so far I've gotten along fine. It's nice not to have to worry about parking and the upkeep of a car."

"No TV set and no car. You are living a revolutionary American lifestyle," David teased. "Speaking of Austin." He took his hand from the wheel to insert a cassette tape that was already in the player. The mellow sound of Willie Nelson's voice filled the car.

"You bought a Willie Nelson tape!" Ruth was surprised, pleased and yet taken aback that he had gone out and purchased music she'd mentioned liking.

"I thought it was only fair to bring along some of your favorite music today, as well as mine. It's a real habit with me to play music when I drive. You can check the tapes and play whatever you want."

"Willie Nelson's great, if you don't mind listening to him."

"I'm turning into a Willie Nelson fan myself. I've been listening to him as I drive to and from the hospital. I'd only heard occasional hit songs on the radio before."

Ruth was gratified that he might share her musical taste. She couldn't resist looking through the tapes he'd brought along and didn't know quite how to react when she saw that he hadn't just bought the Willie Nelson tape that was playing but several other cassettes by Austin City Sound country and western music artists she'd mentioned, plus a couple of tapes, obviously brand-new, that were collections of popular hits from musicals. He'd gone to some expense to provide her with music for a single day.

"You've certainly expanded your music collection for my benefit," she remarked awkwardly. "It was nice of you to go out and buy tapes that I would like, but you really shouldn't have."

"I have no self-control when it comes to buying tapes and records," David claimed lightly. "I always leave a music store with a big shopping bag crammed full." He couldn't explain to her, since he didn't know, why he'd wanted to own the music she'd said she liked, why going out specifically to buy the tapes had given him a disturbing pleasure, been *significant* somehow, beneath the surface.

"Well, I don't feel so bad, then," Ruth said, relieved and yet oddly let down, too. What had she wanted him to say? she asked herself as she sat back, relaxing. That he had bought music she liked because there would be more opportunities besides today for them to listen to it together?

Well, there wouldn't be. There *shouldn't* be. But there was today, so why not enjoy it to the fullest?

David outlined his plans for her on the way to the harbor and the ferry landing. He thought they'd cross Elliott Bay to Bainbridge Island, cross over the bridge at Agate Pass onto the Kitsap Peninsula and stop for breakfast at Poulsbo, a quaint little Norwegian town. From there it was a short distance to the longer bridge over the inlet of the Hood Canal. Once they crossed it, they'd be on the Olympic Peninsula.

"It sounds perfect!" Ruth approved, filled with anticipation. "It's just such a perfect day!"

As the car pulled up the ramp onto the ferry, she felt a thrill of exhilaration. Minutes later, as the cumbersome vessel detached itself from the shore with a slight shudder and an increased vibration of its engines, she seemed weightless, totally unencumbered, *free*. Behind her was the city, her new apartment and job, her new life. Gone for the day were responsibilities, worries, goals and plans.

David obviously shared her carefree mood and gradually shed his reserve, becoming more attractive to her as he let down his guard and showed her a more outgoing side of himself. They drove along with their windows down, inhaling the spicy scent of evergreen forests and absorbing the majesty of the mountain ranges that came into glorious view. Off to the right lay the Strait of Juan de Fuca, and occasional vistas of sparkling blue sea competed for their attention.

Conversation was easy and spontaneous, full of exclamatory interest over the passing scenery as they followed Highway 101 through tiny isolated settlements to the small town of Sequim, nestled in the arid rain shadow of the Olympic Mountain range, and on to Port Angeles. David played guide, relaying bits of information from his store of knowledge, like the theories on why Sequim was pronounced "Skwim" by the locals. He also couldn't resist mentioning places off the main route that he'd like her to see, such as Dungeness Spit, near Sequim.

Ruth changed the tape periodically, and the music played in the background, providing an accompaniment to their journey to somewhere beyond the boundaries of their real lives. She didn't have to wonder if he had the sensation, too, of being captive in a delicate, magical spell. She could see for herself when her eyes met his, hear in the tone of his voice the same light joy that she was feeling, the same helpless fascination with what was happening between them.

There was no fear, no caution, just a spiraling, breathless exhilaration that paralleled their ascent as they left Port Angeles and drove the steep, winding highway up to Hurricane Ridge, the air becoming razor sharp as they climbed higher and higher, with heart-stopping vistas of the world falling away.

"I've never been so *high* before!" Ruth cried out. "I feel like I could just take wings and fly!"

"Isn't it incredible!"

David grinned, able to spare her only the quickest glance, but the glimpse of her animation was enough to deepen his own exultation until he felt on the verge of bursting with a sharp-edged joy.

"On a day like today, I feel like I'm literally on top of the world up here on Hurricane Ridge," he said softly, and felt her quick gaze at his tone, which was so intimate and tender he might just as well have spoken an endearment, such as darling or sweetheart. He didn't attempt to sound any different minutes later when he announced unnecessarily, following a charged silence, "Here we are, at the lookout station."

"David . . ." Ruth spoke his name helplessly as he parked the car and killed the engine.

"Ruth," he said, smiling at her. "Let's go take a look at the glaciers. They have telescopes down on the viewing platform."

Ruth sat there for a dazed moment as he got out of the car and then she opened her own door and started to get out. He came around quickly and helped her, offering her his hand and lightly grasping her upper arm. They both were intensely aware of the touching and stood there for just a second, reacting to the physical contact, before they walked down an incline toward the visitors' center.

"The altitude must be making me short-winded," Ruth said, taking in a deep breath to calm her rapid heartbeat.

"Walk slower. There's no hurry." David reached for her hand and linked his fingers with hers in a warm, firm clasp that did nothing to restore Ruth's normal breathing despite the snail's pace he enforced.

He didn't relinquish her hand, not even when they had reached the concrete terrace of the visitors' center, where the telescopes were being used by earlier arrivals. Once he'd led her over to stand at the stout parapet rimming the platform, he finally did release his clasp, but only to slip his arm protectively around her waist.

Ruth sucked in another deep breath of the air, which tingled sharply in her lungs but didn't seem to provide the needed oxygen. "The glaciers look so close, don't they?" she observed breathlessly, gazing out at the mountaintops, which seemed such a short distance away. "They're beautiful, but almost blinding, sparkling in the sunlight."

"They're magnificent," David agreed softly, sparing a glance for the distant peaks before he turned his attention back to Ruth's face. He smiled at her as she gave up the pretense, too, and turned her head to look at him with another indrawn breath. "Feeling light-headed?"

"A little," Ruth admitted. "But it's not a bad feeling. More like I've had a glass of champagne on an empty stomach." Her last words were a whisper as she almost lost her train of thought, aware of his eyes dropping to watch her lips form the words. For a moment she was mesmerized by the absolute certainty that he was about to kiss her. "How about you?" she asked when he closed his eyes briefly, his arm tightening around her.

"Me?" He smiled ruefully, opening his eyes again. "I feel like I drank the whole damned bottle, but I don't think it's the altitude. That's never affected me before. Maybe we'd better go for a very slow walk and sober up."

His gaze dropped to her lips again, making a light travesty of the solution and awakening a delicious longing in Ruth. She wanted him to kiss her.

"Yes . . . why don't we?" she said.

David guided her outside to the pavement in front of the building. They held hands as they walked, following signs directing them to several nature trails.

"Have you ever seen a marmot?" Ruth asked him as they paused to read a sign explaining that the small furry animal native to the area gave a high-pitched whistling sound.

"Only once. They're shy little fellows. But we're almost certain to hear them. Listen! That was one just now."

"Oh, I heard it!"

Ruth smiled back at him, thrilled beyond all reason, feeling his hand squeeze hers tightly. "Maybe we'll see one, too," she suggested in a soft, dazed voice.

"If we're very quiet and look closely, we might."

Ruth blushed at his faint, amused skepticism that said he doubted he'd be concentrating very hard on catching a glimpse of the elusive wild creature. She doubted she would be, either.

Chapter Six

The trail they chose took them from the wide-open, tree-less landscape of the visitors' center and paved parking area into a dense growth of shaggy fir trees whose interlocking branches formed a canopy overhead, blocking out the blue sky and filtering the bright sunlight. After being so nakedly visible under the huge bowl of the sky, Ruth was intensely conscious of the sudden, hushed privacy.

"It's so much cooler out of the sun," she remarked, her voice coming out too quiet, as though she were speaking in an empty church.

"If you need your sweater, I can go back to the car and get it," David offered softly, squeezing her hand and slow-ing his steps slightly. "Cold?"

His caressing note sent warm, delicious shivers through Ruth. "No," she whispered, looking at him, her steps lag-ging along with his until they were barely walking. "I'm not cold."

He took her other hand and clasped it, too, as he brought them to a complete stop, facing each other.

"We'll be out in the sunlight in a few minutes, anyway," he said in the same, devastating tone, and then, holding both her hands, brought his lips slowly to hers and kissed her. Ruth went weak with the brief, sweet contact and kept her eyes closed, hanging on to his hands for a long, drugged second after he'd ended it.

When she looked at him, drawing in a breath, his dazed expression matched exactly what she felt.

"You think it's the altitude?" he asked huskily.

"I guess it must be," Ruth murmured, and smiled into his eyes, inviting him to succumb to the sweet, magnetic pull between them again. He did, kissing her the same way, with a kind of chaste hunger. Ruth returned the brief pressure of his mouth, savoring the touch and warmth and intimacy, which were enough, for her and for him. What was happening between them was much too delicate to rush and possibly ruin.

With a deep, indrawn breath, David freed one of her hands and started walking again at a leisurely pace. Ruth felt as though she were drifting along beside him, buoyed by a light, dreamy sense of happiness. Maybe the altitude was having a strange effect on her.

"These trees look ancient, don't they?" she mused. "Something about them makes me think of old men with scraggly beards."

David grinned at her. "I hope they're old men with faulty eyesight and poor hearing. Otherwise, I could easily feel uncomfortable."

Ruth laughed, delighted with the quick, humorous play of his mind. "I'm trying to remember the name of a book I read in high school, with trees that were personalities. It was strange but interesting, kind of a grown-up's fairy tale...."

"Tolkien's *Lord of the Rings*, perhaps?"

"That was it! Have you read that?"

They talked lightly and companionably as they walked with no sense of destination, holding hands, carrying on a thrilling, different conversation with their exchanged glances, the inflections of their voices. No matter what the subject, the real communication was devastatingly personal: they found each other fascinating.

Ruth halted in the middle of a sentence as the path took them from the edge of the forest out onto a high bluff overlooking a broad, deep network of valleys. The evergreens decorating the tiers of grass-covered slopes diminished in size until those far into the distance were like perfect miniature Christmas trees. Wildflowers added patches of delicate color, and again overhead was the vast blue sky.

"Oh, my!" she exclaimed, gripping David's hand tighter as she ventured closer to the edge and stopped to gaze at the view with rapt appreciation. "What a beautiful place this is!" She breathed in the wonderful crisp air and smiled at him, sharing her exhilaration.

"Yes, it is beautiful . . . in all seasons," David said softly, his abstracted tone and the warm admiration in his eyes making his words a personal compliment to her, not the scenery. Ruth colored with a pleasurable self-consciousness under his scrutiny of each feature of her face. Her lips parted on an indrawn breath as he focused on her mouth.

"David . . ." She murmured, urging him to kiss her, and freed her hand to slide both arms up around his neck as he brought his lips to hers. Kissing wasn't enough now. She wanted him to hold her.

"Ruth," David whispered, taking her into his arms as his mouth covered hers.

Embracing added a new element of sensual delight to the meeting of their lips. As she kissed David, Ruth was conscious of the sheer delight of hugging him around the neck and molding her body to his within the warm, strong circle of his arms. Her breasts felt perfectly placed to nestle against his chest. Her hips and pelvis and thighs were shaped to form an intimate, ideal contact with his.

It didn't surprise her that she fit so well into his embrace, not today in this idyllic setting, where being together and touching placed them on a magical plane where everything was perfect. The pace was natural, inevitable, not to be slowed or hurried, each step to be fully savored and enjoyed. Ruth knew when she parted her lips and offered him the tip of her tongue for the first warm, wet introduction that his mouth would be opening, too, and his own tongue there, eager and waiting, but not urgent, not yet.

The sound of voices and laughter penetrated her sweet languor, but she and David ignored it for several seconds as they tasted their way toward greater depth and passion until it was an effort to stop kissing. He tightened his arms around her as their lips parted, and he and Ruth looked at each other with dazed wonder. Then they kissed again, lingeringly. He took in a deep, audible breath and released her reluctantly, an inch or so at a time.

"Shall we walk along farther?" he asked huskily.

Ruth sucked in a big lungful of air. "I guess we'd better," she said with dreamy regret.

"We should come to a big open meadow up ahead," David promised, taking her hand again as they started along slowly. "We'll find a place to sit in the sunshine, off the main path."

"That sounds like a good idea," Ruth approved, smiling at him. She felt weightless, loosely coordinated, incredibly happy. "It's hard to believe that I lived in Seattle for four years within easy driving distance and never came up here," she mused, glancing off at the glorious vista over on their left.

David squeezed her hand. "I'm glad you didn't." He met her quick questioning glance with a rueful smile. "I know it's selfish of me, but I'm glad you're seeing one of my favorite spots in the world for the first time with me."

Ruth held his gaze for several steps, thrilling to the warmth in his eyes. "I'm glad you brought me," she replied softly. "I suppose you've been here quite a few times yourself." Her faint trace of wistfulness made her blush and concentrate on the view while she waited for him to answer. She knew it must be painfully obvious to him that she was thinking this wasn't the first time he'd brought a female companion to Hurricane Ridge. Was today any more special than the other occasions?

David tightened his fingers on hers, reassuring her with his touch even before he spoke quietly. "I've been up here at least a dozen times, at different seasons, with various weather conditions. Several times on days as nice as today. This is the first time I've ever felt in tune with someone else here. Usually I feel alone, whether I am or not." He brought her hand up to his lips and kissed it.

"Thank you for telling me that," Ruth murmured, feeling deeply honored.

The sight of other people ahead of them on the path served as an interruption but didn't disrupt the close harmony. They walked in silence, exchanging comprehending glances in response to the remarks they couldn't help overhearing as they overtook two couples, one young and the other older, who were obviously together.

It was readily apparent from the conversation that the elder pair were the parents of the young man and had come from out of state to visit him and their daughter-in-law, whom they barely knew, judging from the questions and comments and excessively polite tones. All four seemed faintly ill at ease, but the young woman especially was nervous. She sounded too bright and cheerful, laughed too quickly and too loud.

"Poor girl," Ruth murmured feelingly when she and David had passed the foursome and were safely beyond earshot. "I know just what she's going through."

"She isn't having a very good time, is she?" David said sympathetically. "But then I doubt the others are, either, especially not the young guy, who's caught right in the middle." He met her glance with an apologetic grin. "Naturally my sympathies would be with him. But seriously, it must be a frustrating situation for him. I would imagine that he's wishing she would relax and just be herself and that his parents would act their usual selves, too, so that the people he cares about could all get to know one another."

"I'm sure she'd like to relax, but she feels on trial," Ruth pointed out. "Plus, out of the group, she's the outsider, the one who has to prove herself, not the others. He was their son and they were his parents long before she happened on the scene."

"There's no changing the biological relationship," David agreed. "But turnabout's fair play. He'll be faced with the same family alliance, I would assume, when he's with her and her parents. It's impossible not to feel like an outsider in any group when you're the one who doesn't know all the favorite stories and background relationships. The situation's awkward for everybody. Nobody wants to be rude, and the conversation gets bogged down with explanations. Passing along a piece of current news like 'Aunt Mary's been burglarized again' turns into a boring, hourlong production."

"Did you just make up that example, or do you have an Aunt Mary who's been burglarized?" Ruth asked. From her own experience, she could have challenged his idealistic assumption that both sets of in-laws would get equal visiting time with a young married couple, but she had no desire to continue the discussion, which was so irrelevant to the two of them.

"She's actually a great-aunt and my most colorful relative." David grinned, shaking his head.

"How many times has she been burglarized?"

"I don't know the exact count, but at least eight or ten times."

"Does she leave her doors unlocked?"

"No, but you'd have to see the house she lives in. It's a big old Gothic mansion out of a horror flick—but you don't really want to hear about my eccentric great-aunt," he broke off skeptically.

"Please, you have to tell me, now that you've aroused my curiosity," Ruth begged. She was intrigued by his amused tone of voice.

David relented without any further urging. After he'd given an entertaining description of his great-aunt's home, which was actually a large estate, and an affectionate character sketch of her, he recounted the series of burglaries, some of which were comical incidents where the burglars had fallen prey to booby traps devised by the old lady. "She had to administer first aid and call an ambulance for her latest victim," he ended up, chuckling. "Then the guy brought a lawsuit against her. She was outraged."

"I can imagine! That whole story would make a wonderful comedy play!" Ruth exclaimed. "Your great-aunt sounds like a real character."

"She is definitely that."

The awkward foursome they'd passed minutes earlier was forgotten. There was no further talk of visits with in-laws. Ruth would never meet David's Aunt Mary or his parents, nor would he ever meet any members of her family. The pleasure and interest they had in each other was purely a matter of the present, the here and now.

They clearly had no future together, and yet there could be no regret for anything—past, present or future—as the path opened up into the broad meadow David had promised. Here, high above the world with the sun shining down, warm and brilliant, leisure was tangible. Time slowed to a standstill as they found a secluded spot away from the main pathway and sat on the grass, holding hands, talking and gazing out at the view when they weren't looking at each other.

Ruth felt compelled to share with him her combination of buoyancy and serenity, knowing even as she spoke that she'd fall short of expressing herself. "This is such a fantastic day!" she exclaimed with a sigh. "I don't have anything to compare it to. I've never, well, done what we're doing now with anyone before."

"Never sat on the ground and held hands with a guy? Come on," David chided in a pleased voice. "You must have been invited on dozens of picnics in high school. You already admitted to me, at lunch on Monday, that you were popular."

"Sure, I've been on picnics and had a great time. But I've never had this strange, nice feeling of just stopping and letting the world go on by."

"Not with anyone?"

His unexpected soft, serious note made Ruth catch her breath. "Not with anyone," she answered, looking deep into his eyes. Her heart beat faster, and delicate tension spread through her as he moved closer to kiss her. She touched her fingertips to his face and closed her eyes as his mouth covered hers, thrilling to the sensation of stepping with him deeper into intimate territory. There could be no caution or fear, not in a magic realm apart from reality.

Their tongues had already met and coupled. The familiarity bought their lips together with an instant sweet hunger, an urgency to resume where they'd last broken apart. They fed the hunger by testing out the angles at which their lips could meet, the range of pressure, the sensuous points of contact for their tongues. Alternating roles of asking and giving, demanding and submitting, they found every combination a rare delight and yet a torment, because kissing couldn't possibly satisfy them.

It made them want more of each other. Ruth ached for David to touch her body, to caress her and know her with his hands. She wanted to touch him, too, know him. When the need was too strong to ignore, she stroked her palm along his neck and shoulder and felt his hand moving up her back at the same moment. Her little shiver of response corresponded with his hard tremor, and they stopped kissing to look at each other, sharing the exquisite aftermath of a simultaneous caress.

"I wish the other people up here would have realized the world was going on by and climbed on, don't you?" David's voice was low and unsteady, sending little thrills up Ruth's backbone to the warm spot where his hand rested.

"Yes, that would be nice...." She smiled, seeing the similar reaction her soft, dazed voice had on him, and then considered the reality of his whimsical comment. "Can you imagine ...."

"Being up here alone, just the two of us," David completed for her. "What an incredible privacy that would be. We could walk around naked, like pagans, if it weren't for your ancient old men, the trees, leering at us." He smiled at her, and Ruth's heart raced at the expression in his eyes that told her he was visualizing her fantasy. Ruth visualized it, too, and increased his heartbeat, she suspected. His hand pressed against her back before he reluctantly slid it free in a caress of withdrawal.

"We'd better put our clothes back on," he suggested with a pained cheerfulness and took her hand from his shoulder as he sprawled sideways, facing her. Ruth shivered with the delicious sensation as he kissed her palm and then nuzzled it.

"Most of the time I use both hands to dress," she teased softly, and freed her hand to caress his face, touching the sensitive, intelligent features and stroking his fine, sandy-colored hair away from his forehead. Her liberty to touch him filled her with a sense of luxury.

David closed his eyes with the pleasure her light exploration aroused in him. "I can explain to you in scientific terms the whole sequence of what you're doing to me," he told her, grasping her hand and holding it against his cheek-bone.

"Tell me," Ruth prompted, and listened with fascination and almost no comprehension as he complied without defining his terminology. She was vaguely familiar with a few terms related to the brain makeup, like *hemisphere* and *cortex*, but it was all mumbo jumbo and she didn't have an inkling as to the meaning of words like *neurons*, *axons*, *synapses*, and *neurotransmitters*.

"That was very enlightening," she teased when he'd finished. "Now that I understand, I'd like to do it again." Gently she tried to free her hand.

"What I can't tell you—" David released his grasp and waited while she stroked her fingertips on his face again. "What I can't tell you," he said softly, "is why one woman's touch is more special than another's, despite the fact that they both set off the same electrical impulses. For all our technological knowledge about the brain, physical preference is a mystery.''

"Maybe there are some things we aren't meant to understand, just enjoy," Ruth suggested in a light, happy voice. "I can't think of one good reason I'm here at this moment having this conversation with you, but I'm glad. And since it was your idea, I won't worry my head about it." She molded her palms to his forehead playfully. "After all, you are supposed to be a genius."

David brought her hand down to his lips, kissed it and then sat up to lean close and kiss her on the lips. "There's a big difference between intelligence and wisdom," he told her softly, and kissed her again, more deeply, cupping his hand around her neck. "That has about the same effect on my brain as a frontal lobotomy."

"A 'frontal lobotomy,'" Ruth repeated with feigned horror. "How terrible. That's a cruel operation, isn't it? The one that was done on patients in mental hospitals, like the poor guy in *One Flew over the Cuckoo's Nest*?"

"Actually it can be a very kind operation," David contradicted. "It's been refined and isn't quite as drastic as Kesey depicted it in his book and the film."

"Is it still being used, then?"

"Not much in this country because of all the adverse publicity, but in other countries it's performed in cases where no other treatment is successful in easing a patient's torment."

"I think it's the idea of a person not having any say over whether his personality is going to be changed that bothers people."

"Altering the brain is irreversible. It's the center of emotion as well as intelligence, but not the heart." David made the conversation intimate again with his smile and his tone, making them both aware that they were sitting close, talking between kisses. "I guess it's too late, though, to clear up that inaccuracy. Can you imagine a love song with lyrics like 'Be careful with my head, my love'?"

"Or 'Please don't break my head'!" Ruth offered laughingly.

"How about 'Since my lover left me, I'm suffering with head pain.'"

They entertained each other and bypassed the issue of David's impaired judgment where Ruth was concerned. It wasn't a day for probing, serious discussions, for clearheaded thinking or sound perspective, all of which would have put into question the intimate pleasure they took in each other.

Following the leisurely schedule that had dictated the pace of the day from the time they'd driven onto the peninsula, they abandoned their grassy slope after a while and continued walking, venturing out at one point onto a narrow high spit of land with plunging depths on both sides.

David stood behind Ruth with his arms around her waist, holding her against him. She shivered, gazing out at the awesome view, and thrilled in the sense of danger.

"Imagine jumping out of an airplane at this height." David's comment revealed that he was in tune with her.

"And hoping that your parachute opened."

"That must be a very exhilarating feeling."

"Yes, it must," Ruth agreed softly, and felt his arms tighten in response to her message: *No more exhilarating than what she was experiencing at the moment.*

Retracing their steps, they picked up the trail again and took it to lower terrain, coming eventually to a bare hilltop with the visitors' center in view some distance below. Holding hands, they descended, heading toward the two-story building where they'd begun their walk.

"I could use a snack," David remarked.

"So could I. I'm starving." Ruth smiled back at him.

"Then maybe we can take a turn at the telescopes. There's a nature film on the peninsula, too, or at least there was the last time I was here."

There was an ease between them now, an intimate rapport that only heightened the newness. Everything was fun and sensual—ordering food at the lunch counter, eating it at a table outside overlooking the glaciers, dropping the quarter for the telescope and having it roll away to the feet of a small boy, who scooped it up and put it in his pocket, sitting in the darkened little theater and watching the nature film, David's arm around her shoulders.

When the shy little marmot was shown, they smiled at each other, remembering their earlier conversation at the outset of their walk.

"I forgot all about him," Ruth whispered.

"So did I," David whispered back. He couldn't appreciate the film, because he was glancing over at her to catch her expressions. Every time she murmured her appreciation for a beautiful scene, he wanted to promise to show it to her. "That's not too far from here," he bent over close to her ear to tell her when shots of Lake Crescent brought an audible intake of breath. "We have time to take a drive there, if you'd like to."

Ruth smiled at him and nodded, eager at the idea. "I'd love it!" she whispered.

The return trip back down to sea level was exhilarating in its own way, as the drive up had been, with roller coaster dips and turns and spectacular vistas. David pointed out the San Juan islands and the city of Victoria, across the Strait of Juan de Fuca in British Columbia.

In Port Angeles they picked up Highway 101 again and, once out of the city limits, were soon driving through stretches of forest with little evidence of human habitation.

"Would you like to hear some music?" Ruth asked.

"Sure," David replied, and left the selection to her when she didn't ask him for a request. He waited, his curiosity growing, as she looked through all of the tapes and chose one. When the music of Vivaldi filled the car, he looked over at her wonderingly. "How did you know that was exactly what I was hoping you'd play?"

Ruth smiled at him, openly pleased. "I thought you might be in the mood for something classical. And that's the only classical tape you brought." She listened with a rapt expression and then hummed along a few bars. "I've heard this before and always liked it, too. It's a beautiful piece of music."

David reached for her hand, and she gave it to him. He squeezed it and then linked his fingers closely with hers and found a comfortable resting place on the center console. They enjoyed the music together in silence for several minutes.

"There's a lodge at Lake Crescent," David said quietly.

"I know," Ruth replied just as quietly. "Friends of mine have stayed there."

They looked at each other searchingly.

"There isn't likely to be an available room, not this time of year."

"Especially not on a weekend," Ruth agreed regretfully.

Neither of them said any more about staying together that night on the peninsula, but the clasp of their hands was more intimate and their glances at each other continued the communication. They were both deeply reluctant to return to Seattle and have the magical day end.

At Lake Crescent Lodge, they stopped in the public parking area. It was adjacent to the grounds but separated from the cluster of buildings visible in the distance by an open field, so that the noise of car engines and slamming doors wouldn't intrude upon the serenity of the lodge's setting. As they got out of the car, David pointed out the sign, across the paved road, that marked the entrance of the trail to Marymere Falls.

"It's a beautiful walk, but steep and rugged in places." He tucked Ruth's hand in the crook of his arm. "I think you'd enjoy it better starting out fresh and energetic."

Ruth's cheeks colored with faint embarrassment as she met his eyes. It was easy to follow his train of thought. If there were a room available at the lodge, they could walk the trail together in the morning after they'd spent the night together.

"I'm not in the mood for a strenuous hike right now," she admitted.

"Good. Neither am I."

The lodge itself was a mammoth old two-story wooden building with a kind of homely dignity, a matriarch presiding over twin rows of tiny cabins. The cabins were spaced apart, and each had a front porch facing the steel-blue lake, which was shadowed by dark green mountains on its northern and eastern shores. It was an utterly peaceful, secluded setting with a deep sense of quiet and yet not eerie. Here and there people were moving about, but no one seemed to pay any notice to David and Ruth as they approached, arm in arm.

Two elderly men on the wooden pier near the main lodge caught their attention. They were tossing bits of bread into the water, feeding a fast-growing flock of wild ducks.

"Let's go watch!" Ruth suggested. David immediately agreed, walking with her out onto the pier.

"Evidently the news is out that there's a free bread banquet," he remarked with dry humor and pointed. "Here come three more."

He and Ruth watched the new arrivals as the ducks zoomed in and skidded to a fast halt on the surface of the water, not wasting a second joining the splashing, raucous competition for the bread bits coming in generous handfuls.

"What a landing technique!" David marveled. "Although 'landing' doesn't seem like the appropriate word, does it?"

Ruth smiled in agreement. "But I can't think of another one." She drew in a deep breath, feeling the air in her lungs, and glanced around, approving of everything, the bright-painted wooden rowboats at the shore's edge nearby, the little storybook cabins, the lodge, the placid dark lake and evergreen-forested mountains. "I'm not at all great with words," she murmured wistfully, knowing that she could never express her sense that their surroundings were exactly right in every way. "All day I've been wishing I'd been a better English student," she added ruefully.

"I know what you mean," David said softly. "There are times when we all wish we were poets. The peninsula has a way of bringing out the need for eloquence."

They smiled at each other and then glanced simultaneously toward the lodge entrance, where several people were emerging. "Let's go and have something to drink," David suggested.

The main room of the lodge was enormous, high-ceilinged and somber with a great stone fireplace and various sitting areas designed to accommodate a large number of guests. Taking up a relatively small portion at the front was the check-in station, with a hotel clerk, who was occupied talking on the telephone. David glanced at him but didn't pause, taking Ruth on a tour of the big chamber instead.

She gazed around, intrigued and slightly overwhelmed. It was totally unlike the usual hotel lobby. The vast amount of wall space was covered with a profusion of pictures and memorabilia. Ruth got the impression that the collection had grown over many years and not been dusted often. Glass exhibit cases contained Indian artifacts. Taking up a rear corner was a bar. Through a door near it they entered a long, narrow sun porch used as a lounge, with white wicker furniture and colorful cushions. Its windows overlooked the lake, making it a very inviting room.

David guided her toward one end, where no one else was sitting, before Ruth could voice her wish that they might have the drinks there, in the cheery room. He seated her on a comfortable settee but remained standing himself, saying quietly, "If you'll excuse me, I'll be right back."

Ruth met his gaze, answering the question in his eyes and assenting to his mission to go to the front desk. "What if the waitress comes?" she asked. "Do you want me to order for you?"

He smiled ruefully. "A glass of white wine. Possibly followed up by a cup of coffee."

She didn't have to ask him when he returned minutes later and sat next to her what he'd learned. His face and his body language told her there hadn't been any available rooms for the night.

"I didn't think there would be," she said sadly, reaching for his hand.

"Neither did I, but I hoped luck might be on our side."

Ruth didn't question his sense of finality. She didn't need for him to explain why he wasn't suggesting they look for other overnight accommodation along the route they'd driven that day. Surely there was an available room in one of the motels or even in a quaint bed-and-breakfast establishment.

But to embark on a search and take whatever they could find might cheapen and spoil the magical accord that had grown between them all day. If there had been a room, they would have made love. Taking that final step of physical intimacy would have been as delicately suspenseful, as inevitable and as beautiful as their first kiss.

Neither of them wanted anything less. It would be too disappointing.

Chapter Seven

The moment they emerged from the lodge and began to walk to the car for the drive back to Seattle, Ruth had to deal with an awkwardness that had been missing all day. She didn't feel free to express her poignant thoughts and feelings, for fear of bringing up the future.

"It's odd to think that I passed so close to this lodge once," she reflected wistfully, wishing that she could say what was in her heart: Thank you for bringing me here today. I wish we could come back again someday.

"With your ex-husband," David said quietly after a pause.

"Yes. The day we drove around the peninsula."

Ruth regretted having said anything at all as they walked along in silence. It was the first "wrong" conversation all day, where they hadn't communicated but just spoken words. Now she had no idea what he was thinking.

He hadn't once referred to their ever seeing each other after today, and, of course, neither had she. Until now, focusing entirely on the present hadn't seemed conscious or restricting to Ruth but simply natural. Each moment of the day had been all-absorbing, taking them on a journey into a microscopic realm of personal discovery where time had no meaning, where an indrawn breath, a smile, a flicker of expression, were significant, delightful.

Now they had to go back, face up to reality. The necessity seemed tragic somehow to Ruth, even though she didn't question it. She wanted to cry when they reached the car, where the sign locating the trail to Marymere Falls seemed like a symbol of all they'd never do together, all they'd never share. David glanced at it with a somber expression that hinted that his thoughts weren't happy ones, either, but he said nothing.

As soon as they were in the car, Ruth started looking through the tapes, desperate to destroy the serious, suspenseful mood that had come over them. She wanted to talk openly, and yet she didn't trust herself, not until she'd gotten a grip on her emotions.

"I think we both need to hear something cheerful," she said, feeling his eyes on her. "Any suggestions?"

"Play whatever you want to hear."

He sounded disappointed, as though she'd let him down. There was none of the curiosity or indulgence that had been in his voice all day when he'd given her the same choice.

Ruth swallowed at a lump in her throat as he started the car and backed out. "Would you rather just hear this same tape again?" she asked uncertainly, reaching to push the Vivaldi tape back into the player. David had ejected it when he'd stopped the car.

"No, play something else."

Ruth put the Vivaldi tape back in its case, inserted her selection and sat back, tense and unsure. She'd picked a collection of popular tunes from movies and plays and was glad she had when the music of the first number filled the car. It was a favorite of hers from *My Fair Lady*. She relaxed, listening to it, a sad perspective easing away her uncertainty and awkwardness.

"I love that movie," she told David, and smiled at him when he glanced over with a sober, questioning expression. "I watch it over and over when it plays on TV. It would almost be worth buying a television and a VCR just to have my own video tape and be able to see it when I wanted."

"I've never seen the movie. I've seen the Broadway play."

His reply was faintly grudging with the same undertone of disappointment. He didn't realize, Ruth reflected, how the answer emphasized the gulf between them, showed how he took for granted a cultural background that was so entirely different from hers.

"I guess the story is the same," she went on. "It's a complete fairy tale, of course, as much as Cinderella. A girl from the lowest level of society could never improve herself enough to be the wife of a man like the professor, who's educated and cultured."

David's quick glance was penetrating. "Plus there's the age difference," he said with a note of irony. "No, I doubt there's any realistic basis for the plot of *Pygmalion*."

"No more than there was any realistic basis for today," Ruth said gently. "But it was a wonderful day." Please, let's not spoil it, she pleaded silently.

"Yes, it was," he agreed tonelessly, and was silent a moment, concentrating on the road ahead. Ruth didn't dare say anything, wondering what his next words would be. "I don't quite see where the story of Professor Higgins and Eliza Doolittle or the original Pygmalion myth it's based on is apropos to you and me," he said finally. "In both instances, a man creates the woman he falls in love with. The sculptor literally carves her out of stone, and the professor educates and refines the human raw material."

"I didn't mean to draw any comparison!" Ruth protested, mortified that he'd made that interpretation. "It was the fantasy element I was pointing out. I wanted you to know that I understand completely why we could never be seriously involved. You're much too nice a man to say outright that I'm not the right woman for you, even though it's true."

"Is that a reverse way of saying that I'm not the 'right man' for you?" he asked quietly.

Ruth stared at his profile, completely taken aback that he might in any way feel rejected by her effort to state the truth. "I don't dare even think about that," she said earnestly. "Otherwise, I run the risk of not being satisfied with any of the men I meet who are nice, ordinary guys. I've already experienced that," she added, remembering her date with Larry Osborne.

David looked over at her closely. "Have you met someone?"

Ruth experienced another little shock wave at his intensity. It wasn't a casual inquiry. "No one special," she replied, and felt compelled to explain. "Larry Osborne, the same man who waited on you Monday at the store, has asked me out a couple of times. I've been out with him once."

"Was that on Monday night?" David met her surprised glance. "When you said you'd been out for beer and pizza, I assumed it was with a man."

"Have you met anyone?" It was Ruth's turn to dread his answer, which didn't come at once.

"I've met a couple of women I could probably enjoy seeing."

Ruth waited a moment for the constriction in her chest to ease before she asked, "What kind of work do they do? Or do they work at all?"

"They're both career women. One is a neuroscientist, and the other one is a stock broker."

"A neuroscientist," Ruth repeated bleakly. "She must be very intelligent. I guess you two would have a lot in common." He wouldn't have to explain to a woman with similar knowledge of the human anatomy what effect touching his face had upon his nervous system.

"Professionally we do, but then so do you and your co-worker."

"Did you meet her at the party you went to last night?" After he'd already invited me to go with him today, she thought silently.

"No." David's sideways glance was perceptive. "I'd already met her when I saw you at the store on Monday. You said Osborne had asked you out a couple of times. Did he want you to do something with him today?"

"Yes. There was a party at his apartment complex. He invited me to come."

David nodded. "You'd have gotten to meet some people. But you'd already agreed to today with me."

"I figured there'd be other parties at his complex," Ruth said softly. "But no other chances like today."

David reached out his hand, and Ruth linked her fingers with his in a warm clasp that felt thrillingly familiar. "I'm glad you didn't cancel out on today. I'd have been terribly disappointed. All week I've been looking forward to spending the day with you here on the peninsula."

"So have I." Ruth's emotion tightened her throat and made her voice come out husky. "I felt so sad when we were leaving the lodge, knowing that the day would soon be over. That's why I said and did all the wrong things.''

"I guess I want too much," David said quietly.

Ruth's heart hammered with a strange blend of hope and dread. "What do you want?"

He didn't answer at once. "I want you to feel, as I do, that seeing each other isn't a matter of rational decision. But you obviously don't feel that way."

"But you haven't said anything all day to make me think you intended for us to see each other again!" Ruth protested, stirred with the deepest regret that she'd fallen short of his expectations.

"*Intent* has little to do with it," David admitted hesitantly. "I never intended to be attracted to you in the first place, but I am and have been, from the first time I saw you."

"And I'm very attracted to you, but that still doesn't change the way that nurse looked when she saw you standing with me outside the store on Monday. Or how you looked, either," Ruth added with gentle reproach. "But, please, do we have to talk about it? Today isn't over."

"No, it isn't," David squeezed her hand in acquiescence.

They rode several minutes in silence. Ruth sneaked looks over at him and finally got caught when he glanced her way.

"What does your ex-husband look like?" he asked, taking Ruth completely off guard.

"Tom?" She had to adjust to the question. "He's about six feet tall and has brown hair and brown eyes. Most women would say he's quite attractive."

"Is he the same physical type as Osborne?"

"I guess. What does the woman you've met who's a neuroscientist look like?"

David frowned at the transition. "Evelyn Payne's her name. She has short blondish streaked hair and blue eyes, a

different shade of blue from yours, without the gray."
Ruth's gaze wavered under his scrutiny of her irises. "Not
nearly as pretty, in my opinion," he added.

"Is she thin?"

David smiled at the morose note. "Yes. She's small, actually."

Ruth nodded. "Petite. She sounds cute. How many degrees does she have?"

"Three, I assume, unless she skipped a master's and went
straight for a doctorate."

"She must have a high IQ, too. I guess the two of you
would almost be guaranteed to have children who were ge-
niuses."

"Then I'd definitely pass on being a father," David said
feelingly. "I'm pretty much decided on that anyway."

Ruth regarded him questioningly and with a hint of dis-
approval. "You're serious? I'd think you would consider it
almost an obligation to have children and pass along your
genes."

"The only way I'd want children was to know that they'd
be of normal intelligence. I wouldn't want to inflict my kind
of childhood or adolescence on my own offspring."

"Were you very lonely?" Ruth asked with a rush of sympathy.

"Extremely lonely. I felt isolated much of the time,
growing up. My parents spared what time they could for me,
but they both had medical practices. Probably they
shouldn't have had a child, although I'd never tell them
that."

"My parents probably shouldn't have had eight." Ruth
felt faintly disloyal as she offered the rare confidence and
knew from his quick inquiring glance that he'd picked up
immediately on her guilty undertone. "You'd never have felt

isolated or lonely growing up in a family the size of mine, crammed into a small living space.''

"I suppose you had a total lack of privacy."

"Total. I'd never say this to my parents, either, since I wouldn't hurt their feelings for anything, but I feel pretty much the way you do. I'd never want to see a child of mine grow up the same way. That's something I've never said to anyone before," she admitted.

"I wondered if being an older sister in a large family had turned you against having children," David commented thoughtfully.

"Maybe it did. It's just as well, though, considering how my marriage turned out. Have you ever been even close to getting married?"

"No." His answer was completely without hesitation.

"Haven't you been in love?"

Now he did hesitate. "I was infatuated once, but she was married. There was no affair, even. Actually she was completely unaware that I was smitten."

Ruth's pulse quickened with the outlandish intuition that he was talking about her. "It sounds as though you just created a fantasy."

He smiled faintly. "That's what I told myself. But like our good professor and talented Greek sculptor, I was so taken with my creation that no other woman could compare."

Ruth had to make two tries before she could muster her voice. "You got over her, of course."

"I thought I had. Until recently I hadn't consciously thought of her in years."

"David!" Ruth tried to pull her hand free as she murmured his name in protest, but he tightened his clasp as he continued in the same, quiet tone.

"Now I find she isn't married, and not only is my old fantasy intact, but it doesn't seem to be a fantasy. In reality she's much as I imagined her."

"I don't know what to *say*." Ruth's voice conveyed her confused emotions. She was deeply flattered on the one hand but just as deeply disturbed at the idea of her being some kind of romantic ideal for him. "Why, of all the women you must have seen and noticed...?"

"I can't answer that. And I have wondered," David admitted gently.

For the first time he was indirectly agreeing with Ruth that they weren't suitably matched. For all her insistence on the subject, she felt a dull wave of rejection wash through her.

"Things make more sense now," she told him, looking unseeingly out through her window. "The fact that you remembered me, invited me to lunch Monday, made this date for today...." And had been the perfect, romantic lover all day, she thought.

"It wouldn't be honest or fair not to tell you and then ask to see you," David said quietly. "And I do want to see you."

Ruth squeezed her eyes shut briefly, summoning strength, and then turned her head toward him with a wan smile. "Give yourself a month and see if you still feel that way after you've been out with some other women, like those two you mentioned, had time to make friends and get settled into a routine."

"During which time you'll be going out with Osborne and other men you meet."

Ruth shrugged aside the jealous note in his taut response. "I'll be doing the same things you are," she said earnestly. "Working at my job, meeting people, making a new life. I'm hoping that coming back to Seattle will turn out to be a good move for me. I want to give it every chance."

David was silent for a long moment, waging a mental argument he kept to himself. "A month, then," he said finally, then squeezed Ruth's hand and gently unlaced his fingers.

Ruth consoled herself joylessly that she'd done the right thing for both of them. In a month's time he might not have forgotten her, but he would have changed his mind by then. He'd be busily involved in a life that wouldn't and shouldn't include her.

"Is something wrong with the engine?" she asked dully, becoming aware that they'd decelerated.

"No, I'm just slowing down, making today last as long as I can."

He smiled over at her, coaxing her to lighten the mood with him. Ruth had to hang on tight to her judgment as her lips curved in a bittersweet response that started deep inside her. Humor lighted his clear intelligent eyes and was reflected in his face, giving a boyish attractiveness to his sensitive features, but he couldn't quite hide his disappointment. There was just the faintest hint of the lonely quality she had detected in him years earlier. It tugged much more strongly at her now.

She braced herself, knowing that if he asked her at that moment to back down on the time restriction she'd imposed, she might weaken. But he didn't mention it again, not even humorously. He could have undermined her fears with playful complaints, tried to wear her down with light pleas and been successful in having his way, she suspected, but he made no attempts.

Apparently he intended to abide by her decision without any further word. Was it a combination of pride and respect for her wishes? she wondered, illogically hurt. Or deep down was he secretly relieved for the reprieve she'd granted him?

They talked about a variety of topics, alternated tapes to play as an accompaniment and had comfortable periods of silence when they looked out at the scenery and listened to the music, but there was an element of anticlimax. The excitement and the magic were gone. David was just as attentive a companion, managing to make Ruth feel as though her opinions and thoughts were of real interest to him, but he'd drawn something of himself back.

Returning to Seattle by a different route, they took the Edmonds-Kingston ferry to the mainland. Darkness was falling as David drove up the ramp. Ruth remembered with a pang of sadness her rush of exhilaration that morning when they'd driven onto the Bainbridge ferry as they started out.

"You'll probably get chilled standing outside," David remarked as they got out of the car. "Why don't we go up to the snack bar and have a cup of coffee?"

"Okay." Ruth agreed against all her deepest instincts, which cried out for a different passage. She wanted to stand with him at the rail and shiver with the bite in the sea breeze, watch the receding shoreline, *feel* the day coming to its conclusion.

"Or would you rather stay outside?" David's offer seemed plainly hesitant.

"Not if you don't. You're probably right. It'll be cold outside."

The ferry was filled to capacity, many of the passengers, like Ruth and David, returning from a day's outing on the peninsula, others permanent residents of Kingston or the surrounding area who were going to the mainland for more sophisticated dining or entertainment. She took irrelevant notice of the fact that some of those abandoning their cars

GIVE YOUR HEART TO SILHOUETTE®

FREE!

Mail this heart today!

AND WE'LL GIVE YOU
4 FREE BOOKS,
A COMBINATION
CLOCK/CALENDAR
AND A FREE MYSTERY GIFT!

SEE INSIDE!

⊷ IT'S A ⊱

SILHOUETTE HONEYMOON

A SWEETHEART

OF A FREE OFFER!

FOUR NEW SILHOUETTE SPECIAL EDITION® NOVELS—FREE!

Take a ''Silhouette Honeymoon'' with four exciting romances—
yours FREE from Silhouette Books. Each of these hot-off-the-press
novels brings you all the passion and tenderness of today's greatest
love stories . . . your free passport to a bright new world of love and
adventure! But wait . . . there's <u>even more</u> to this great offer!

COMBINATION CLOCK CALENDAR—ABSOLUTELY FREE

You'll love your new LCD digital quartz clock, which also shows the
current month and date. This lovely lucite piece includes a handy
month-at-a-glance calendar, or you can display your favorite photo
in the calendar area. This is our special gift to you free with this
offer!

SPECIAL EXTRAS—FREE!

You'll also get additional free gifts from time to time, as a token of
our appreciation for being a home subscriber!

MONEY-SAVING HOME DELIVERY!

Send for your Silhouette Special Edition novels and enjoy the
<u>convenience</u> of previewing six new books every month, delivered
right to your home. If you decide to keep them, pay just $2.49 per
book—26¢ less than what you pay in stores, plus 69¢ postage and
handling per shipment. Great savings plus total convenience add up
to a sweetheart of a deal for <u>you</u>!

START YOUR SILHOUETTE HONEYMOON TODAY—
JUST COMPLETE, DETACH & MAIL YOUR FREE OFFER CARD!

SILHOUETTE BOOKS

FREE OFFER CARD

FREE CLOCK/
CALENDAR

MONEY-SAVING
HOME
DELIVERY

PLACE HEART
STICKER HERE

4 FREE BOOKS

PLUS AN
EXTRA BONUS
MYSTERY GIFT

YES! Please send me my four SILHOUETTE SPECIAL
EDITION novels, free, along with my free Clock/Calendar
and Mystery Gift as explained on the opposite page.

335 CIL 81ZT

NAME _____
(please print)

ADDRESS _____ APT _____

CITY _____

PROV. _____ POSTAL CODE _____

Business Reply Mail

No Postage Stamp
Necessary if Mailed
in Canada

Postage will be paid by

Silhouette Books®
P.O. Box 609
Fort Erie, Ontario
L2A 9Z9

Canada Post
Postes Canada
125

CLIP AND MAIL THIS POSTPAID CARD TODAY!

were well dressed, while others were in casual clothing. As she filed ahead of David up a narrow series of stairs and walked with him into the snack bar, it didn't cross her mind that she would encounter anyone she knew.

They were standing in line for coffee when she spotted Neil Frazier, who'd been their neighbor when she and Tom had lived in the same apartment complex. He was immediately recognizable, even at a distance, a swashbuckling figure several inches taller than any of the men near him, with broad shoulders and a rangy build, a full dark beard and the inevitable camera bag slung over his shoulder.

"I see an old friend!" Ruth exclaimed, a smile breaking over her face. "If you don't mind, I'll go and say hello to him."

David followed her gaze. "No, of course I don't mind."

Neil spun around in surprise as Ruth spoke his name when she was several steps away.

"Ruth, sweetheart!" he boomed in his deep voice, and threw his arms wide. Embracing her in a bear hug, he picked her up off of her feet. "Where's that lucky son of a gun Tom?" he demanded, glancing behind her when he'd put her down, keeping a big arm loosely around her shoulders.

Ruth brought him up to date on her current status, including how she happened to be on the ferry, and then asked him questions, learning that he still worked for Boeing, had the same apartment and was still devoted to photography.

"Still a bachelor, too, I take it," she speculated.

"Hell, yes," he said, grinning. "I've been waiting for you to shake loose of ole Tom. Seriously, I'm sorry to hear about you two, but his bad luck is a stroke of good luck for us single guys. You and me'll have to get together, bend an elbow—" He broke off as David joined them, holding two Styrofoam cups of coffee, his expression scrupulously polite.

Ruth took the one he held out to her, thanking him, and performed the introductions, identifying Neil as a former neighbor. Neil took his arm from around her shoulder to shake hands with David.

"Not a relative, I take it," he remarked affably, and grinned at Ruth. "Hell, it looks like I'd have to change my name to ever get in on the ground floor with you. So where'd you two go on the peninsula today? I was over on the Pacific side myself." He patted his camera bag tenderly. "Got some great beach shots for a magazine spread I'm hoping to sell."

David replied that they'd gone to Hurricane Ridge and Lake Crescent.

Neil whistled. "Must have been some view up on the ridge today." He looked pained when he inquired whether they'd taken any pictures and learned they hadn't.

"I didn't even think to take my camera," Ruth spoke up regretfully, vivid mental pictures flashing through her head of beautiful scenes with her and David in the foreground. "But then it's only an instamatic." She blushed, meeting David's eyes and reading his question: What pictures was she thinking that she'd like to have on film for keepsakes?

"I have several cameras. You would have been welcome to use one," he told her. "Personally I find that it requires too much dedication to try to capture a day on film. You have to take a hundred pictures to get one good one." And he'd been busy today with more enjoyable pursuits than photography, he added in another silent communication with Ruth.

Neil asked David what cameras he owned and came alive with interest when David told him, naming off the various lenses as well. After conducting a rapid-fire test conversation with David on lenses, film and photographic technique, Neil was soon unzipping his bag and taking out a camera for David to examine and admire.

Ignored for the moment, Ruth watched and listened with interest, her admiration for David growing. It was obvious, even to her, that he had an enormous store of technical knowledge on the subject of photography, and yet he didn't try to impress Neil or show him up but let Neil take the lead and responded courteously.

The delicate, sure manner in which David handled the camera called Ruth's attention to his hands. She thought of the skilled, complicated surgery he performed and had doubts that this moment or today was real. Then she remembered the strength of his fingers interlocked with hers, the exquisite gentleness of his palm stroking along her back, his fingertips caressing her face. The recollections were so vivid she had to suppress a shiver of warm, delicious pleasure.

"What line of work are you in?" Neil broke off to ask David, interrupting Ruth's sensuous reverie.

"Medicine," David replied.

"A doctor, huh?" Neil didn't show any surprise. "Specializing?"

David handed Neil's camera back to him. "Surgery."

"That takes a lot of years of hospital training, I understand." Neil sounded sympathetic.

"A year's internship and then four to six years of hospital residency, depending on the subspecialty. The average is five years total, I'd say."

Neil whistled. "When we're complaining about our doctor bills, most of us don't stop to think what a long haul it is, becoming a doctor. That's how many years altogether, counting four years of college and three years of med school?" Neil did the mental calculation. "Twelve years?"

He shook his head. "And then you have to study and pass boards, right?"

David hesitated almost imperceptibly. "Right."

"You guys deserve to make those big bucks that you can expect to earn when you finally hang all those medical certificates on the wall and start building a reputation."

Ruth realized that Neil assumed, based on his guess at David's age and the fact that he was with her, that David either hadn't finished his medical training or wasn't established. Before she could get past a moment's indecision and speak up to correct his error, David asked Neil what kind of work he did and the opportunity was lost.

To Ruth's disappointment, they ended up chatting with Neil for the entire ferry crossing. He seemed glad for their company, and when David didn't excuse them, she didn't have the nerve. Now and then her attention drifted to the large windows, but outside it was dark. There was only the vibration of the engines to indicate that they were moving through the water.

Neil gave Ruth an affectionate hug around the shoulders when he told her goodbye after the ferry had landed. "It was great luck, running into you like this, kid. You're just as pretty as ever. Give me a ring sometime, and we'll get together and talk over old times." He unwrapped his long arm and extended his hand to David with genuine friendliness. "Nice meeting you, Bradford. Hope to see you again—on a nonprofessional basis, of course. Take care." He raised his hand in a casual salute and strode off.

"It's impossible not to like the guy," David remarked as he ushered Ruth toward the stairs.

"Everyone likes Neil," Ruth replied, finding David's remark puzzling. "Did he look like someone you wouldn't like?"

"He has that blatant kind of masculinity that most men wish they had."

"Neil's a lamb. Any time I had a little crisis at the apartment and Tom wasn't there, as he usually seemed not to be, I could always bother Neil if he was around."

"I got the distinct impression that he'd be readily available as your handyman now, even if he had to drive across town," David said sourly.

"That's just his way with women. He makes a big show, but he'd actually rather spend time in his darkroom than with a woman. You notice he didn't have a date today. It's his dream to be a full-time professional photographer. He has a real dead-end job with Boeing that he's hoping to quit."

"So I gathered. How long has he been trying to establish himself in photography?"

"I would guess at least ten years. When Tom and I first met him, seven years ago, he'd apparently been seriously into photography for some time. He'd sold a picture to a national magazine and was all excited, hoping that it was a big break."

"Ten years. That's a long time to work at a job you don't like and keep your hopes alive."

"Not many men ever know what it's like to be among the top in their field, like you are," Ruth told him as they were reaching the stairs. "I hope someday Neil does make it big, poor guy," she reflected, walking down ahead of him.

"I hope so, too," David said from behind her. "I'd like to see him get a big assignment, preferably somewhere far away from Seattle."

Chapter Eight

Ruth was conscious that time was short as the wheels of the car rolled onto solid land. The drive from Edmonds, north of Seattle, to the city and her apartment wouldn't take more than an hour. Since this was her last opportunity to get a glimpse of David's professional side, about which he hadn't talked all day, she plied him with questions, asking about the hospital training Neil had referred to and his work as a surgeon.

His answers were clear but without any enthusiasm, his tone indicating that his mind wasn't fully on the conversation. She could tell he was occupied with other thoughts while he explained the residency system to her, telling her briefly how it had originated almost a hundred years ago and was still in effect, with minor changes.

"It's basically an apprenticeship plan with on-the-job learning and graded responsibility. The first year, you scrub in and mainly observe and assist, accompany the chief of surgeons and the various attending surgeons on rounds, follow their diagnostic procedures and postoperative patient care. By the fifth and sixth year, you're actually performing complicated surgical procedures with the attending surgeon standing by to assist.''

''Isn't it frightening, that first time you have a person's life in your hands?'' Ruth drew upon her limited knowledge, based on TV and movies, and imagined David in surgeon's garb in an operating room.

''Yes, but by then you've been through a necessary depersonalizing kind of process. The operating room itself is a clinical environment with various team members doing their jobs—the technicians, nurses and whole pecking order of assisting operatives, from beginning resident to perhaps the chief of surgeons. The patient is draped in sterile sheets so that only that part of the anatomy that's being operated on is exposed. His or her vital signs are responses on sophisticated instruments. There's never a moment when you're unaware that a human being's life hangs in the balance, but you have to concentrate totally on the procedure that you wouldn't be performing if there weren't a dire necessity.''

Ruth hesitated, gathering her nerve. ''How *do* you operate on the brain?'' She reached up and touched her head, feeling the hard bone of her skull. ''How do you . . . get to it?''

''Neurosurgery involves more than the brain. The spinal cord and the entire nervous system come under the neurosurgeon's domain,'' David pointed out, suppressing a sigh. It was hardly the conversation he wanted to be having with her, but she obviously wanted to steer clear of personal talk at this point. He was first and foremost a prominent doctor to her, anyway, not a man with needs and emotions.

"When it is necessary to gain open access to the brain, we have to do a craniotomy," he went on, and briefly explained the process, glossing over details she might find gruesome. "Actually only the preliminary and final stages of the surgery require anesthetic, since the brain itself has no sense of pain. In some instances a local anesthetic is used and the patient is awake—when he or she is an epileptic, for example, and it's necessary to determine what portion of the problem area in the brain that is causing seizures can safely be removed without impairing speech or thought or other major functions."

"You mean, you don't already *know* when you operate?" Ruth asked, horrified and yet fascinated.

David glanced over at her with a faint smile. "Not precisely. Every human brain is different, unique." He was silent, his amusement fading. "We know a lot, but there's even more we can't explain. How personality forces like motivation, willpower and ambition originate in the brain, for example. Why some people have them more than others and some seem to lack them altogether. Emotion is largely an enigma. We can observe outward behavior and measure body changes, like heart rate, but we can't scientifically define feelings such as hatred. Or envy, shame, pride, contentment, love, disappointment." His voice lowered on the final two examples, setting off a whole range of disturbing body changes in Ruth.

"If you could come up with an operation to implant willpower, you'd certainly make a fortune with all us dieters who don't have any resistance to food," she joked desperately, avoiding his glance.

"Resistance to temptation is yet another mystery," he said quietly, after a pause. "We all have weak points in our armor. I hope this doesn't seem like inopportune timing, but

I was about to ask if you'd like to stop somewhere along the way for dinner."

"Are you hungry?" Ruth asked miserably. His inquiry was clearly nothing more than politeness. He wanted to get the final parting over with.

"No, not especially."

"Neither am I," she admitted, and sighed, wishing that the day didn't have to end on such a down note.

"Temporary loss of appetite isn't a serious cause of concern," David chided her gently. "You'll need to see a good doctor, though, if it persists. Seriously, please do call on me if you should happen to have a health problem of any kind," he added earnestly. "I can always make inquiries and refer you to someone highly respected."

"Thank you. I certainly will," Ruth said bleakly. "Knock on wood, but I'm usually healthy as a horse." His sincere offer seemed to finalize what she assumed, that after tonight she wouldn't see him again.

"You have the telephone numbers I gave you."

"Yes, I do."

Conversation lapsed, and Ruth felt separated from him by miles. When they entered the outskirts of the city, about to make full circle of the day's journey, their intimacy and closeness over on the peninsula seemed like a dream.

Even their good-night kiss was a disappointment, calling into question the magic of their kisses and even the slightest touch up on Hurricane Ridge.

"Don't bother to get out. I can walk to the door by myself," she told him when they arrived at her apartment. "Thank you. I had a wonderful day."

"So did I."

He leaned over to kiss her on the lips. Ruth met him partway and kissed him back, closing her eyes, but she was tense, braced for these last moments, and so, she sensed, was he. Neither offered to deepen the kiss. David ended it, resting his forehead against hers briefly before he drew back with an air of apology.

"I guess it was the altitude affecting us," Ruth said with a wan smile. "Good night, and thanks again."

"Good night." David touched her on the cheek with the back of his fingers.

It was a tender farewell caress and brought the smarting pain of tears to Ruth's eyes. He was saying *goodbye*, not *good night*. She opened the car door and got out quickly before she made a fool of herself. With a little wave, she headed blindly up the walk.

She didn't hear his car engine start until she'd reached the door. By the time she'd gotten upstairs to her apartment, he was gone. She stood at the window where she'd watched for him that morning and felt empty and sad, looking out at the deserted curb.

David braked for a stop sign several blocks from Ruth's apartment. Searching through the tapes, he chose one he'd bought for her and played it. The music vividly brought back her presence and eased his loneliness and sense of letdown.

His reason told him Ruth had been right to put him off. David couldn't honestly argue with her that having an affair with him was a good idea, for her or for him. If he'd been surer, he might have tried to undermine her judgment.

It stung him that she could be clearheaded when he couldn't resist the sweet, wonderful attraction between them. The fact that she wasn't willing to gamble meant that it was stronger for him than it was for her. She had an appeal for him that no other woman had ever had, but he didn't touch a corresponding chord in her. She was more impressed with him than drawn against her will by his personal qualities and delight by his physical presence.

He would definitely keep the pact with her, try to put her out of his mind, try not to be encouraged that she hadn't ruled out a relationship with him altogether.

The next morning when Ruth awoke, a faint depression lingered, but she shook it off impatiently, determined not to mope. Her philosophy had always been to accept what couldn't be changed and live in the present.

After she'd had a cup of coffee, she went out for the Sunday paper. Back inside, she postponed reading it until after she'd called her mother. Listening to the distant ring of her parents' phone, she prepared herself for hearing all of her mother's worries. In a large family, there was sure to be one or more problems at any time, and her mother carried them all around on her shoulders. Ruth felt obligated to get in touch often and listen. The calls seemed to mean so much to her mother, and they soothed Ruth's conscience a little for the fact that she was glad, deep down, that she was too far away to do more than sympathize.

"Hi, Mamma. How's everybody?" She spoke cheerfully into the receiver when her mother, sounding harried, answered the phone. In the background was the noise of a loud video game and boyish shouts and laughter.

"Brian and Billy, you turn that racket down! It's Ruth Ellen calling long distance," Betty Cook scolded shrilly, making Ruth flinch and hold the receiver away from her ear. "I was hoping that was you when the phone rang," Betty said in a voice that was more normal but that still held a telltale undertone of anxiety. Something more than usual was wrong. "I'm terribly worried about your daddy. He's been having pains in his chest this last week, and I can't get him to go to a doctor. He insists it's just indigestion."

"Maybe it is indigestion," Ruth suggested, trying to keep her own voice clear of her immediate concern. "Has he been eating a lot of heavy fried food?"

It was a silly question, Ruth knew. Frying was her mother's main method of preparing food. Any vegetables she didn't fry were seasoned with bacon grease. Ruth's weakness for fried, fattening foods could be traced to her diet when she was growing up.

"He's been eating normal. Naturally I'm scared it's his heart. He don't want to take off from work, spend the money to see a doctor and then find out it's really nothing serious."

"Peace of mind would be worth a lot."

"That's what I been telling him, night and day. I thought I almost had him talked into going, but then Leonard Purser told him how his brother-in-law went to a doctor for chest pains, got examined and hooked up to a special machine to test his heart. Everything looked normal, and he paid his bill, which amounted close to a hundred dollars. It's a crime these days, what doctors charge. Anyway, he walked out the door and fell dead on the sidewalk with a heart attack. That story pretty well killed any chance of your daddy going to the doctor."

"You can't force him," Ruth pointed out sympathetically. "The pains must not be severe, or he'd be worried. I'm sure he'll go if they continue."

"I guess you're right." Her mother sounded heartened. "So how's everything with you? We all miss you something terrible. I don't know why you had to move off so far."

"I miss everybody, too. How's Heather? Does it look like she'll be able to carry the baby full term?" Ruth evaded what was too delicate to try to explain and diverted her mother's attention to Ruth's sister-in-law. Heather and

Kevin, Ruth's twenty-five-year old brother, were expecting their second child.

"Her doctor says so, but I'm doubting it. Kevin's bringing Kevin Junior over in a little while for me to watch him. He's a handful, spoiled rotten, and just can't understand why his mommy can't pick him up." Her mother chattered on, touching on every member of the family before she broke off on a note of self-reprisal. "But here I am, doing all the talking, as usual. Tell me about you. Everybody'll want to know."

Ruth gave a cheerful, positive account of her week, mentioning that she'd been out with a nice man who worked at the store. She eliminated any mention of David or yesterday's trip to the peninsula.

At the end of the call, her father's health came up again, reviving her concern. After she'd hung up, she sat a moment, coping with her usual aftermath of emotions, a mixture of nostalgia, guilt and relief, which was stronger today than usual because of the added fear that something serious might be wrong with her father.

Ruth knew that chances were that the pains would have gone away next week when she called, and her mother would be concentrating her worries on another member of the family.

If Ruth were closer, she would be just as helpless to do anything, she reminded herself. She could only add her nagging advice to her mother's, and her father still wouldn't buckle under. He was a strong-willed, stubborn man. Not that he meant to be unreasonable. He just couldn't justify an outlay of money to see a doctor for himself, when there was never enough money to go around. She knew he would have a different attitude if something were wrong with his wife or one of his children.

She thought of David's well-intentioned offer. "I hope you'll call me if you have a health problem of any kind," he'd said. "I can inquire and recommend someone highly respected." For him, health care was simply a matter of consulting a qualified medical expert. He couldn't conceive of a world in which seeking medical attention was a financial decision.

That was the kind of world in which Ruth had grown up, the world to which she had strong family ties. Despite her need for distance, she could never reject her background or be disloyal. Tom hadn't been able to understand that. His contempt for her upbringing had turned out to be one of the basic problems undermining their marriage.

The telephone conversation with her mother strengthened Ruth's awareness of the great gulf between herself and David Bradford. She took a small consolation in knowing that she'd acted wisely in denying herself further contact with him. In time she'd be able to think about him and yesterday without a dull sense of loss.

During the next week, her problem was that time dragged and hope lurked somewhere inside her, against her judgment and will. While she didn't doubt that David would abide by her wish and not try to see her, whenever she glanced around in the store and caught a glimpse of a man who vaguely reminded her of him, her heart would pound wildly. Then she'd droop with disappointment when a closer look showed that the man was a stranger. On the infrequent occasions when her telephone rang at her apartment, she'd undergo the same panic and the same letdown after she'd answered and heard some voice besides his.

By the second week her vigilance had dulled and changed. When she noticed a slender fair-haired man with a casual air of distinction, her heartbeat seemed to slow with her despairing certainty that he wasn't David, who wouldn't appear or call her during the month she'd stipulated or after it, either. Still, without realizing it, she was marking time. As she woke on the Saturday two weeks following the day on the peninsula, her first thought was *Today's the halfway point.*

A call to her parents put everything immediately into clear perspective again, evoking her home environment. Her mother was thankful to report that her father's chest pains hadn't gotten any worse or more frequent, even if they hadn't disappeared. Betty had slacked off pressuring him to see a doctor, with other worries dominating. Heather had been ordered by her doctor to remain in bed for the duration of her pregnancy, another two months. Betty had to babysit for little Kevin Junior, plus do Heather's housework and cooking. Ruth didn't bother to suggest that her brother take on those woman's chores. She knew the answer: Kevin was a man and worked hard all day.

Adding to Betty's state of frayed nerves was the fact that they were waiting to hear bad news on twenty-three-year-old Jimmy's job situation. He expected to be laid off any moment. Married and with two children, he was head over heels in debt, with a mobile-home mortgage, automobile financing and credit card bills he and his wife, Trixie, had run up. Both were extravagant and spent every penny he made.

"Me and your daddy will have to try to keep up his trailer payment," Ruth's mother lamented, sighing. "Otherwise, they'll lose it and won't have a place to live. We don't have the room for them to move in here."

"Jimmy hasn't been laid off yet," Ruth pointed out soothingly. "If he is, he might get another job right away." She knew from experience that suggesting that Jimmy and Trixie should learn the hard way to manage their own finances would fall on deaf ears.

"It never fails to give me a lift to talk to you," her mother said gratefully. "You always look on the bright side of things. You've been like that all your life. You were even a happy little baby, hardly ever cried. It's pure selfishness that makes me wish you lived closer, but I hope everything works out real good for you way up there and you find what you want out of life."

Ruth had to contend with a big lump of emotion in her throat before she could speak. "Everything's fine with me, Mamma. My job's great, and I'm busy."

"Becky said to tell you she plans to write off for a catalog from that big university in Seattle." Becky was Ruth's seventeen-year-old sister, who would be a high school senior in the fall. She was a straight-A student and had aspirations for being the family's first college graduate.

"The University of Washington. I'm sure the out-of-state tuition would be high," Ruth warned mildly, knowing what was coming. The uneasiness her intuition stirred made her feel vaguely guilty.

"Naturally she's thinking that she could live with you and give your address. She said she didn't know why you didn't think about taking classes part-time and getting a degree yourself. You're plenty smart enough. But then that girl has college on the brain," Betty scoffed fondly. "I told her you have a good job and make a nice salary without any college education."

"I guess I could go to college now." Ruth was shocked to hear her own words. She'd never even consciously considered the idea of going to college. It was having a degree that appealed to her, and the reason was immediately and disturbingly clear. With a college degree she'd be more on an intellectual par with an educated man like David. "It would take twice as long, going part-time," she pointed out to her mother, trying not to sound deflated by her reasoning.

"And I don't know what I'd study. Business, I guess." She sighed silently. By the time she'd earned a degree, David would have gotten over her completely. Besides, a college education wouldn't remove all the other barriers between them.

The rest of the morning as she cleaned her apartment and did chores, Ruth mulled over the idea her mother had planted. Even if she didn't get a degree, she could take college courses, improve her mind as well as possibly enhance her job potential. It would boost her morale, if nothing else, to prove to herself that she could have gone to college, had things been different.

She'd passed her high school courses easily, despite the fact that she'd never applied herself. There had simply been no motivation to excel. She hadn't grown up in an environment where college was the next step after high school. It was assumed that she'd marry and have children, as her mother had done. Her peers had all been in favor of sliding by and having a good time, and studying was all but impossible at home.

Thinking back to her high school classes, Ruth remembered the old stir of restlessness at having to sit at a desk while a teacher droned on and life passed outside. She'd been too full of energy to want to read textbook assignments and concentrate on memorizing dry, meaningless information. Life still beckoned to her too strongly for her ever to be a scholarly type, and yet now there was an appeal in learning that was a by-product of her brief association with David. He made being educated attractive to her in a way it hadn't been before.

In the afternoon she went to a branch of the public library, trying to remember the last time she'd been in one. After applying for a card, she browsed, feeling overwhelmed and discouraged by all the volumes of information. She found herself in the medical section eventually, and her attention focused and she stopped fooling herself. She'd come to the library for more than just to absorb the atmosphere of stored learning.

On the bus as she took her stack of books home, she understood the curious, sympathetic expressions of several other passengers who noted the titles, all relating to surgery, hospitals and the brain, and then glanced at her head. They evidently wondered if she wasn't doing research because of some alarming personal condition.

She guessed she was, in a way. It seemed she had a hopeless case of fascinated interest in a man outside her sphere.

The next week she suddenly seemed besieged with social opportunities, and Ruth was actually torn, regretting the loss of her reading time, but she forced herself to go out with Larry Osborne and accepted invitations for lunch and dinner from several of her former married friends. At Jane and Bob Zimmerman's she met a divorced male friend of theirs, Tony Freeman, who promptly asked her out.

Meanwhile, chance encounters with her neighbors led to introductions and friendly chats, opening up avenues for future friendships and making her feel more settled in and at home in her apartment house. She got to know some of her female co-workers better and through them met other single or divorced working women, several of whom were taking college courses and encouraged her to do the same.

As she neared the end of a month with no contact with David, Ruth's life had opened up and promised to be full. She already knew enough people so that she didn't have to be alone when she wanted company, and she would continue to meet others, make friends, build a whole network of relationships. It bothered her that she didn't feel more buoyant about her prospects for a busy, happy life.

By choice she had no plans for the weekend when David would be free to see her again, if he still wanted to. Larry had invited her over to his apartment complex on Saturday afternoon for a cookout with neighbors. Tony Freeman had suggested a drive on Sunday to Mount Rainier National Park, located to the east and south of Seattle. Ruth had made excuses to both men.

She just felt like a quiet weekend, she told herself, knowing deep down that she was lying. Even though she didn't expect to be hearing from David, she just couldn't take the risk that he might want to see her and she wouldn't be free. Come Monday, she'd put the whole encounter with him behind her and resume the business of living in the present.

On Friday she found herself glancing around hopefully as the noon hour approached and realized that she'd been harboring the possibility that he might appear and take her to lunch a day before the month had ended—to Ivar's, of course. She went there alone and ate, discarding her futile yearnings along with her empty plate when her solitary meal was over.

David wouldn't call or want to see her this weekend. He'd come to his senses. It was time Ruth came to hers.

The store was swarming with customers on her return. She plunged into work gratefully, deciding that she'd offer to trade shifts with someone and work the next day. Saturdays were always busy, and she would go home tired. Sunday she'd figure out something to do, and the weekend would be over.

Two hours passed before there was a lull. She finished handling a purchase and glanced around, the smile she'd summoned for her customer lingering on her lips as she looked for Jeanie Cooperman, who was scheduled to work the next day. But all thought of Jeanie and volunteering to work vanished at the sight of David heading toward her, his eyes searching her face. For a second she went numb with surprise and then she was flooded with an overwhelming rush of joy.

"David!" She spoke his name as she came quickly from behind the counter to meet him. "What a nice surprise!" She smiled at him, knowing that her gladness was transparent, but it didn't seem to matter. He looked equally happy to see her.

"How are you?" he asked softly, sticking his hands into his pockets. The warmth in his eyes and his voice told Ruth he would have taken her into his arms if he'd followed his true inclinations.

"I'm fine. What about you?" she returned eagerly, trying to register the incredible fact that he was there.

"Everything's going well professionally. How are things here with your job?"

"Great. Just great."

"I'm one day short of your deadline," he said apologetically, and hesitated. "But I've made plans to camp on the peninsula this weekend, and I wanted to see you."

Ruth's heart plunged at his serious tone and expression, as well as at the disappointing news. Had he come to tell her that he'd found a suitable companion? "What's a day?" she said, trying to sound light. "I envy you. A weekend camping on the peninsula sounds wonderful."

David took a breath. "I'm planning to camp at a really beautiful spot, right on the shore of Lake Quinault. The rain forest is there, with beginners' hiking trails, and the Pacific beaches are within driving distance. Lake Quinault Lodge is nearby and has an excellent dining room. It isn't even necessary to cook." He faltered under Ruth's wide-eyed comprehending gaze.

"Cooking outside sounds like part of the fun of camping," she replied faintly. *He wanted her to go camping with him on the peninsula this weekend.*

David looked intensely hopeful. "You'll love the location," he urged.

"I'm sure I will," Ruth said softly, giving herself as well as him her answer. Without delving into any of the implications of accepting his weekend invitation, she just couldn't say no to spending two days and a night with him on the peninsula.

"You'll go." David reached for both of her hands and held them in a tight grip, his face showing his struggle to believe she'd accepted. He obviously hadn't been optimistic.

"If you're sure you want to take a chance on a complete novice," Ruth demurred, suddenly unsure of his reaction. What if she hadn't said yes? Did he have someone else in mind to take instead?

"I made the plans with you in mind, knowing I'd more than likely be camping alone," David confided softly. "I didn't dare let myself believe the weekend would work out the way I imagined it. For one thing, I knew it was highly unlikely that you'd be free. In a month's time I expected you to have weekend invitations from other guys you'd been seeing."

Ruth was awed and touched by the yearning in his eyes and his voice. He really wanted to know whether she'd kept her weekend free for him, she realized. "I wasn't in the mood for socializing this weekend," she confessed, giving him the answer he desired.

"Then I didn't know either whether you were scheduled to work," he continued, thanking her with his eyes.

"No, but when you showed up just now, I was just about to volunteer to work in someone else's place tomorrow."

Ruth glanced around self-consciously, aware suddenly that she was standing in her place of employment, holding hands with him, totally oblivious to being observed.

"Another case of split-second timing," David mused thoughtfully, and squeezed her hands before he released them. "Can I call you later and discuss specifics for tomorrow? Will you be at home around six-thirty?"

"I should be home all evening," Ruth replied, and blushed at the hopeful note in her voice.

"I have a dinner party," David said regretfully. "It's not something I could cancel out on at the last minute, I'm afraid."

"Of course not. I wouldn't expect you to," Ruth protested quickly before he could add the obvious: Nor could he take her along as his date. The number of guests would be fixed. He'd already be matched up with someone, whom he might be escorting. "You'll call about six-thirty, then?"

"Without fail," David promised. "Whether I'm home, at the hospital or in transit. I can't tell you how much I'm looking forward to this weekend."

Ruth knew from the concern in his expression that she hadn't been able to hide her feeling of slight at having been excluded from his evening. He was much too perceptive.

After he'd gone, she mulled over her fleeting perception unhappily. Had there been just the faintest suggestion of guilt mixed in with his apology? There was no doubting his gladness at seeing her, his sincerity in anticipating a weekend in her company on the peninsula, but was she someone he could envision taking to a dinner party with his social equals and medical friends?

Ruth was besieged by all her former doubts about a relationship between her and David, and yet she knew she wouldn't back out of the weekend with him. She just didn't have the strength of self-denial.

Chapter Nine

The next morning Ruth phoned her mother early, before David came to pick her up. She hadn't called the previous weekend and knew her mother would be answering every ring eagerly all morning and Sunday, too, in the hope that it was Ruth. Ruth would be selfish not to call, just to avoid being reminded of her home environment and depressing family problems as she set out on the weekend with David.

Her brother Jimmy's job situation was still tenuous, and Heather was bored and restless, having to keep to her bed with four weeks of her pregnancy remaining, but Betty Cook's main concern once again was Ruth's father. He continued to have the chest pains and had even admitted to some fear himself that his heart might be the source of the problem.

"If he's still having pains by Monday, he's promised me he'll see a doctor," Ruth's mother told her worriedly. "I just hope he doesn't have a heart attack in the meantime."

It was an effort for Ruth to be upbeat and offer a soothing blandishment when she was forced to cope with her own stab of dread at the thought of her father stricken with a heart attack. Aside from her deep concern for him personally, there were chilling practical considerations, too.

He was the breadwinner, with three of his eight children still living at home. Betty Cook had never held down a paying job and was ill equipped to take over her husband's role of supporting the family if he were disabled or—Ruth shied away from even thinking about the other frightening possibility: death.

Her usual pragmatic reasoning, that she might as well not worry about something she couldn't prevent, failed her today. When David arrived, she hadn't been able to clear her mind, and he immediately detected that something was wrong even though she greeted him smilingly.

"What's the matter?" he asked hesitantly, taking her small suitcase from her hand. "I hope you aren't having second thoughts."

"No, it's just a family matter," Ruth assured him. "I called home this morning, and I'm a little worried about my father's health." If David hadn't made the assumption that she was disturbed about going away for the weekend with him, she wouldn't have confided in him, but once she had, it was a tempting thought to get his reaction as a doctor to her father's symptoms.

"I'm sorry to hear he's ill. What's the problem?" David asked sympathetically, guiding her down the brick walkway to the car.

"He isn't exactly ill. He's been having chest pains, actually, for more than a month." It was easy for her to remember the time span, since she'd received the first news of her father's condition on that Sunday following her day with David on the peninsula. "He's put off seeing a doctor, insisting that it was nothing serious. My father's never been a great believer in going to a doctor for every ache and pain. The fact that he's decided to go is what worries me."

"In the majority of cases, chest pains are not an advance warning of a heart attack," David said gently.

"They aren't?" Ruth asked, relieved.

"No, but your father definitely should consult his primary-care physician and check into the symptoms he's having."

The conversation was halted at the car while David opened the passenger door for her and stowed her suitcase in the trunk. He resumed it as soon as he'd slid under the wheel and started the engine.

"There may be other important symptoms besides the chest pains that will indicate the nature of your father's problem," he informed Ruth calmly, checking for traffic before pulling out onto the street. "His doctor will know what questions to ask. To be on the safe side, he'll undoubtedly order a cardiogram, which shows whether the patient has already suffered a mild heart attack. He may also have your father wear a heart monitor for at least a twenty-four-hour period. If an irregularity shows up, then the next step is for your father to consult a cardiologist, who can order further tests and make a diagnosis."

"A cardiogram, then, doesn't tell whether a person is in danger of having a heart attack."

David smiled at her, picking up at once on her knowing tone. "No, it doesn't," he replied. "A cardiogram shows whether a patient has suffered a previous heart attack. It's the test that's featured in all those stories about patients walking out of the doctor's office with a clean bill of health and then keeling over with a massive coronary."

Ruth's answering smile was a confession that he'd read her thoughts. "My father heard a story just like that from one of the locals. I feel a hundred percent better now, just talking to you," she told him gratefully. "It was selfish of me, I know, to bring up a medical topic when you're on your off time."

"I don't mind in the least. Although I wish you'd called me, instead of worrying for a whole month," David admonished. "Not that I'm in a position to put to rest your fears about your father's health. He might have a cardiovascular problem, but there's a great deal of medical knowledge and expertise in that field, and certainly there should be excellent care available in Texas. I'll do some checking. Which major city would be the most conveniently located for him?"

"Dallas is the closest really big city," Ruth replied, merely to be cooperative. David didn't understand that her family wasn't in the income bracket to go off to a big city and seek the best medical help.

"I'll make inquiries about the best hospital facilities in Dallas and find out who the top men are, just in case your father should need the information."

"Please don't go to a lot of trouble," Ruth protested.

"It's no trouble. But it wouldn't matter if it were. I'd want to do anything in my power to help you in medical matters," David said quietly. "That extends to members of your family, since you obviously have very close ties."

"That's taking in an awful lot of people," Ruth told him, deeply touched by his sincerity. "I do have very close ties to my family," she admitted. "Despite the fact that I like living some distance away from them."

"Which causes you to feel guilty?" David asked with quick perception.

"Yes. I'm sure you don't feel that way about living in a different part of the country from your parents."

"No, I don't," he agreed without hesitation. "They're very busy with their own lives, and even though I'm sure they'd be glad to see me more often, my absence doesn't leave any gap for them at this point. I've been gone from home since I went away to college at sixteen."

"Do you keep in contact?"

"More or less. Either they call me or I call them every couple of months or so."

"Do they expect you to come home for big holidays, like Christmas and Thanksgiving?"

"I'm welcome to, but, no, I can't say that they 'expect' me to or that it's especially important to them. My parents aren't big traditionalists where holidays are concerned."

"Our situations are about as much alike as daylight and dark," Ruth marveled with a note of envy. "I've been gone from Baker ten years, and I never call home or visit when my mother doesn't put a guilt trip on me because I don't live closer. She's already started pressuring me about when I'll be home for Christmas. Maybe it's a southern custom to make a big deal about the whole family getting together at holidays and especially Christmas. Tom's mother felt the same way about him coming home, too."

"How did you work that out?" David asked, his curiosity overcoming discretion. "Did you alternate years or split the visits, spending part of the time with your family and part with his?"

"The first year we were supposed to spend an equal number of days with both our families, but it ended up that we spent most of the time at Tom's house, including Christmas Day. After that I went home by myself. The two following years, when we were living here in Seattle, we'd fly to Houston and he'd stay there with his folks while I used one of his father's cars to drive to Baker. After we moved to Houston, well, then I used my own car, of course."

David was quiet, managing not to speak his thoughts. She'd just told him Dallas was the closest large city to Baker, and yet they'd flown to Houston, accommodating Tom, rather than her. "Tom did go with you at other times besides Christmas to visit your family, didn't he?"

"No." Ruth's answer was prompt and matter-of-fact. "He visited my parents twice, once before we were married and then that first Christmas. After that he didn't want to go, and I didn't insist. It would just have put a strain on everyone if he'd gone and been miserable."

"But that must have been terribly awkward for you." David was unable to keep from sounding a little outraged on her behalf. Tom Bradford sounded like a completely self-centered jerk to him.

"Yes, it was awkward," Ruth admitted. "I felt very bad for my parents' sake. Plus I couldn't help being resentful that I was expected to fit into Tom's family. But fortunately that's all past history now and not worth talking about. Tell me about Lake Quinault. Quinault must be an Indian name."

David wasn't really ready to drop the subject yet. He wanted to express his low opinion of her ex-husband and suggest in a tactful way that she shouldn't generalize from her admittedly rotten experience and assume that all men would be as insensitive of her feelings as Tom Bradford evidently had been.

But seeing that such a discussion could become very personal, he took her conversational lead. "Quinault is the tribal name of the Indians whose reservation bounds the lake on the southwest end. The Quinaults have control over the use of the lake—they issue fishing permits and so on. The Olympic National Park owns the northern shore of the lake, and the southern shore, where we'll be camping, is a national forest. Aside from the old lodge I mentioned and a ranger's station, the whole area is virtually unpopulated.''

Ruth asked him interested questions and put aside every care as they left Seattle behind and took a southern route to the campers' paradise he described. When they'd been driving about an hour, they stopped for breakfast in Shelton and then looped down through Elma, Montesano, Aberdeen and Hoquiam before turning north on Highway 101 and driving through miles of forests with few human habitations.

David had brought along a variety of tapes, including some new ones he'd bought by recording stars who were favorites of Ruth's. With the music in the background, she and David talked about one subject and then another, smiling at each other more and more often as the peace and remoteness of the peninsula worked its special magic.

''I missed you,'' David told her softly, reaching out his hand when their common need to touch each other could no longer be denied. ''I thought about you a lot.''

''Same here,'' Ruth admitted in the same tone. ''I've even been reading books I'd never have opened in a hundred years, thanks to you.''

David glanced over, openly curious. ''What books?''

Ruth told him about her trip to the library and her self-conducted study in his medical field. ''I'm finding it very interesting reading,'' she said a little uncertainly. She found his reaction difficult to judge. He didn't seem especially pleased. ''The more I learn about what you do and how much you have to know, the more I'm impressed.''

''Maybe you won't be when you hear how far behind I am in reading my medical journals,'' David caressed her hand with his fingertips, arousing little shivers of pleasure with his touch as well as with his soft, intimate tone. ''I take a whole stack of medical journals to bed, but I find myself fantasizing about you instead. I'm lucky if I get through one technical article.''

"It sounds as though we're having opposite effects on each other,'' Ruth observed ruefully. "Here I'm getting inspired and thinking of going to college at this late date, and you're losing your concentration.'' She was slightly disappointed that he hadn't responded seriously to her admiring interest in his profession, but it was impossible to feel slighted and meltingly warm with pleasure at the same time.

"Are you thinking of going to college?'' David asked with mild surprise.

"I thought I'd take some courses, as much to prove to myself that I could pass as anything else.'' Ruth tried to sound offhand and not show how much his reaction mattered to her.

"If that's the only reason, don't bother,'' David advised her indulgently. "There isn't any doubt that you can pass. I'm sure, for that matter, that you could be an A student if you wanted.'' He squeezed her hand and gave her a teasing sideways glance. "Even if you had a lady professor.''

"You don't seem to think it's a good idea for me to get more education.'' Ruth couldn't keep a note of hurt from creeping into her voice.

"I'm sorry,'' David said quickly. "I didn't mean to treat the idea lightly. Certainly it isn't too late for you to go to college, get a degree even, if that's what you want to do. Or just take courses that might be helpful or interesting.'' He paused reflectively. "Were you thinking of going to school part-time or quitting your job and becoming a full-time student?''

"I wouldn't quit my job,'' Ruth replied positively, rejecting the idea instantly. "I had in mind taking night or weekend classes.''

"Not weekend classes," David objected swiftly, and then coaxed her with a guilty smile, "Save your weekends for me and chances like this when we can get away. You can bring along your books and study." He grinned at his magnanimous offer. "I'll bring along something to read, too. Or I could quiz you for an upcoming exam." He brought her hand to his lips and kissed her knuckles one by one, raising delightful warm sensations in Ruth and blatantly undermining the notion of her concentrating on anything but him in his presence.

They dropped the subject of her furthering her formal schooling. Ruth didn't know how to interpret his apparently neutral attitude. He'd neither encouraged her nor been in any way negative. It didn't seem to matter to him whether she sought more education or stayed the way she was.

Later she would wonder about his reaction, she knew, and try to come up with an interpretation, but now she was too caught up in being with him. He had shed his reserve and was relaxed and fully attentive, as he'd been on their day's outing to the peninsula a month ago.

Ruth's anticipation had built to a level of bubbly excitement by the time they reached Lake Quinault at midday, checked in at the ranger's station, and then drove to the camping sites, located on a high wooded bluff with glimpses of blue water through the trees. David pointed out the bathhouse as they drove past it on an asphalt service road. The small concrete-block building was neatly painted a soft green that made it blend into its forest background. Entrances at either end were designated Women and Men.

"This is strictly tent camping," David explained as Ruth looked eagerly at the occupied sites, noting the variety of tents. "No RV's or electrical hookups, but as tent camping goes, it's pretty luxurious, with a picnic table, a cooking pit, a level tent bed and a paved parking pad." He pulled into a vacant site, killed the engine and smiled at her, excited, too, beneath his comparative calm. "Ready to help me set up camp?"

"You'll just have to tell me what to do!"

He drew in a deep breath of the evergreen-scented air that filled the car through their open windows. "It's been so long. I hope I remember the procedure." He grinned. "Actually I have to confess that I've done some practice pitching the tent."

"Where?" Ruth demanded, delighted with the sheepish sound of his confession.

"Would you believe in my living room?"

Laughing lightheartedly, they got out of the car and proceeded with setting up camp. "This is *fun*!" Ruth pronounced while they were erecting the tent, her exhilaration more than she could possibly contain. "And I love this place. It's just *perfect*!"

David stopped in the middle of what he was doing and looked at her. The moment suddenly became intense. "Yes, it is perfect," he agreed softly, smiling at her. "Thanks to the fact that you're here. I'm very glad you came with me this weekend."

"I'm glad, too," Ruth said, her voice almost a whisper. The yards separating them seemed filled with powerful magnetic currents pulling them toward each other. She wanted to move across the distance, succumb to the need for them to touch, kiss, make love....

David gave his head a little shake and grinned with an obvious effort, breaking the tension. "Do you know it took me a lot less time to put this tent up in my living room without any help?" he remarked ruefully. "But then I was only going to take it down again. Since tonight is your first time sleeping in a tent, I definitely wouldn't want it to collapse, not when I'm hoping to sell you on camping this weekend." He wanted everything between them to be perfect and not rushed, he added silently. Including sex, which should come later, culminating naturally, not taking priority.

"You're off to a good start," Ruth told him, smiling and holding his gaze in a warm, intimate communication that made words unnecessary.

He was as stimulated as she was by the knowledge that tonight they'd share the tent they were now setting up. He looked forward with intensity to making love, taking down all the physical barriers and sleeping together in naked intimacy, but he hadn't brought her to the peninsula just for that. There were other pleasures he wanted to share with her.

"You haven't lost your knack," she praised him warmly a few minutes later when they'd finished putting up the tent and stood admiring it, David's arm around her shoulders and her arm encircling his waist. "That didn't take long at all. I expected pitching a tent to be more difficult."

"It is, with the old-fashioned type of tent," David replied, looking proud and happy and utterly relaxed in a way she'd never seen him. "This tent is so well-designed that a couple of well-trained chimpanzees could handle it." He smiled at her teasingly.

"Thanks a lot!"

He hugged her shoulders. "I couldn't have asked for a better helper—or a prettier one." He kissed her lightly on the lips and then again, not so lightly. "Now, how about some lunch? I'm hungry. Are you?"

"That's a silly question," Ruth retorted cheerfully.

David looked her over possessively, noting the fit of her yellow plaid blouse and navy slacks. "I'm glad to see you haven't had any success with your dieting," he said, his gaze returning to rest on the rounded fullness of her breasts again before he looked at her face and smiled to see that she was blushing.

"I managed to lose five pounds, but then I gained most of it back again."

"And I managed to put on about the same and then got busy and skipped enough meals to drop it right off again."

"But you really don't need to gain weight!" Ruth protested. "I like you just the way..." She colored a deeper pink. "Your build is exactly right for you. I like the way you look," she said with soft determination.

"And I like your figure, very much." David took his arm from around her shoulder and clasped her hand. "For now, though, I think we'd better drop this discussion and take it up again later." His glance at the tent was eloquent. "It's a beautiful afternoon for taking a walk in the rain forest. I'd like for you to see it with the sun filtering through, and then maybe tomorrow morning the weather will be gray and misty, which gives an entirely different atmosphere."

"It sounds beautiful. I'd like to see it both ways." *With you,* Ruth added with her smile. "Do you want to have something to eat here, then, and go?" David had brought along a cooler packed with food, as he'd told her.

"No, why don't we walk along the lake to the lodge and have lunch there in the dining room? I think you'll enjoy seeing the lodge. Directly across from it are several beautiful hiking trails that we can take from there."

Agreed on their plans, they left the remainder of the camping equipment and supplies locked in the car and set out on foot. Hand in hand, they strolled along, following a pathway through the trees that led them to the highway. Once they'd crossed the highway, they picked up the path again and followed it along the edge of the lakeshore. A placid blue expanse of water unfolded to a distant green shore on their left and a wooded hillside on their right. Small frame houses were perched here and there among the trees, only their roofs and eaves visible from below.

"Look—over on that floating pier." David stopped Ruth to point out a sleek brown otter basking in the sun. They stood watching it.

"I wish I had a picture of it!" Ruth lamented.

David cursed mildly. "I brought a camera for you and forgot to mention it. Speaking of cameras..."

Ruth smiled at him indulgently. "I haven't seen Neil Frazier since that day on the ferry," she told him, willingly supplying the answer to the question she assumed was in his mind.

"I have seen him."

"*You've* seen Neil?" Ruth blinked at him, surprised. "What a coincidence that you should happen to run into him again."

"I didn't run into him," David corrected her. "I called him, and he invited me over to his place to see some of his photography."

"You went over to Neil's apartment?" Ruth tried to adjust to the idea that he had been to the same apartment complex where she'd lived with Tom. "I didn't think you were that interested in photography."

"It depends on the subject matter." David started them walking slowly again, and Ruth didn't give the slumbering otter a parting glance. She'd forgotten it. "Neil mentioned on the ferry that he had some good pictures of you. I managed to acquire some of them."

Ruth didn't know what to say. "He usually had his camera with him and was always taking pictures. I got to the point where I didn't pay him any attention."

"You're very photogenic." David's sideways glance was warmly caressing. "Your face isn't just pretty but expressive. Some of Neil's pictures of you are works of art. I think his real talent is photographing people, anyway, not scenery."

"Did you tell him that?"

"Yes. He's assembling a portfolio. I don't have a lot of contacts, but maybe I can at least get him in some doors."

"That would be just great if you could help Neil get a break!" Ruth exclaimed. She was still amazed that the two men had gotten together. It was impossible to visualize David in the surroundings that had been a familiar part of her past, but not wanting that past to intrude at all into the present, she didn't comment on her imaginative failings.

For now the past had no importance, and the future didn't exist. There was just that utter leisure of the moment, which she'd experienced only with David their last time together on the peninsula. Her one concern was the human inability to absorb the full range and depth of pleasure available to her in his company as she walked along with him, soaking in the sights and sounds and atmosphere. She'd never been happier or more carefree. It didn't matter whether her euphoric state of mind was reasonable or that it was surely transient.

They approached the lodge from the rear, crossing a gracious expanse of sloping green lawn. The large, main building was dark and severe, its architecture bringing to mind a huge gathering hall for Vikings.

"You'd think it was a library," Ruth murmured to David, glancing around at the guests. They all seemed to be engrossed in books, whether they sat in groups in the sunshine or were en route from one place to another, walking slowly but apparently with an instinct for their destination.

"It looks like a reading convention," he agreed in a low amused voice. "No name tags, though."

Virtually unnoticed so that they felt free to smile broadly at their own humor, they entered the capacious main lobby and guest reception area that was reminiscent of Lake Crescent Lodge with a somber, dignified atmosphere and a huge stone fireplace. In contrast, the dining room was bright and cheerful, with windows overlooking the lawn and the lake beyond it, each table draped in crisp linen and adorned with a little vase of fresh flowers.

Lunch was superb and elegant. They both ordered Lake Quinault salmon broiled in herbed butter, which their waitress, a plainspoken local woman, proudly recommended, explaining that the lake had several species of salmon that were unique to its waters. Exchanging secret smiling glances as they politely took her advice, both remembered Ivar's and the conversation about their preference for a common fish over salmon.

"Were you really intending to order fish and chips that day you bought me lunch at Ivar's?" Ruth demanded to know after the waitress had left.

"I was going to order whatever you did," he admitted. "It didn't really matter. The fish and chips was always my favorite, just as I told you."

"I don't know when I've felt more awkward and ill at ease," Ruth confided. "But then I'm sure I don't have to tell you that. It was obvious." Just as today she didn't have to tell him she felt relaxed, secure in the knowledge that she was there because he wanted her, and no one else, as his companion.

"I kept trying to read your reactions and coming up with wrong answers." David reached across the table to clasp her hand.

"And I felt like a pane of clear glass."

They smiled at each other, their present close sense of accord making the glance back in time seem pleasantly irrelevant. What mattered was now and how right it felt to be exactly where they were, together.

Their salads were served, interrupting the conversation, and they didn't resume it, concentrating on the meal instead and the present.

"That was the best salmon I've ever eaten," Ruth declared contentedly, after she'd swallowed the last bite of the food on her plate.

"I was thinking the same thing. But then the broccoli tasted outstanding, too, and I'm not a big broccoli fan." He smiled at her. "I think your company has a positive effect on my taste buds."

"I don't care for broccoli, either," Ruth confessed, and followed his amused glance at her empty plate.

"Will you have dessert and coffee? I'll bet their fruit and berry pies are good here."

"I think I'd better pass on dessert," Ruth replied with a note of regret. "But you go ahead."

"We'll be walking off the calories this afternoon," David pointed out, but he didn't insist. He did ask the waitress to bring two pie forks, though, and Ruth ended up helping him eat his blackberry pie à la mode.

"That's sinfully good," she murmured.

David smiled. "The best I've ever eaten."

They left the lodge through the front entrance and crossed the narrow black ribbon of highway to the dense woods opposite, where a painted sign marked the beginning of a nature trail through rain forest.

"I'm glad it's sunny today for your first time to see the rain forest," David told her. "The light is impossible to describe. Although I enjoy the atmosphere on an overcast day, too."

"I'm looking forward to seeing the rain forest," Ruth replied eagerly.

Privately she thought there was nothing special about the thick woods they entered, but she didn't speak the thought aloud, content to walk with David anywhere. A stroll down the quiet asphalt roadway would be delightful after the long drive and the leisurely, satisfying lunch.

Within minutes, though, she was wide-eyed with awe, clutching David's hand while she tipped back her head and tried in vain to see the tops of towering trees that soared out of sight, lost in the thick canopy of branches far up above. David pointed and mentioned the names: Sitka spruce, Douglas fir, hemlock.

"They must be a hundred years old! Look how *huge* that one is!" As much as she'd looked forward to seeing the rain forest, she was as unprepared for its primeval majesty as she'd been for the aerial splendor of Hurricane Ridge. She felt like a small child in a cool, dim forest cathedral. After the civilized comforts of the lodge, nature left to its own devices from time immemorial was all the more impressive.

Their footsteps were soundless on the path thickly carpeted with needles and moss. Everywhere was greenness and silence, the floor of the forest thickly grown with lush ferns and tangled vines. The sunlight pierced the heavy ceiling of vegetation with an occasional shardlike ray, but was otherwise diffused and filtered through the green, causing a mellow golden illumination.

"Do you see what I mean about the light?" David's voice was hushed, like hers, unashamedly reverent.

Ruth nodded and groped for a comparison. "It's kind of like you'd imagine being down at the bottom of the sea would be on a sunny day. Gosh, it's quiet, isn't it? It's hard to believe the lodge is just a few minutes away and those people are all reading their books. I keep feeling like I should whisper," she whispered, smiling at him sheepishly.

"Like you're an intruder."

"Yes."

They walked along a minute or two in silence, two intruders in perfect accord. "That's called a nurse log," David explained, following her curious glance at a huge decaying log with a line of stately trees growing out of it in a straight, orderly row. "As you can see, there isn't any exposed soil to speak of. Rotting tree trunks provide a soil medium for tree seeds that otherwise wouldn't germinate."

"A 'nurse log,'" Ruth repeated, intrigued with the term. "It sounds so kind and motherly. You just don't think in those terms with trees and plants, usually."

"No, you don't. I have this odd sense when I'm in the rain forest that I never have anywhere else, that I can *feel* the forces of creation at work, the natural harmony of life and death." David looked at her for a hint of understanding.

"Things growing and dying at the same time," Ruth said softly.

David gripped her hand tighter. "Precisely."

They walked for a while in close, comfortable silence, absorbing the solitude and sense of remoteness from civilization. After a while the path led into an open, parklike area that was dappled with sunshine, and then wound back into thicker forests with a hilly terrain. They paused to catch their breath periodically at the end of a steep climb.

The distant sound of rushing water gradually grew louder and then its source became apparent as they approached a rustic bridge over a narrow, deep ravine.

"A waterfall! Isn't it wonderful!" Ruth stopped on the bridge beside David, enchanted.

He slipped his arm around her shoulders, and she automatically encircled his waist and hugged him. "Lovely," David agreed softly, his eyes on Ruth's radiant face.

Ruth looked at him, smiling, and then caught her breath at his expression. He looked . . . *adoring*. The thought that she'd been about to share with him fled, and her heart started beating fast with the sudden emotional tension.

"When we were putting up the tent at the campsite, it was a temptation just to stay there," David said, his voice caressing her. "But then we wouldn't have had all the rest of this afternoon. And I wouldn't have missed a minute of it."

"Neither would I," Ruth whispered, and they kissed, with the joyous tumbling and gurgling of the little waterfall playing a natural lyrical accompaniment. Ruth reflected, there was still tonight ahead of them and more magical hours of pleasure leading up to it.

Chapter Ten

Most of the campsites were taken by the time they returned from their walk. Ruth glanced discreetly at the activities of her fellow campers. Supper preparations were in progress with charcoal fires burning in some of the cooking pits and saucepans heating on campstoves. She and David exchanged friendly hellos with several people they encountered.

Ruth found it a quietly communal kind of atmosphere with the knowledge that there were others enjoying their own little spaces of privacy, located some distance apart and separated by trees and natural screens of vegetation. She sniffed the aroma of someone's barbecuing food and met David's astute glance with a guilty smile.

"Smells good, doesn't it?" he commented.

She nodded. "After that lunch, I was sure I wouldn't be hungry again for twenty-four hours."

"You've had a lot of exercise. We've walked a number of miles."

They had hiked quite a long way and up and down hilly terrain in some areas. Ruth was pleasantly fatigued and glad to be arriving back at their campsite, where she had a feeling of homecoming at the sight of David's car and his tent.

"Why don't you go ahead and have a shower while I finish unloading the car and start a charcoal fire?" David suggested.

Ruth found the idea extremely tempting. "I should help you finish setting up camp," she demurred.

"You can help cook supper." Putting his arms around her, he held her while he kissed her, leaving them both a little breathless. "By the time you get back I'll be finished with everything else, without distractions. Then I'll go for a shower, too."

He wanted to ready the tent without her, for obvious reasons, still not wanting to rush anything. Ruth took the hint. She didn't want to make love feeling grimy either.

The bathhouse was functional and clean, reminding her of the shower room in the high school gym. Feeling refreshed by her shower but a little self-conscious at her clean-scrubbed appearance, she walked the short distance back to the campsite. It seemed intimate, somehow, to be returning to David without makeup but perfumed and powdered beneath her changed clothing.

He had everything done, the car unloaded, a charcoal fire going in the cooking pit with foil-wrapped packets of food on the grill, one end of the picnic table set, even with plastic place mats and stemmed plastic wineglasses. A butane lantern sat in readiness for lighting when darkness fell.

"It doesn't look as though you've left anything for me to do," Ruth said lightly, aware of his admiring scrutiny.

"Just relax. I won't be gone more than five minutes, I promise." He kissed her lightly on the lips and inhaled her clean, feminine fragrance. "You smell wonderful and look pretty, too." He caressed her cheeks with his fingertips and traced her full lips.

"I don't have makeup on," Ruth said lamely, suffused with weak pleasure at his touch and his nearness.

David drew in a sharp breath and stepped away with a reluctant expression on his face. "I've opened a bottle of wine. It's in the cooler. Would you like me to pour you a glass?" he asked in a caressing tone that did nothing to calm her quickened pulse.

"No, I'll wait for you."

After he'd left, Ruth stirred herself to movement and hung her damp towel to dry and packed away her soiled clothing. Then she sat at the picnic table, feeling utterly serene, looked around at the campsite and reveled in the tangible proof that she was there with David. She should have some sense of incredulity over the whole set of circumstances, she knew, but there was none.

Everything seemed so wonderfully *right*, though unlikely. The thought of his return in a matter of minutes filled her with expectation.

The first sight of him destroyed her complacency. She hadn't been prepared for the informality of seeing him fresh from the shower, his hair damp and neatly combed. The sandy color was darker and he looked more vulnerable somehow. Then there was the onslaught of clean male scent when he walked over to the picnic table and kissed her, smelling of soap. Plus the awareness that he found the whole situation disturbingly new, too.

"I never realized that taking separate showers could be this erotic," he remarked wryly.

He took the bottle from the cooler, poured pale golden wine into the two glasses and handed her one. Holding his gaze, Ruth tasted her wine while he tasted his, the silent communication more meaningful than any toast could ever be.

"This is a marvelous wine," she murmured, holding the coolness and light flavor on her tongue.

David smiled. "It is superb, isn't it? I think some worker messed up and put a common label on a prize bottle."

Ruth smiled back at him, taking another sip. "I think you're right. I love your sense of humor," she confided warmly.

"Careful, or you'll bring out the clown," David cautioned dryly, and then grimaced at the remark. "Humor can be a form of cowardice," he told her simply. "It's easier and safer to fall back on the light touch than to risk being open. Just now, for example. To hear you say you 'love' something about me has quite an effect, even if you do just mean an extreme form of 'like.'"

Ruth held his gaze, momentarily tongue-tied by her own confused emotions, among which was alarm at his unexpected seriousness. He smiled at her expression and stroked his fingers along her face in a tender caress. "I'll check on the food and then I'll sit down with you." Putting down his glass, he went over to the cooking pit and dropped to a crouching position, commenting, "The chicken's starting to smell good."

Stirred with misgivings, Ruth watched him as he began to unwrap one of the foil packets with care. Getting up with quick decision, she went over and squatted next to him.

"Why don't you let me do that?" she suggested, concerned that he might burn his surgeon's hands. "You said I could help with the cooking," she added when he glanced at her keenly.

"Don't worry. I'm being careful," he chided her gently. "I'm the old camping expert, remember?" Laying open the package with deft movements, he exposed the contents. The two chicken breasts, sprinkled with herbs, emitted a savory aroma. "Another thirty minutes or so and they should be done, I'd say." He glanced at her for confirmation.

Ruth had been admiring his hands, enjoying the physical proximity and wanting to touch him on her own initiative. So far she had always responded, never made an overture. "I should think so," she said agreeably, and rested her palm on his back as he proceeded to turn over the two other foil packets, which contained corn on the cob and potatoes, if Ruth judged from their shape.

"You should use tongs," she scolded, patting his back admonishingly and then gently rubbing the spot. "In your profession, you really can't risk injuring your hands."

"No, but a few scorched fingertips seem a reasonable price for all this solicitous attention I'm getting," he countered, smiling at her. "I'm almost wishing for leaping flames."

Ruth hugged him, loving the physical liberty. "This is fun, cooking over a rock pit in the ground," she reflected, sighing happily. "Camping out is kind of cozy, isn't it? I can see why you enjoy it so much."

"There's a simple domestic quality about it that's always appealed to me, but never quite this much before," David told her softly, leaning over to kiss her on the lips. "Enough food-tending."

He refilled their wineglasses and they sat close beside each other at the picnic table. "I'm getting a whole different view of you," Ruth commented. "You don't seem at all the domestic homebody type."

"Except for camping, I'm not," David admitted. "But, then, to be a homebody, you'd have to have a home, and that's rather an alien concept for me. I think more in terms of residence, I suppose."

"You probably always have maid service," Ruth speculated enviously, drawing an amused smile from him.

"Yes. I take it you're not fond of housework?"

"I don't mind doing it when I'm in the mood for it, but I don't like the drudgery element. The same with cooking." She made a self-derogatory face. "I was no prize as a homemaker. Have you ever lived with anyone?" She returned to more interesting subject matter.

"Not on any long-term basis. The times when I have shared my living quarters temporarily, I've always been glad when I was the sole occupant again."

"You sound like a confirmed bachelor to me. Maybe you've lived alone too long to adjust to living with someone."

"I don't think it's just that. How do you like living alone? You hadn't before your divorce, had you?"

"No." Ruth elaborated without enthusiasm, wanting to pursue his theory behind the preference for his single lifestyle. "When I left home, I had apartment mates until I got married. Living alone took some getting used to, but I've adjusted. If the right opportunity came along to share an apartment, though, I'd consider it, for the sake of economy as well as the company."

"How about sharing a condominium, with regular maid service?" David asked lightly.

"Don't tempt me," Ruth warned him, laughing. "I meant sharing with another female, of course. Half of your rent wouldn't be economical anyway, I'm sure."

"I'm not renting. I'm buying."

"Are you? What's your condominium like?"

"Is that idle curiosity or an interested inquiry?"

"Interested curiosity," Ruth retorted.

He described his condominium for her. They drank more wine and then ate supper in the soft twilight. With nightfall, a deeper quiet seemed to descend. Ruth could hear fish splashing out on the lake, as well as an occasional voice or laugh. When she shivered with the growing coolness of the night air, David went to the car and got sweaters and a blanket, which he spread on the ground next to the glowing embers from the charcoal fire.

"Sit here, where it's warm, while I clean up," he urged her. "It won't take me long."

"But I want to help," Ruth objected. "You've done everything."

"You can put the throwaway stuff in a garbage bag," he conceded, and began washing the few dishes himself with water from a plastic jerry-can. The whole cleanup took a minimal amount of time.

Afterward they sat very close on the blanket, his arm around her, and finished drinking their wine while it grew fully dark. He had lit the lantern earlier and turned it to a low setting, and it provided a dim illumination from the table, along with the embers in the pit.

"What are you thinking about?" Ruth asked him softly, sensing his abstraction.

David didn't hesitate. "I'm wondering when I last felt this happy," he said simply. "So far I'm coming up with 'never.'"

"I feel very happy, too," Ruth whispered, touched to the core and humbled by his sentiment. "It's been a marvelous day. I love being with you here on the peninsula."

"It's incredible how good together we are here," he reflected quietly. "I've never experienced anything like it. Did you want more wine?" The intimate note in his voice and his hand caressing her back and shoulders pressed her for a refusal that would be another kind of affirmative.

"No," Ruth said, her answer soft and definite. Her heart beating faster, she got to her feet with him. "I would like for you to go to the bathhouse with me."

"Of course. I'll get a flashlight."

It was an intimate prelude, walking together in the darkness, David keeping the flashlight on a low beam and training it just ahead of them, out of consideration for other campers. Whatever slight awkwardness there was in accompanying each other to take care of bathroom needs only added to the stimulating newness of camping overnight together.

Ruth was wondering what the procedure was for retiring for the night in a tent. Did they undress on the outside or inside? Either alternative was provocative as she thought of being naked with David, of exploring his body intimately and having him do the same with her, taking liberties with each other for the first time, really. For two people who were about to make love, there had been little sex play, she reflected. He'd fondled her breasts only with his eyes, and she couldn't wait for him to use his hands.

The lantern on the picnic table shed a dim glow over the campsite when they returned.

"Do you leave the lantern burning all night?" Ruth asked.

He smiled at her. "It'll be out of fuel in a couple of hours. Without it, it would be pitch black. Our bedroom isn't wired for electricity." At the tent he took her into his arms and hugged her tight against him. Then he opened the flap of the tent and fastened it so that the soft light from the lantern could illuminate the interior.

Ruth stepped out of her shoes and crawled inside over the sleeping bag, which took up most of the floor. "Gosh, this feels comfortable, almost like a mattress," she declared in surprise, sitting and bouncing up and down. David crawled in after her.

"You didn't think I had brought you off to the wilderness to sleep on the hard ground," he chided her, stripping off his sweater.

Ruth started to pull her sweater off, too, and he helped her, then tossed it over on top of his and combed her ruffled hair with his fingers.

"Do you know the sensible way for two people to take off their clothes in a tent this size?" he asked, framing her face and kissing her deeply before she could answer.

"No, how?" she murmured breathlessly.

He kissed her again, dropping his hands to unbutton her blouse, and then explained. "One person enters the tent first and undresses. Then the other follows and does the same." Ruth sat erect with her arms out a little, letting him tug her blouse free of the waistband of her slacks.

"You should have told me," she said, pretending to scold him. "You know I'm a complete novice at camping."

"I was counting on that." He slipped her blouse off her shoulders and slowly down her arms, his eyes on her breasts rounding out the cups of her lacy bra.

Ruth sucked in her breath audibly as he stroked the tender exposed curves with his fingertips. "Do you know you haven't touched my breasts before?" she murmured, aching for him to take all her fullness in his hands.

David smiled at her faintly accusing tone. "Not in reality. Nor seen them bare, either." He unclipped the center closure and gently peeled away the bra. "But I knew you would be a delicate pink here." He caressed the satiny aureola of one breast with the tip of his forefinger, making the tight little bud of her nipple protrude. "And I knew that your breasts would be beautifully shaped, and firm and lush."

"You knew?" Ruth breathed, and went weak with the sensual devastation of his hands lightly stroking her breasts and conforming to their fullness, like the hands of a sculptor admiring his handiwork.

"Cold?" David asked, responding solicitously to her shiver. He ran his palms over her shoulders and arms and back, warming them.

"A little." Ruth hadn't actually been aware of the chilly air against her bare flesh.

"We'll be warm inside the sleeping bag." He took off his shirt, baring his upper torso. When he unbuckled his belt, Ruth proceeded with her own undressing, turning to sit sideways so that she could extend her legs.

But taking off slacks from a sitting position turned out to be more of a problem for her than for him. "You're better at this than I am," she told him, amused at her own difficulties, which were caused in part by distraction. She was watching him more than paying attention to what she was doing.

"That's because I don't have hips." David came to her aid, kneeling beside her. Ruth dropped back on her elbows and let him take over, helping him by raising her hips. "And a sexy bottom," he added, tugging the slacks down around her thighs. She held the position for him while he stopped a moment to mark possession of her buttocks, caressing and squeezing through the silky fabric of her bikini panties.

"I don't have beautiful thighs, either," he continued, pulling the slacks down farther around her calves and taking a few pleasurable seconds to slide his palms up her thighs and then down again along the sensitive insides.

"You have beautiful hands," Ruth murmured, almost too weak to lift one foot and then another for him. "I love your hands. I knew they'd feel wonderful on my body. I've wanted you to touch me. *Like that*," she whispered helplessly as he stroked the shape and length of her, warming and claiming and admiring her responsive flesh, her shoulders and arms, her breasts and stomach and hips, her thighs and calves and feet, and, finally, the aching hub of her femininity, which was still hidden beneath her lacy briefs.

"You're so warm and vital and alive." David lay down next to her and kissed her with tender passion. Ruth put her arms around his neck and kissed him back, willingly giving him her tongue and the moist pressure of her lips. She moaned when she felt his hand slip under the waistband of her panties, and opened her thighs, granting him intimate possession. "I want you, Ruth," David whispered against her mouth, and kissed her more hungrily, locking her own words in her throat: *I want you, David.*

But her hands were free. She stroked his back and chest and flat belly, delighting in his warm, taut flesh, which quivered in response. Then she slid lower for a gentle exploration. David groaned and stopped kissing her, going absolutely still while she discovered him.

"Ruth, *darling...*" he murmured when she made a delicate capture, his voice expressing his sensations of exquisite pleasure and pain.

Rolling onto his back, he brought her on top of him and hugged her tight, his desire for her causing little convulsions in his muscles. "Let's get under the sleeping bag before you get chilled," he said in a husky voice.

"All right," Ruth agreed softly, although she wasn't cold. His whispered endearment had set off a whole succession of fireworks inside her, leaving a flush of warmth behind.

They finished taking off her underwear together and then shared the utter intimacy of both being completely naked before they got inside the downy cocoon of the sleeping bag. David lay on his back and drew Ruth up over him so that he could caress and kiss and suckle her breasts. She reveled in her own feminine generosity and couldn't hold back sounds of pleasure at the delicious sensations he aroused with his mouth and his hands, also his voice, because he repeated his earlier compliments, telling her she was lush and beautiful.

The sensations became more urgent when he cupped and squeezed and kneaded the aching fullness of her breasts and then nipped the tightly contracted buds of her nipples with his teeth. Ruth moaned and moved her lower torso against his side in an instinctive search before she voiced her need.

"Make love to me, David."

He rolled over on his side, bringing her close to him, and stroked her back and hips and buttocks while he kissed her, hard and deep, his touch less gentle now and arousing her more.

"I want you more than anything," he told her in a voice resonant with his passion but also with an intense yearning that touched Ruth deep inside, springing something loose.

"I want you, too," she whispered, her need deepening and becoming more than sexual.

The union of their bodies was simple and perfect, the culmination of a perfect day, and brought complete fulfillment. "I love you," David told her in a quietly exulting tone as he entered her, having sheathed himself for her protection. Before Ruth could cope with her mingling of answering emotion and physical pleasure, he kissed her deeply, the statement of his feelings an offering with no strings attached.

She hugged him tight and kissed him back, joy coursing through her and becoming a part of her passion. The rise to a shattering climax was swift for both of them. Lying close together afterward was sweet and companionable. David didn't tell her again with words that he loved her, but his voice and his touch were tender and caring.

"Do you think you'll have any trouble sleeping?" he asked after he'd gotten up to drop the flap of the tent, shutting out the light.

Ruth snuggled closer to him. "No," she replied drowsily. "This sleeping bag is heavenly." As was lying close to him with his arm circling her waist protectively, she added silently. "Camping really is cozy, isn't it?"

"Very cozy," David agreed softly, combing his fingers gently through her hair. He smiled when he heard her breathing become regular, then he lay there, not ready to join her in sleep. There was too much to savor consciously; her warm, relaxed body close to him, the nighttime tranquility of the campsite, the remoteness of the peninsula, with its huge core of untouched wilderness beauty, only the fringes of it easily accessible to man.

Sleep seemed like a waste to David. No dream could offer him more happiness than the waking reality of the moment. It was only the practical need for rest that made him close his eyes. Tomorrow he would want to be fresh when she awoke. He would awaken before her, see her come to the consciousness with him that they had more wonderful hours together here on the peninsula. . . .

"Sleepyhead," Ruth taunted David when he took a deep breath and opened his eyes. She was lying on her side, facing him, and smiled at his consternation. "Remember me?"

He framed her face, smoothing back a rumpled lock of hair. "Have you been awake long?"

"About an hour," she lied cheerfully, and then confessed her deceit with a smile. "I just woke up a couple of minutes ago. I must have gone out like a light last night."

David raised up on his elbow and bent to kiss her on the lips. "You didn't show any evidence of insomnia," he remarked dryly, smiling.

Ruth caressed his face, rubbing his beard stubble. "You look cute sleeping, more like a David than a Dr. Bradford."

"Does that mean I sleep with my mouth open?" he demanded, pleased by her observation. Kissing her again, more thoroughly this time, he let his hand rove over her warm nakedness inside the sleeping bag.

Ruth arched her back in languorous response to his caresses, her breasts and hips, stomach and thighs all coming alive to his touch. "You have such talented hands, Dr. Bradford," she murmured.

"David," he corrected, kissing her neck.

"And such a nice-looking, scratchy face," Ruth added, giggling.

"Sorry." David lifted his head to look into her face, which was alight with her merriment and awakened sensuality. "Good morning, my love," he told her softly. "I'm glad to see that camping out agrees with you. You're looking very beautiful after a night of sleeping on the ground."

"I'll bet I'm an absolute mess," Ruth jeered weakly, melted by the warm light in his eyes and his possessive, tender tone. She put her arms around his neck and pulled his head down to kiss him.

They made love, the soft morning light brighter in the tent than the faint illumination of the lantern had been the previous night. It was more intimate, seeing each other's faces clearly, reading the passion and pleasure and emotion. With the lowering of physical barriers had come a sweet familiarity and a new confidence that made her more at ease with him. She could be herself and not risk losing favor with him.

"Do you always wake up early?" David asked with a tender note that gave her a little thrill. They were lying close, their passion satisfied.

Ruth made a lazy affirmative sound. "I'm a morning person. What about you?"

"I wake up early, by habit," David replied. "But it could just be years of discipline. How can you tell whether you're a morning person?"

"I can only speak for myself. My whole life I've liked waking up. When I first open my eyes, I have this feeling that something nice is going to happen. You know the way you felt when you were a kid waking up on a special day like your birthday?" She pushed away so that she could see his face. He was smiling indulgently. "You're thinking I've never grown up!" she accused.

"I'm thinking that I hope you never lose your love of life," he contradicted gently. "It's what drew me to you in the first place." He kissed her. "What made me fall in love with you."

Ruth caressed his lightly stubbled cheek and smoothed back his hair. "I think you must have been ready to fall in love," she speculated fondly, visualizing the younger David.

"I was," he admitted. "I wanted a romantic fling with a fun-loving girl, and there you were. It was like a scene out of a love story, instant recognition. Only all on my side. To you, I was just another customer." He touched the tip of her nose with his forefinger.

"Not just another customer, or I wouldn't have remembered you!" Ruth protested. "You made an impression. I thought you were sensitive, attractive, highly intelligent and very nice. I figured that whatever profession you were in required an advanced education. And all my impressions were right." She smiled at his rueful expression. "But I have added to that recently."

"That's good," he said dryly. "I feel fairly certain that you regard me as a safe driver, also prompt, since I've arrived to pick you up on time twice now. Oh, and you have mentioned that you like my sense of humor.''

"I said I loved your sense of humor," Ruth corrected him, smiling. "And so far everything about your personality. You're the most interesting man I've ever known. I love being with you. The simplest conversation turns out to be fascinating. I feel very complimented, you know, that you would want to spend time with me."

"I wouldn't trade places with any other man in the world today," David told her quietly, hugging her tight.

Ruth stayed snuggled in the sleeping bag and took a possessive pleasure in watching him while he dressed quickly, shivering with the cool morning air. Then he kissed her before he left her alone in the tent to don her clothes as hastily as possible. Ruth could hear him whistling outside while he moved around, and when she emerged, he had a portable campstove set up on one end of the picnic table and was putting a coffeepot on to perk.

"Hot coffee coming up soon," he promised, holding out his arms to her. "And then bacon and eggs for breakfast. How do you like your eggs?"

"You don't have to bother cooking breakfast on my account," Ruth demurred. "Coffee is enough."

"Wait until I start the bacon cooking and tell me that," David scoffed.

"There's nothing that smells better than bacon," Ruth agreed.

"Especially when you're camping and get up on a cool, crisp morning in the out-of-doors."

Ruth smiled at him. He was so visibly relaxed and in a good mood. "I think maybe you are a morning person," she suggested fondly. "Or at least when you're camping."

David still held her in his arms, and he tightened his embrace while he answered her in a happy voice. "Today when

I woke up and you were there in the tent with me, I was definitely a morning person. But then last night I felt like an evening person and could have stayed up until dawn."

"Did you have trouble falling asleep?" Ruth thought of him lying awake beside her while she slept. What had he been thinking?

"I just didn't want to go to sleep and let go of my state of mind. I've never been in love before, and I wanted to hang onto the feeling. But then I decided that it was a good risk that it would come back in the morning." He kissed her tenderly on the lips. "And it did."

Ruth was flooded with sweet emotion. "I'm honored," she told him softly. "Falling in love is the most wonderful feeling in the world. I'd forgotten." She smiled at him, stirred by the intense light in his eyes at her admission that she had been falling in love with him, too. "We're having the romance you wanted seven years ago. I'm glad you waited and didn't find someone else to take my place."

"I don't think anyone could." David kissed her lingeringly, as though removing any doubt.

The faint smell of cooking bacon was unmistakable as their lips parted, and they sniffed and then smiled at each other.

"Now aren't you glad I had the foresight to bring along bacon and eggs?" David demanded.

"You seem to have thought of everything," Ruth commended him. "In fact, you're a very handy guy to have around, considering that you're a genius," she teased. "I thought people with high IQ's were absentminded and lacked common sense."

"That's a popular misconception. We have the advantage of being able to commit whole lists to memory. However..." He grinned at her, rubbing her hand lightly over his growth of sandy beard. "You didn't happen to bring along a razor, did you?"

"Yes, and you're welcome to borrow it, but I think you look cute, needing a shave."

"I have a seedy charm, you mean?"

They walked to the bathhouse together, holding hands, carrying on lighthearted conversation in low tones, smiling at each other, unconcerned that to anyone who passed or saw them they were visibly lovers. When they got back to the campsite, the coffee was made, and they sipped from mugs while they prepared breakfast together.

Ruth felt free to touch him whenever she wanted, and the impulse seemed almost constant. She was under no constraints of any kind with him. He took such obvious pleasure in her spontaneity that she was encouraged to be her most outgoing, enthusiastic self.

Everything was fun about the camping routine: cooking breakfast and then eating it out in the open, the clean-up afterward, even breaking up camp and repacking the car after they'd gone for a walk along the lake. But there was a moment of poignance when it came time to get into the car and drive away.

"We'll come again," David promised when they stood together, taking a final look around. He hugged her around the shoulders.

Ruth managed a smile, but she didn't try for a cheerful remark. Her throat was too tight to speak until they were out on the highway and had gone at least a mile. "I didn't take any camping pictures," she reflected. "You mentioned bringing along a camera, but I forgot." She'd been too busy being happy with him, and it suddenly seemed tragic that she would have no tangible evidence.

Chapter Eleven

David reached for her hand, squeezed it and then held it tight. "I'll be sure to get the camera out when we get to the beach at Kalaloch," he said quietly, and Ruth knew he understood the real nature of her regret, that what they'd shared at the campsite couldn't last forever.

The drive from Lake Quinault to the Pacific Ocean took them along the northern boundary of the Quinault Indian Reservation, which was shaped like a wedge on the map and tapered to a point inland at the lake. After the wooded beauty of the forest they had left behind, it came to them as a shock to pass through large open sections where all the trees had been clear-cut, forming ugly gashes in the landscape. Weathered stumps served as reminders of the large trees that had once stood tall.

"What a shame!" Ruth lamented, horrified. "Why did they have to cut all of them? And it doesn't look as though there's been any effort to replant, does it?"

"You'll see the same destruction in some of the land controlled by the National Forest," David remarked grimly. "There's all the difference in the world between the National Forest Service and the National Park Service. The Park Service is dedicated strictly to conservation, whereas one of the major activities of the Forest Service is selling off timber, selectively or otherwise. Fortunately, almost a million acres of the Olympic Peninsula is national park and protected from lumbering and from hunting its wildlife. A fifty-mile strip of Pacific coastline is part of the park, too, beginning at Kalaloch and extending up to Cape Alava. I think you'll agree when you see the beaches, that it would be unthinkable to ever allow them to be exploited by commercial interests and ruined as so much of our country's shoreline has been."

Ruth had heard about the Pacific beaches and seen pictures of them, but she wasn't prepared for their grandeur, which was almost overpowering. The surf thundered ashore, creating a furor of leaping foam and noise. All along the shore as far as the eye could see were strewn great bleached drift logs, testament to the power of the sea in a storm. Silhouetted against the horizon, stark and lonely, were sea stacks, sheer-sided monoliths that had once been a part of the land.

"I don't think I'd want to come here by myself," she confided, glad of David's arm around her as they walked along the beach at Kalaloch. Other people were in sight, but the crashing of the surf and the grand scale of nature ensured a sense of privacy. There was no need for them to lower their voices.

"It's a powerful scene, isn't it?" David marveled. "Can you imagine the Indians along this shore putting out to sea in small craft to hunt whales?"

Ruth shivered at the thought, and he hugged her tight, not to reassure her but to share her perception of human frailty and smallness.

Driving a few miles farther north, they came to Ruby Beach, where Ruth became absorbed in searching along the pebbled shore for the rosy-hued pebbles that gave the beach its name. The day had been overcast, and suddenly the sun came out. David got a blanket from the car, and they found a warm niche among the drift logs, where they could hear but not see the ocean.

They sat close, resting comfortably against a log and holding hands. Whether they talked or lapsed into peaceful silences, being together seemed a palpable joy.

After another walk, this time in the opposite direction, they picnicked on the blanket, eating cheese and crackers and fruit. David opened a bottle of wine, but they each had only one glass, mindful of the alcohol intake and the necessity for safe driving. The sun went behind the clouds, and they held each other, the return to Seattle looming as a necessity they both regretted as the afternoon wore on.

"Here on the peninsula, hospital facilities are limited. There isn't a great demand for neurosurgeons," David remarked when they were getting into the car. "I guess I overspecialized."

Ruth returned his smile sadly, able to follow his train of thought without an explanation. The peninsula was an ideal place to get away for a weekend or holiday or even a long vacation, but its very attractions made it an unlikely place to live. They had to go back to civilization and their separate worlds.

"I have the advantage over you there," she replied with an attempt at lightness. "As long as there's a little general store that needs a good clerk, I can get a job."

"I guess I could set up practice as an old-fashioned country doctor. Set broken bones and do minor surgery."

"What about delivering babies?"

"I'd forgotten about babies," David admitted. "I'd definitely have to do some reading in obstetrics and call in a good midwife to assist."

Ruth smiled at his lack of confidence. "It would be a terrible waste," she reflected, returning them to seriousness. "All your skill and knowledge not put to use for people who need it."

"I have a spinal cord injury first thing in the morning. A man about my age, a construction worker who fell on the job. He has eighty-percent paralysis and no hopes of regaining his mobility without surgery, but there's only a fifty-percent chance that removing the vertebra fragments in his spinal cord will bring improvement. The surgical procedure is highly delicate and subject to being halted at any moment, to prevent the patient from suffering total paralysis."

Ruth tried to conceive of the responsibility and pressure but couldn't. "Are all your cases that crucial?" she asked, and he told her of other patients and answered her questions, explaining the medical terminology in layman's terms. Glancing over at him, she imagined him in surgical garb and tried to place him in an operating room environment, which was familiar to her only from television and movies.

"In stories about hospitals there's always a room with a glass wall overlooking the operating room, where people can watch," she remarked, and realized when David looked at her questioningly that she sounded as though she were hinting that she'd like to watch him performing an operation. "I just wondered if that was based on fact," she added quickly.

"In a hospital that's connected with a medical school, an operating room is a classroom theater," David replied. "There's usually a whole crowd of medical students and doctors looking on, plus technicians operating cameras for close-up views on TV monitors. The conversation in the operating room is picked up by microphones and played on speakers." He paused. "I'm afraid you'd find it a very disturbing scene. Most nonmedical people would."

"I never even watch those TV programs where they show close-ups of operations," Ruth declared, trying to hide that she was hurt by his response, which was perfectly reasonable and yet still seemed like a rejection. He clearly didn't welcome the thought of her coming to the hospital. "Doesn't it bother you to have a lot of people looking on while you're doing surgery?" she asked, busily selecting a tape to play.

"I'm used to it," he replied. She sensed him glancing at her. "I can't afford to be distracted."

"No, of course you can't."

When Ruth didn't continue the conversation, he seemed content to let it lapse and think his own thoughts. For her, the exchange was like a tiny wedge driven into their closeness. It wasn't so much what had been said, but what hadn't. She'd made her interest in his professional life plain by asking questions, but he hadn't even casually mentioned that she might want to visit him at the hospital some time and get a guided tour when he wasn't busy. He could have offered her a glimpse of the operating room when it wasn't being used.

Memory of his expression when the nurse had walked outside the store and spoken to him while he was standing with Ruth came back vividly to her now. Did he privately react the same way to the thought of introducing Ruth to the other hospital personnel with whom he associated on a daily basis? The possibility cut deeply.

"I won't be able to take off next weekend." David spoke up quietly, reaching over for her hand.

"I'm scheduled to work this Saturday anyway," Ruth replied hollowly, slow to link her fingers with his. She yearned for the clasp and yet knew she should hold back, feeling such doubts.

"We can see each other in the evenings. Maybe I can get downtown for lunch occasionally."

"I'd like that."

David's sideways glance was penetrating. "You don't sound very convincing," he said, and frowned. "You're not about to suggest another trial period of separation while we get some perspective on being involved with each other, are you?"

Ruth sighed. "No. I think we both have perspective. We're great together on the peninsula, but we probably won't be great together in Seattle. There's too much going against us. But I will see you, whenever you want to see me. I just don't intend to build false hopes."

David was silent for a long moment. "In other words, if we agree right now that it isn't a good idea for us to feel the way we do about each other, you can just go back to Seattle tonight and forget the whole thing?"

"Of course I won't 'forget' anything," Ruth protested miserably. "And I'm not doubting that you're sincere, but I just know that I'm not right for you. You'd only end up being not satisfied with me." It was an unbearable thought for her, more unbearable than not seeing him.

"Like your ex-husband," David said grimly. "Because one man from a different kind of background didn't love you for yourself, you're assuming that I won't, or can't, either. You know, it's just possible that all your ex-husband

and I have in common is a name." He sighed and went on, sounding hurt and reproachful. "I can't promise that what you and I have is lasting, since I've never experienced it. But I want to give it a chance. You have to be willing, too, though."

"I'd like to believe it would work, but it wouldn't!" Ruth said desperately. "And I'd be the one taking the big risk." The last words slipped out before she considered them. His fingers went lax on hers, and she numbly withdrew her hand to her lap while he returned his to the wheel.

"How do you figure that I'm any less vulnerable than you are?" David asked quietly. "Unless you doubt my feelings for you. Do you?"

Ruth swallowed to ease the painful tightness in her throat, wishing that she didn't have to answer him. "I think you're romantically in love with me. It's very exciting and beautiful—"

"But you don't trust it."

She didn't answer, letting her silence affirm his bleak analysis.

"And what about what you feel for me? Is that 'romantic love,' as well?"

"I don't know," Ruth murmured unhappily. In her heart she was all but sure that it wasn't.

They rode for miles after that in silence.

"Would you like for me to play anything in particular?" Ruth finally asked with a note of pleading.

"Play Willie Nelson," he replied, sounding defeated, and waited until she found the tape and started it. "Now tell me about you and Bradford. Start from the beginning."

Ruth complied. David listened, showing no reaction. Occasionally he would summarize what she'd told him, as though double-checking to be sure he'd comprehended accurately.

"Your main failings in Tom's eyes were that you didn't manage a household to his satisfaction or measure up to his expectations as a hostess when he entertained clients. You didn't take to country club life and play golf and tennis, and you insisted on working when your income wasn't needed. In short, you were totally unlike his mother."

Ruth had concentrated on her own shortcomings deliberately, to reinforce for herself as well as convince David that she wasn't suitable for him, either. Paraphrased briefly like that, Tom's complaints sounded like a flimsy basis for the break-up of a marriage.

"It caused a lot of friction that I liked Seattle and he didn't," Ruth said defensively. "Then when I didn't want to move back to Texas, he accused me of not wanting to live close to my family. He called them 'trashy' and showed what a low opinion he had of them and of me."

David didn't say anything for several seconds. "You've told me how you didn't measure up to Bradford's standards. It wasn't all one-sided, was it?"

"No," Ruth admitted. "I lost respect for Tom when he didn't do well in his job at Boeing. He made all kinds of excuses, but I just don't think he was well qualified enough. He was only an average student in college. Other guys who started in his department when he did were promoted over him." She made a guilty face. "I'm afraid that when we were having all our fights, I made that point to him and his ego never recovered.

"After we moved back to Texas, I saw that he was more like his father than I had ever realized—and I don't like his father at all. His father loves to brag about what a shrewd businessman he is, and he talks about money constantly. Nothing is important unless it's expensive. People don't matter unless they're in at least the same income bracket as he is. I would never have married Tom if I'd known he would turn out like that, although the signs were there all along. I was just blind at first and then didn't want to see them.''

''What did you admire about Tom initially?''

''Admire?'' Ruth repeated skeptically, giving the question deep thought. ''I liked his looks. We were very attracted to each other physically. He was lots of fun that year when we were dating. He'd come to Austin to see me, and I'd go and visit him at Texas Tech. We partied both places and had a great time. We slept together, of course, and had good sex. I don't suppose I did admire Tom,'' she concluded. ''Not the way I admire you. I didn't find him interesting in the same way, either. He isn't at all imaginative and has just average intelligence, like me. We didn't actually carry on long, deep conversations. He watched TV a lot. He'd never have been able to stand a weekend like this one. He'd have been bored and restless.''

David was silent again. Ruth cast curious, faintly anxious glances over at him.

''What are you thinking?'' she asked finally.

''That from everything you've told me, you apparently made a poor choice in a husband. Tom Bradford didn't deserve you.''

Ruth went soft and warm inside at his tone, which was grim on her behalf. ''I guess I gave a slanted view.''

''I also don't see any similarity between Bradford and me, other than the name.''

''You and Tom aren't alike in any way!'' Ruth assured him quickly.

''Then I fail to see how you can conclude on the basis of your marriage and divorce that you and I would find it impossible to work out problems arising out of differences in background and education. I'd hope we would confront em with more honesty and sensitivity than you and Tom did and not try to destroy each other, even if we can't succeed."

"I guess it doesn't sound logical," Ruth admitted, desperately wanting to believe him. "But then I'm not on the same level with you in thinking."

"Level of thinking has nothing to do with our problem," David said with a quiet finality. "It's a question of trust and caring."

After having undermined her doubts and given her a weak ray of hope, he wasn't going to suggest that they try to make a go of a relationship, Ruth realized with despair. She wanted more than anything to protest that she did trust him and she did care for him very deeply, but what would be the use? Despite a whole multitude of regrets and wishes, she still knew that there wasn't a prayer it would ever work out between them in the end.

And would he have given in without any real efforts to convince her if he himself were truly sure of their chances?

"Would you like for me to drive?" she offered in a small, unhappy voice when several minutes had passed and she'd found the silence unbearable. "It's been a while, but I haven't forgotten how and I have a valid license."

"You can, if you like. I know it can be tiring just to be a passenger."

He slowed and pulled over on the shoulder of the road. They got out and exchanged sides.

"You're still not finding it inconvenient without a car," he remarked when they were under way again.

Ruth was quick to reply, glad for any conversation. They talked politely, easing some of the strain so that occasional silence wasn't tense and uncomfortable. Ruth turned the wheel over to him again an hour from Seattle. He asked if she'd like to stop for something to eat, and when she refused, he didn't insist.

"By Tuesday or Wednesday I hope to have that medical information I promised to get you for your father," he told her when they'd arrived at her apartment house.

"Thank you. I'd appreciate it." It meant they'd be in contact at least one more time.

He kissed her goodbye, standing with her beside the car, a bittersweet kiss that brought the sting of tears to Ruth's eyes. Then he handed her her suitcase.

"I'll be in touch in a few days. Meanwhile, should some emergency arise and you need me, you know how to reach me."

"I have the numbers you gave me."

There was nothing more to say. Ruth trudged up the walk with feet of lead and stopped to turn around and watch as he drove off.

David switched off the car stereo and rode in silence, thinking ahead dully to unpacking the car, putting away all the camping gear. He couldn't fathom using the equipment again anytime soon. The idea of sleeping in the tent by himself in some campsite brought an aching loneliness, and the thought of sleeping in it with some other woman besides Ruth was inconceivable until the memory of this weekend had faded. That would take some time.

It hurt damnably that she didn't share his feelings that what they had together was precious and rare and not just a passing infatuation. She didn't sense as he did that for reasons he couldn't begin to explain, they completed each other somehow. For Ruth, being with him wasn't *necessary*, as being with her was for him, or there wouldn't have been a question of whether they would see each other.

Was this the end of it? Would he stay away from her? In his present state David couldn't answer either question for himself. All he knew was that despite his disappointment in her, he would take advantage of the excuse to contact her next week, even though he could easily mail her the medical information.

He'd call, talk to her, with the hope that she would make an overture. And if she didn't . . .

He just didn't know.

Ruth awoke the next morning and lay in bed, hugging her pillow and remembering the conversation with David about being a morning person. The scene in the tent came back vividly, arousing bittersweet emotions and uncertainty.

Was she wrong in not hoping?

Getting up with none of her usual energy, she went about her morning routine and got dressed for work. When the phone rang just as she was leaving the apartment, her heart leaped with a foolish anticipation. She went to answer the call but told herself that it wasn't David. He would be in surgery by now.

Without any premonition of bad news, she picked up the receiver and a nightmare began. It was her mother, crying and hysterical.

"Ruth Ellen, it's happened! Your daddy's had a heart attack! They called me from down at the station a few minutes ago—" Betty Cook broke down into gasping sobs.

Ruth started to tremble with an icy chill that spread through her whole body. "Mamma, is he . . . is Daddy . . ." She couldn't say the terrible work, *dead*.

"He was still alive when they took him away in the ambulance. Your Aunt Trudy's coming to drive me to the county hospital. I'm so all to pieces I wouldn't dare get on the highway—I just keep *praying*—" Her voice broke despairingly. "You'll come home right away, won't you? No matter what . . . *happens*?"

"I'll get the first flight I can."

Ruth tried to question her and get more information, but her mother was completely distraught and, if she had been told more, she hadn't absorbed any of the details. Ruth terminated the conversation and set about making the necessary travel arrangements. She was able to get a seat on a flight that left in two hours. Next she reserved a rental car to pick up on her arrival at the Dallas-Fort Worth airport and then called the store.

Only the tasks of packing and getting to the Seattle airport remained, but Ruth stood by the phone, consumed with a longing to talk to David. He wouldn't be home, of course. She called his home number first anyway and listened to the ring before she called the hospital.

"Dr. Bradford is in surgery," she was informed by a brisk and professional female voice. "I can take a message."

Ruth gathered her nerve. "This is Ruth . . . Cook calling to tell Dr. Bradford that it won't be necessary now for him to get the information about doctors in Texas. My father has had a heart attack and is in the hospital. Dr. Bradford can reach me at my home number or at the airport until an hour and forty-five minutes from now."

There was little hope that he would even get the message before she was airborne, but at least he would know that she was gone from the city. If he tried to call her at her apartment and couldn't get an answer, he wouldn't just think that she was out with someone.

She'd save him the trouble of inquiring about heart specialists and hospital facilities her father might have benefitted from in different circumstances. This very moment in the county hospital, her father was receiving the kind of care that was available to ordinary people. Ruth prayed that it was good enough.

Boarding the plane, she felt utterly alone, and, once in the air, she struggled with the sensation of being a displaced person, suspended between her chosen world, which she was leaving, where she was Ruth Bradford, and the one to which she was being pulled back by the binding cords of family, where she'd always be Ruth Ellen Cook. Those worlds seemed so far apart. How could she ever reconcile them? How could she ever be whole and complete if she didn't?

But now wasn't the time for thinking about herself and her identity problems. What mattered was that her father lived and recovered. She needed to shore her inner strength, which would be needed.

The flight was routed through Denver, where she had an unscheduled layover of several long, frustrating hours but was able to learn through phone calls that her father was still alive though in critical condition after having suffered a massive coronary. She called again from the Dallas-Fort Worth airport and relieved her worst anxieties again before beginning the several-hours-long drive.

It was late afternoon by the time she arrived at the county hospital which was thirty miles from Baker. Her mother broke down at the sight of Ruth, making Ruth's own self-control a necessity. There had been no worsening of her father's condition, but he remained in an intensive care unit and wasn't allowed visitors.

Her Aunt Trudy, who had stayed with Betty all day, went home to her family, leaving Ruth to sit with her mother, who calmed down and took comfort in relating the whole ordeal in detail, beginning with the phone call from the gas station.

"Did you contact Tom from Seattle?" she asked Ruth absently at one point. "He called the house and talked to Becky, asked about Jack's condition, what hospital he was in, who his doctor was and so on. He said he wanted you to call him as soon as you got here. Naturally it came as a surprise. I didn't know you two were on such good terms."

"No, I haven't talked with Tom since our divorce was final. Was Becky sure that it was Tom?" Ruth's mind whirred. Had David called and Becky missed out on his first name, just picking up Bradford?

"Why, yes. He explained who he was and said he was calling from Houston. He left some numbers. I've got them written down here in my purse."

"Will you be okay by yourself for a few minutes while I call him?" Ruth asked, mystified.

"I feel a hundred percent better now that you're here," Betty replied, smiling gratefully at her daughter. "Somehow I just know everything's going to be all right."

Tom didn't waste time with pleasantries or pretend sympathy. He explained immediately that Ruth's doctor friend from Seattle had telephoned him and asked him to contact Ruth's family and inquire about her father. Ruth felt a surge of warm emotion at the evidence of David's concern on her behalf. The anxiety that had had her in its grip since her mother's phone call that morning eased ever so slightly.

"So you hooked yourself a doctor, huh, Ruth?" Tom was grudgingly admiring as he made the conversation personal. "The name business is quite a coincidence. How'd you latch on to this guy? He sounded high-powered."

"I knew David before, when you and I were married and lived in Seattle." When Tom's silence at the other end seemed reproachful, she added, "He was a customer at the store, and I waited on him a couple of times."

"I see. Well, I hope I haven't thrown a monkey wrench into your chances for landing him. I gave him the rundown on your parents' financial situation. I wanted him to understand that they're in no position to pay for VIP medical treatment. We're talking major expense, transferring your father to a Dallas hospital and having a big-name heart man take care of him."

Ruth cringed to think of the telephone conversation between David and Tom. Tom wouldn't have thought about sparing her pride. She understood the faint defensiveness in his voice. He was prepared for her to mention her small divorce settlement and perhaps ask him for money.

"Whatever you can do in cooperation with David to help my father's chances for recovery, I'd appreciate it, Tom," she told him quietly. "He has hospital insurance, and what that doesn't cover, the family will manage to pay somehow."

After she'd hung up, Ruth impulsively tried to call David at his home number, on the slim chance that he might be there, even though the time difference made it unlikely. It was earlier in Seattle. She felt humbly appreciative and wanted to thank him. Even when he didn't answer, the sound of his telephone ringing in his condominium was soothing somehow. She didn't feel nearly as alone now, nor as afraid. Like her mother, she had a blind optimism that everything would work out.

That evening there was a constant flow of family and friends and neighbors dropping by. The small waiting room at the hospital was like the scene of a somber reunion, with everyone greeting Ruth. Her brother Kevin was on hand when the family doctor, in company with a consulting physician, reported on Jack Cook's condition and the diagnosis. He would need bypass surgery. The hospital had been informed of the family's likely preference for transferring the patient to a Dallas hospital into the care of an eminent specialist. A legal confirmation was needed.

Ruth's brother and mother looked helplessly at her. All three had gone pale at the mention of bypass surgery. Only Ruth had made any sense of the rest. Her mother hadn't thought yet to ask about her telephone conversation with

Tom, and it had all seemed too complicated to explain, since Ruth had never mentioned David.

"Transfer Dad to Dallas?" Kevin murmured.

"Yes," Ruth told the two doctors decidedly, taking the decision on her shoulders. "That's what we'll want to do."

Betty Cook nodded in agreement, her eyes frightened. "Whatever my daughter thinks best," she whispered.

Late that night Ruth managed to talk her mother into going home to get several hours of rest, to prepare for the next day. Everyone was still up, anxious about their father and waiting to greet Ruth. Besides Becky and the two youngest boys, Ted still lived at home. A high school dropout, he earned enough to pay for his clothes and entertainment and buy gas for his souped-up car, his pride and joy.

With one glance around the cramped interior of the Cook residence, Ruth knew that her mother had been interrupted in the midst of her housework and no one had been there to issue orders to pick up clothes and shoes, empty glasses and evidences of snacks. The television blared in the living room, and from the boys' room came the loud throb of the stereo. Window air-conditioning units added to the noise.

It was all instantly familiar to Ruth, the sense of being close and crowded and a part of a large family. With worried pride Betty pointed out the set of new living-room furniture.

"Don't you think it's beautiful? Now I wish I'd held off on getting it, what with this happening to your daddy, but the old set was falling to pieces, and he told me to go ahead and get a new one. I'll just have to talk to them at the furniture store and see about lowering the payments."

Ruth didn't need to have it explained to her that her parents had bought the furniture on credit. It would be well worn by the last payment, when they owned it free and clear.

"Billy spilled soda on the—" Brian was cut off in the midst of his tattling by his older brother, and a fierce tussle ensued on the living-room floor.

"You dirty little sneak! I'll get you," Billy threatened. "I told you not to tell!"

"Boys! Now, stop that fighting this minute!" Betty implored. "Now look what you've done! You've knocked that glass off and could have broke it! Think about your father in the hospital and have some consideration."

The mention of their father had the desired effect, though the truce was uneasy, and Billy made it clear to Brian with his menacing expression that he'd exact revenge later.

"I washed up all the dishes and cleaned the kitchen today, Mamma," Becky informed her mother in a self-righteous tone. "I told them all they had to clean up whatever they messed up after that, because I wasn't their mother, but, of course, they didn't pay me any attention."

"Guys don't wash dishes," Ted jeered. "That's women's work."

"Turn off the TV, and let's all go to bed. I'm dead on my feet," Betty said tiredly, evading the issue.

Ruth slept in her sister's room, sharing the double bed. "I put clean sheets on," Becky told her, her whole attitude toward Ruth a little shy but admiring. "I'm getting out of Baker, like you did," she confided when they were lying in the darkness. "If I do get married, it'll be to somebody educated, and I probably won't have any kids, either. I want to make something of myself, go places, enjoy life, not just worry and wait on other people hand and foot. Mamma gets very upset with me when I say all that."

"Maybe you shouldn't be so outspoken," Ruth suggested, touched and yet disturbed that her sister would set her up as role model, which Ruth had never tried to be. She didn't want the burden. "There's no point in upsetting

Mamma or hurting her feelings. She'll be very proud of you
if you go to college. We all will." Ruth drew in a deep
breath, as though relaxing for sleep. "Good night, Becky."

Long after Becky was asleep, Ruth lay awake, feeling a
deep empathy for her youngest sister. She wished that she
could prepare Becky for the reality of breaking away from
home and family, for the complicated guilt of rejecting one's
parents' lifestyle and wanting distance, but it was all so difficult to put into words, and Ruth didn't want to be an in-
fluence. Becky needed to make her own choices, formulate
her own values.

She was too young for Ruth to talk to her openly about
her marriage and divorce. It was too soon and too risky to
warn her about marrying a man from a different background. Ruth was fearful that any confidence might be repeated, and she'd been careful never to tell her family of
Tom's contemptuous attitude toward them, not even when
her marriage had ended. She'd always made excuses when
he wouldn't visit.

Ruth hoped fervently that Becky never had a Tom Bradford in her life. But what about a David Bradford? If she
met a man like him when she was fresh and undaunted, as
Ruth had been when she met Tom, would there be a chance,
even a slim one, that the match would work despite the disparity in backgrounds? Intense yearning flooded Ruth as
she considered that question, whose answer might be important to Becky someday but was crucial to Ruth in the
present.

And was she making an even worse error in judgment not
to trust David than she'd made in trusting Tom?

Chapter Twelve

Your husband came through like a champ, Mrs. Cook."

Ruth looked on, relief surging through her, as Dr. Nate Benjamin draped his arm around Betty Cook's shoulders and gave her a reassuring hug. A short, heavyset man of about fifty, with a homely face and a shiny bald head, he didn't look or act like Ruth's idea of an eminent heart surgeon.

He divided his friendly attention between her and her mother as he elaborated on the success of Jack Cook's bypass surgery and gave a positive forecast for recovery. When he'd finished, he patted Betty on the shoulder and shook Ruth's hand.

"So you're a friend of Will Bradford's boy, up in Seattle. Chip off the old block, I hear. Will's a good man. Tops in the field. Your father couldn't ask for a better quarterback on the team than him. Or maybe you weren't aware that he consulted with us on your father's case by phone from New York State."

"No, I didn't realize," Ruth admitted, trying not to show how surprised and taken aback she was. No wonder Tom had used the expression "VIP medical treatment."

Knowing her mother was completely at sea over the conversation, Ruth gave a generalized explanation after the surgeon had left.

"He must think a lot of you," Betty reflected. "A doctor." She was torn between motherly pride and distress. "It's selfish, I know, but I hate to think of you marrying somebody so far off. You'd probably never come home. And I don't guess we'd ever even get to meet him."

"I'm not going to marry David." Ruth's certainty gave her a deep sharp pang. "He's just a good friend."

She got to look in on her father in his hospital room early in the evening before she returned to Baker, leaving Betty to sit by her husband's bed. Ruth knew her mother was anxious about her children at home and would feel better knowing she was there.

The sight of her father lying pale and asleep in a hospital bed, attached to tubes and monitors, made his close call with death frighteningly real to Ruth. She felt an enormous gratitude to David for having done everything in his power to help her father sustain life and have the best chance possible for recovery.

Twice she stopped during the drive to Baker and attempted to call David at his home number, but there was no answer, and when she arrived at her parents' home, a private long-distance conversation with him would have been impossible. Her brother Jimmy was there with Trixie and their two children, worked up to a fever pitch of excitement. The telephone rang almost constantly with people calling to inquire after Jack Cook.

Going to bed after midnight, exhausted, Ruth waited until the others were asleep and crept into the kitchen to the wall telephone. David answered on the second ring and the one word—hello—spoken in his quiet, familiar voice touched off an almost overwhelming joy in her. She could hear classical music playing in the background.

"Hello, David. It's Ruth. I wanted to call and thank you." She pitched her voice as low as she dared, not wanting to rouse Becky or the boys.

"Ruth. Where are you calling from? Are you okay?"

His concern brought the prick of tears to her eyes. "I'm calling from home. Everyone's asleep, and I don't want to wake them. I'm fine, just tired. And very relieved and grateful. I can never thank you enough."

"I was glad to do what I could from this distance. It was a matter of making some phone calls. The only problem was establishing communication with you or your family and determining your father's condition and whereabouts."

"I didn't leave you my parents' telephone number, and you only knew they lived in Baker, Texas, which isn't really a town but just a rural community." Ruth voiced the obvious apologetically. "So you managed to track down Tom in Houston. He'd called here at the house by the time I arrived at the county hospital. I'd been delayed in Denver. It was a big mystery how he knew about my father and why he'd have the slightest interest. You went to so much trouble."

"Bradford was actually quite cooperative. He volunteered to contact your family and get the facts, and I agreed that that seemed best, since he wasn't a total stranger. I hope his role didn't cause a painfully uncomfortable situation for you."

"No, it didn't." Ruth's cheeks were burning with embarrassment at the imagined conversation between the two men. She could hear Tom explaining to David the difficulties of communicating with members of her family who were uneducated and backward. "I was glad for help from anyone, even Tom. I just hope that talking to him wasn't terribly unpleasant and awkward for you."

"We didn't strike up a long-distance friendship, but that wasn't to be expected." There was the briefest pause. "Does your father have hospital insurance, Ruth?"

His hesitant tone sent a wave of mortification through her. Based on Tom's financial report on her family, whom he'd probably described bluntly as "dirt poor," David was concerned about whether they could handle the cost of the medical care he'd provided.

"Yes, he does have hospital insurance," she said with a little note of pride. "I've checked, and it pays eighty percent up to a certain point, and then there's a major medical clause, and the coverage increases. Despite what Tom might have told you, my parents aren't on welfare status. They have a good credit rating and can borrow money to pay the balance. I have savings and intend to help, too."

"I'm sorry. I didn't mean to offend you by asking," David said quietly.

"No, I'm sorry," Ruth murmured miserably. "And you didn't offend me. I'm just embarrassed to think of the impression Tom must have given you of my family."

"The fact that you're a member of your family says more to me than anything Bradford could tell me. Your parents must be good people to have a daughter like you."

"*You* must have wonderful parents," Ruth said softly, overcome with a gratitude that had nothing to do with her father.

"They'll be in Seattle next month. My father will be speaking at a medical conference of cardiologists. He told me when I talked to him on the phone yesterday."

Ruth couldn't read into the disclosure any invitation to meet his parents, and her own reaction to the idea was mixed. She was both eager to meet his parents and intimidated.

"Dr. Benjamin said your father consulted with him on my father's case."

"He did, at my request. There'll be no fee. Medical ethics wouldn't allow it. More than likely it was overkill, since your father had very good doctors in Dallas, but an outside expert opinion never hurts. Your father came through the surgery very well and has good prospects for resuming a normal, active life. He's in general good health and still a young man, at forty-nine. He might need to modify his diet and follow an exercise regimen. If he's a smoker, his doctors will undoubtedly order him to quit."

"He is a smoker, and his diet is all wrong. My mother fries everything. And although he works hard, he doesn't do any kind of regular exercise. I just hope he'll cooperate and do what his doctors say." Ruth was wishing while she talked that she could turn the conversation to more personal channels. "How's the weather been up there?" she asked wistfully.

"Like typical Seattle weather. It's been overcast, with mild temperatures."

"Sounds wonderful. It's as hot as blazes down here, and dry. Everything looks parched."

"How long do you think you'll stay?"

Ruth's heart pounded at the question, which she thought might be an opening. "Another couple of days, anyway. I don't want to miss any more time at work than necessary. I'm scheduled to work Saturday."

"Yes, so you said on Sunday. You don't have a return flight reservation yet, then?"

"No, not yet." Ruth waited hopefully, but there was silence at the other end. He didn't suggest that she call again and inform him of the arrival time of her plane so that he could meet her at the airport. "That's beautiful music you're listening to," she said finally, a note of discouragement in her voice.

"Brahms."

She almost thought he sounded disappointed, but with the one word, it was difficult to tell. "I'll let you get back to listening to it," she told him. "And I'll go to bed. It's been a long day. I wanted to call and thank you from the bottom of my heart for everything."

"You're most welcome," he replied quietly. "And I'm glad you called."

Again Ruth detected what sounded like faint disappointment. "Good night, then," she said uncertainly.

"Good night, Ruth."

With the connection broken, she felt separated from him by an unbreachable distance. She'd called for more than to thank him. Surely she had gotten across to him that she'd wanted urgently to talk, to hear his voice, to reach out to him.

But he hadn't responded with any encouragement. He'd come to her aid in a way that she could never repay and yet hadn't said a word to indicate that he wanted to see her on her return.

Had he undergone a change of heart? It had been only two days since Sunday, but perhaps his talking to Tom had had some effect, and maybe looking ahead to having his parents come to Seattle had given him a different perspective, too. Perhaps the thought of bringing them and her together had brought him around to her way of thinking, just when she was trying to convince herself she might be wrong.

Or did he just not want her to think there were any strings attached to what he'd done for her father? Of all the explanations, that was the only one in which Ruth could take any comfort.

She had to know, she realized, and picked up the receiver again with a trembling hand.

The phone rang four times before he answered. Ruth listened with a sinking feeling, thinking that he must have gone out.

"Hello." He sounded resigned, totally uninterested in knowing who was calling. Willie Nelson was singing a plaintive country and western tune in the background.

Ruth's heart leaped with the intuition that the reason he'd had no desire to answer the phone was that he didn't think it could possibly be *her* calling.

"David, it's me again. Ruth."

"Ruth." The way he spoke her name eased seventy-five percent of her anxiety, and then he added, "I almost didn't answer."

"I'm glad you did. I'd have lain awake, wondering where you'd gone and who you were with."

"It's just me and Willie here, both feeling down. Why did you call back?"

"Because I didn't say nearly all I really wanted to say just now when I talked to you."

"Neither did I, but you first."

Ruth gathered her nerve. "I've been doing a lot of wishful thinking the last two days, and if you haven't changed your mind, I'd like for us to see each other when I get back to Seattle. When I called, I was hoping for an opening to say that, but you didn't exactly give me one and I didn't have the nerve just to come out with it."

"This isn't just gratitude talking?" David asked quietly. "What if your father hadn't had a heart attack and you were in your apartment here in Seattle right now? Would we be having this conversation?''

"Not exactly the same conversation, of course," Ruth replied earnestly. "The last two days *have* happened, and they've had an effect on the way I feel about you. Flying here yesterday morning, I felt terribly alone and frightened. You don't know what it meant to me, how reassured I was, when I arrived and learned through talking to Tom that you were taking steps from Seattle to see that my father got the best medical care. I didn't feel alone anymore. I tried to call you and felt good just hearing your phone ring. If you had answered, I probably would have thanked you, like I did when I called just now, and I wouldn't have had the courage to say then either that—'' Ruth swallowed a lump of emotion "—I love you.''

"I'm glad you called back and got those words out," David said softly. "I was choking on them myself during our whole conversation before.''

"Are you choking on them now?" Ruth encouraged him shyly.

"I love you, darling. There isn't anything I wouldn't do that was in my power, as a physician or a man, to protect you from being unhappy.''

"David..." Ruth whispered, thrilled to the core by his warm ardor, but humbled, too. She just hoped she could live up to the image he had of her. It was impossible for her not to feel vaguely undeserving when she considered who and what he was.

"Let me know your travel plans when they're definite," David urged. "If it's at all possible, I'll meet you at the airport. That's something else I had to bite my tongue to keep from saying before," he added with a rueful candor.

"And I was so disappointed when you didn't say it," Ruth confessed, happiness bubbling in her voice. "I can't wait to see you, David."

"I can't wait to see you either, darling." His voice lightened with warm amusement. "It's hard to say which of these two telephone calls would have played the worst havoc with my prospects for a good night's sleep. After hanging up before, I was too dejected, and now I'm too euphoric. In either case, it doesn't help that I can see you in every room."

"What do you mean?"

"I have photographs of you, the ones that I got from Neil Frazier." David's voice lowered intimately. "You'll see them."

Ruth flushed at his tone. "In every room, even your living room?"

"They're works of art, not snapshots out of an advertisement. They could be hanging in a gallery in a grouping titled *Nuances of Expression on the Face of a Lovely Woman.*"

"I don't have a picture of you," Ruth complained wistfully. "I'll bet Neil took some when you visited him."

"He had his camera out," David admitted. "But don't get any thoughts about visiting Neil yourself."

"Neil's an old friend. It would be perfectly innocent if I went to his apartment," Ruth stated earnestly.

"Neil's a man with eyes and all the normal urges," David retorted. "I'm jealous at the idea of you alone with any man in his apartment, but especially a man like Neil, who epitomizes masculinity."

"Neil would never be a threat to you," Ruth assured him. "But I can understand your feelings. I feel exactly the same way thinking of you with other women, and not just alone with them in an apartment. I'm jealous thinking of all those nurses and medical students and doctors you work with and see every day.''

"Don't be. I don't look at any of them the way I look at you."

It brought a deep thrill to Ruth, knowing that he would single her out among all the women available to him, but she still had the same faint anxiety. She hoped she could live up to his expectations.

"I should say good-night and go to bed," she said reluctantly after they'd talked a few minutes longer, opening up their emotions to each other across the miles separating them.

"It's late there. You'll need your rest," David agreed. "Though I hate to hang up. I could talk to you all night. Please call me tomorrow night if you can. And reverse the charges. Which reminds me of something else I wanted very badly to say to you before. I was afraid of hurting your pride or seeming as if I was trying to buy you. As Bradford would point out to you in a second, doctors are in a high-income group. If paying the hospital bill is a hardship for your parents and you would like to pay it for them, I wouldn't miss the money. They wouldn't have to know where it came from. You could even tell them Bradford had an attack of conscience and came through with a decent settlement.''

"That's very generous of you, David, but I couldn't accept money from you." Ruth was touched but also mortified.

She changed the subject quickly. "I gather Tom told you that I didn't have enough business sense to get out of him what I could have. I considered our divorce settlement fair.''

"Bradford was the one who made a poor settlement for himself, in my opinion," David said gently, responding to her note of hurt pride. "He lost you. Now, as much as I hate to be practical, we should say good night and let you go to bed."

"We should." Ruth sighed. "Good night. I love you." She was still shy at saying the words, which felt new-minted.

"I love you, too," he said softly. "Very much."

Neither of them hung up.

"On the count of three?" Ruth suggested laughingly, and they counted together in unison, a note of humor lightening the weight of regret at having to break the connection. Ruth sat in the semidarkness of the kitchen, smiling, and then she remembered the one unresolved issue from that first, unsatisfactory telephone conversation.

His parents' visit. Neither of them had thought to mention it. She assumed he would want her to meet them. Her outlook now was slightly more confident, but the element of apprehension was even stronger. It was more important than ever that she would make a good impression on his parents.

There was all the difference in the world between her return flight to Seattle and the one leaving it five days earlier. On the takeoff in Dallas, she felt a thrill of pure exhilaration. There was none of that sense of being a displaced person. She was heading back to the climate, the job, the life, the man she loved.

Her father was recuperating nicely, and she'd turned over the reins of responsibility to relatives and neighbors. There had been the inevitable sadness of saying goodbye to her family, all of whom she loved, but she found it a relief to escape from all the demands and the constant everyday problems, a relief to leave behind her, until her next visit, the world in which she'd grown up.

Strangely enough, she'd tried to imagine David visiting with her at some future time and not been totally pessimis-

tic at the prospect. She'd looked at the familiar surroundings, visualizing them as he would view them with his
perceptive, intelligent eyes; conjured his expression in reaction to situations and conversations, and not felt es-
tranged from him or defensive, as she'd been made to feel
with Tom when his contemptuous attitudes had come out in
the open.

There was no doubting that David would be completely
out of his element in Baker, around her family and relatives and the local people. Probably he'd be ill at ease and
bored, but it wasn't conceivable to her that he'd ever be
rude, act superior or criticize. Even though such a visit
wasn't likely, her speculations warmed her and deepened her
feelings for him.

On arrival at the Seattle airport, she was eager at the
thought that he'd be there to meet her, but suddenly she was
shy, too. The sight of him as he stood waiting and watching
for her at the airport brought a sense of disbelief along with
a surge of pride and love. His handsome features had an
intense, serious cast, and to her eyes he was so obviously a
man of distinction and high intellect that he couldn't possibly be there to meet her.

But then he spotted her and smiled, his face lighting up
with welcome, and Ruth forgot everything in her buoyant
rush of happiness. She just barely managed to hang on to
her dignity until the last few steps when she dropped her
carry-on luggage and ran into his arms.

"You're back," he said feelingly, hugging her tight.

"Yes, and it's wonderful to be here! When we landed and
I saw that it was drizzling rain, I was so happy I could hardly
stand it!" She smiled at him, telling him with her eyes and
her glowing expression that it wasn't the Seattle weather that
was responsible for her jubilation.

They walked arm in arm amid the stream of other travelers, David carrying her larger bag with the strap hooked over his shoulder. He inquired about the flight and about her father and the circumstances she'd left, and Ruth answered with a lilt in her voice.

"Did you want to go by your apartment?" David asked her when they were in his car, leaving the congested environs of Sea-Tac Airport behind them and driving north on the interstate toward the city. The rush-hour traffic was over, since Ruth's plane had landed in the early evening.

"Not particularly," she replied, meeting his glance with a smile, adding the message that it was irrelevant to her where they went, as long as they were together.

"I thought we'd go to my place. Do you mind not going out?"

"Not at all," Ruth assured him. Aside from the fact that she welcomed the thought of being alone with him, she was curious to see where he lived, eager to see another side of him.

His condominium was in the university area. The half dozen town house units had brick exteriors and an air of quiet privacy. Ruth wasn't at all surprised; she hadn't expected anything modernistic or showy.

"Do you know any of your neighbors?" she asked.

"I've met them. They're all connected with the university or the medical school."

The interior suited him, too, she saw when he took her inside and showed her the first floor. It was restful and spacious, with a minimal amount of furniture of very good quality. The sectional sofa in his living room was upholstered in glove-soft leather a shade darker than the sand-colored walls. Shelving painted the same hue housed his television and VCR and stereo equipment. The only part of the decor that completely took her unawares were two black-

and-white photographs of her, close-up studies of her face, hung side by side on one wall and creating a focal point. In one she was laughing, and in the other she looked pensive.

"You said you had pictures of me in your living room," she murmured, staring. Aside from feeling odd and a little embarrassed, she was fascinated. The photographs were excellent and had captured her moods. "Neil is good, isn't he?" she mused.

"He had a good subject in you," David said, standing with his arm around her shoulders and looking admiringly at the photographs of her. "You're so naturally expressive. I have several other pictures of you upstairs," he warned her, smiling. "I hope you don't mind seeing yourself."

"It is a little strange," she admitted, blushing at his tone. His bedroom was "upstairs," of course. She turned her attention back to him and the room at large. "Is this where you listen to music?"

"Here and in all the other rooms. They're wired for sound. I'll put on some music and show you." He led her over to the stereo equipment and played a CD, turning up the volume at first and adjusting the controls to demonstrate the sensitive range of variations.

"Great sound, isn't it?" He was smiling with boyish enthusiasm. "This is the main control center, but every room has an intercom panel with an on-off switch and volume control. I'll explain how to work all this later. You have a choice of radio, old-fashioned records, cassette tapes and CD. The TV is connected up to the stereo, and there's a recording option on anything that's playing."

Ruth viewed the bank of sophisticated electronic modules with open skepticism. "I wouldn't think of touching that. It looks like you'd have to be a technician."

"No, it's easy. You'll catch on." He took her into his arms and drew her close, his mood undergoing a change. Ruth slipped her arms up around his neck and hugged him, expectation coursing through her at what she saw in his face.

"It feels so good for you to be here with me," he told her softly. "Come and see the rest of it."

His embrace tightened at the invitation, and Ruth moved closer into his arms, murmuring his name in a voice that expressed all of her longing for him to kiss her as he brought his lips to hers.

"David . . ."

His mouth on hers was tender and seeking, the contact sweet and familiar, awakening an aching joy. "I love you," he murmured against her lips, and the words, spoken with urgency and hunger, unleashed passion in Ruth. She returned the harder, restless pressure and moaned softly in her throat, parting her lips for his tongue and welcoming the intimate mating that sent weakness through her.

She clung to him for the support and the pleasure as he ended the kiss, lifting his head to look into her face. His expression, intensely yearning, gave her a tender thrill.

"I love you," she told him, and felt a sense of rare privilege as she watched the effect of her words on him. "On the plane, I was thinking about making love with you again. It'll be our first time in an ordinary bed."

He gave her the whimsical smile she adored. "I thought about setting up the tent here in the living room."

"What is the music you're playing?" Ruth asked him as they went upstairs to his bedroom. "It's so beautiful. I remember you were listening to it the first time I ever talked to you on the telephone, the same night after we had lunch at Ivar's."

"You have quite an accurate memory for music." David smiled at her with a sheepishness she found intriguing. "Yes, it is the same Tchaikovsky piece. *Romeo and Juliet.*

You asked me what it was that night, and I was too embarrassed to say."

"Did you remember that tonight when you chose it?"

"I played it for purely sentimental reasons," he admitted without hesitation.

"No woman in the world could stand a chance of not being swept off her feet by you," Ruth mused. "Aside from being the most intelligent, most interesting and most considerate man I've ever known, you're a romantic."

"I thought I was completely cured," David replied. "I'd about decided that falling in love with a very special woman was either the delusion of poets or something I'd missed out on. Then I came back to Seattle and met you again."

"But why...me?" Ruth asked with a touch of uncertainty.

David stopped her in the open door of his bedroom, framed her face in both his hands and kissed her with deep, tender thoroughness before he replied in a voice husky with feeling. "I can't explain it rationally. All I know is that being with you makes me happy in a way I've never been before."

"Do you see what I mean?" Ruth protested helplessly, weak with pleasure at his kiss, his words, the look of adoration on his face. "What hope do I have of keeping a clear head with you?"

"Don't worry about keeping a clear head," David urged her. "Just be happy with me and enjoy what we have together. We'll work everything out. But prepare yourself for having to put up with a man with romantic tendencies who's overdue for falling in love," he warned, smiling at her. "It might get a little trite—candlelight dinners, flowers, presents...champagne in bed."

Ruth smiled back at him, delighted by her suspicion. "Are we having champagne in bed tonight?"

David shrugged, his smile broadening into admission. He led her into the bedroom as he answered so that she could see for herself two delicate tulip-shaped glasses and an ice bucket with the protruding neck of a champagne bottle. "I thought you might be thirsty after your plane trip. And this is a special occasion: our first time to make love in a bed, our first evening together here in my condo—"

"The first time you've ever picked me up at an airport," Ruth contributed teasingly, putting her arms around his neck. "I'd love to have a glass of champagne—" she drew his head down to hers without any difficulty and kissed him on the lips lingeringly before she ended her sentence "—later."

They undressed each other, and the ordinary mechanical skills, like unbuttoning a button and sliding down a zipper, became a source of intimate pleasure. David made love to her with his eyes and his spoken appreciation of her body as well as with his hands and his mouth.

"I love you," he told her as he entered her.

"And I love you," Ruth replied with a tender urgency.

Saying the words to each other gave the union of their bodies a deep significance, made the giving and taking of physical pleasure an act of caring.

Afterward there was the more relaxed intimacy of sipping champagne as they lounged in bed, naked. Ruth looked around his bedroom with closer attention and saw several more pictures of herself, but she felt no embarrassment.

"Is your condo always so immaculate?" she asked ruefully, noting the lack of clutter. "I haven't seen a thing out of place."

"Today's Friday, the day I have cleaning service," David replied, smiling at her tone.

"Do you have a washer and dryer?" Ruth surveyed him with amused interest, trying to imagine him doing laundry.

"They came with the condo, but I don't use them. The cleaning service takes care of laundering towels and sheets, and I drop my clothes off at a cleaner's about once a week."

"You're a completely self-sufficient bachelor."

David leaned over and kissed her. "But not a self-sufficient man. I don't need a housekeeper, true, but I do need a companion. I have plenty of closet space, and you could have your own bathroom if you wanted."

"Careful," Ruth teased, not taking him seriously. "You might come home and find I've moved in with you."

"I'll help you. How about Sunday? You wouldn't have to give up your apartment right away."

Ruth blinked in surprise. "You are serious. I'm very flattered, but I think you'd better spend some more time with me before you make that kind of offer." To her dismay, he looked crestfallen. "For one thing, David, I don't want you to get tired of me. You told me yourself you've never liked living with anyone."

"Will you stay tonight?"

"Yes. I can go to work from here tomorrow morning. I have clean clothes and makeup in my luggage in your car." She smiled at him. "One morning of waking up with me here and then the two of us both getting dressed and off to work might be enough for you."

David kissed her. "I wouldn't count on it."

Chapter Thirteen

She spent Saturday night with him, too. He took her to dinner at an exclusive hotel restaurant located on a top floor. He'd reserved a choice table with a beautiful view of the harbor lit up at night.

It was a different kind of magic, romantic evening for them. They'd never before dressed up for each other to go out. Ruth wore a blue silk dress that she knew was becoming to her, but he made her feel beautiful in it. She was proud to be his date. He was handsome in a coat and tie, and fully attentive to her, paying her every masculine courtesy, making her feel pampered and adored.

There was nothing stiff or self-conscious about the occasion, though. David was the same interesting, amusing companion, fascinating her with the quick play of his mind. Ruth was hardly aware of the other people in the restaurant. Once when she glanced absently, it came as a surprise to her to see that they were being closely observed from a table across the room.

"Do you know those people over there?" she asked David. "One of the women is wearing red."

David looked and immediately raised his hand in a salute and nodded in greeting before he turned his attention back to Ruth. "That's Lane and Mary Carruthers. Lane's a surgeon, too. The other couple are Harry and Betsy Coleman. He's an attorney with one of the big law firms in the city."

As far as Ruth could tell, the presence of his acquaintances didn't cause him any strain through the rest of the meal, but the knowledge that she could be observed by people who knew him did affect her. She found it impossible to be as relaxed and confident as she had been before.

Then as she and David rose from their table to leave the restaurant, he steered her over toward the foursome, saying, "I hope you don't mind, but I really should say hello. Mary and Lane have gone all out to welcome me in Seattle socially."

Ruth could feel her smile stiffen on her face during the round of greetings and introductions. David clasped her waist more protectively, and she knew he was aware of her discomfort at being scrutinized with polite but frank interest.

"We were about to order after-dinner drinks. Why don't you and Ruth join us?" Lane Carruthers urged David cordially, and the others joined in.

"Thanks, but we have to be somewhere," David said pleasantly.

Ruth felt as though she'd failed a test. "They seem to be very nice people," she remarked miserably in the elevator.

"They're pleasant enough," he agreed, "but I didn't want to spend time with them tonight. I'd rather be alone with you, and I assumed you were of the same mind." His smile had a hint of secretiveness. "Besides, I have entertainment planned."

"Entertainment?" Ruth asked, glad to drop the subject.

"I've rented a movie I've been wanting to see. I thought we'd make microwave popcorn and watch it together."

Ruth was surprised and curious, since he hadn't mentioned a word about a movie. "What's the title of it?"

"You'll have to wait and see. All I can promise is that you're sure to like it."

"How can you be so certain?" Intrigued, she pressed him for clues and forgot about the meeting with his acquaintances.

The movie was *My Fair Lady*, and he hadn't rented it; he'd bought it for her. "You said you'd like to own it so that you could watch it whenever you wanted," he reminded her, and then smiled when she refrained from saying what was on her mind, that she'd have to buy a television and a VCR. "Just a small inducement for becoming my housemate," he added.

"You make it very tempting," she told him, only half-teasing.

They agreed to get comfortable to watch the movie and ended up making love. Ruth put her slip on afterward and David his underwear, and they made the popcorn out in the kitchen, following the instructions. Then, lounging comfortably on the big sectional in his living room, they watched the movie.

Ruth became raptly involved in the story and the music, as she always did, but by the time the movie was over she was drowsy and lying snuggled in David's arms. "Let's go to bed, darling," he said, and she didn't argue with his assumption that she was staying.

The next morning he had to go to the hospital for a couple of hours. Then they spent the rest of the day together outdoors, enjoying beautiful sunshiny weather that was warm but not punishing. David rented bicycles for them, and they rode for miles through the wooded beauty of the University of Washington Arboretum.

By the afternoon Ruth was pleasantly tired by all the exercise. "I don't think I'll have any trouble sleeping tonight," she remarked.

"I'm thinking that a quiet evening with take-out Chinese food and music and catching up on reading would be nice. How does that sound to you?"

It sounded cozy and wonderful to Ruth but was obviously another overnight invitation, as he admitted. "I won't try to lure you into staying with me tomorrow night," he promised reluctantly. "It's very selfish of me, I guess, to ask you to make changes in your daily routine."

"It's no problem for me to go to work from your part of town, and I don't mind," Ruth replied honestly. "It's fun, as a matter of fact, to break the routine, and your condo is roomier and nicer than my apartment. But I don't think we should spend every night together." She didn't want him to get tired of her.

David conceded without expressing any agreement.

The next morning when he was ready to leave for the hospital, he asked Ruth, "Do you mind if I call you tonight?" She wasn't quite finished dressing and stopped to admire him as he came over to her. He looked fresh and clean-shaven and handsome in a jacket and tie, every inch the distinguished professional and yet so endearingly familiar to her.

"No, I wouldn't mind," she protested. "Please do call me. I'll be home."

His goodbye kiss was tender and urgent, as though they were about to be parted for a long time. "It's going to be lonely, sleeping without you tonight," he commented, glancing at the rumpled bed. Then he smiled and instructed her. "Don't make the bed or tidy up before you leave. I want to come home to the evidence that you were here."

"With me there's plenty of that," Ruth retorted lightly, having to hang on to her resolve not to see him that evening.

When he called her, it was almost eight o'clock. She was concerned when she heard the deep fatigue in his voice, which seemed more than physical.

"Did you have a bad day?" she asked sympathetically. "You sound tired."

"I am tired," he said quietly. "What about you? How was your day?"

Ruth ignored the inquiry, some instinct filling her with dread. "Did you lose a patient?" she asked hesitantly.

"Yes. But that's one of the realities of my work. Not every surgery can be successful."

Ruth was silent, trying to conceive of the enormous responsibility. "It must be terrible, having to tell the members of the family."

"It is. Plus the patient is a person, someone you've talked to. In some cases you've gotten to know and like him or her. But it's not the failures on the operating table that are the hardest to deal with. At least you were able to offer the patient hope, if only a glimmer. It's having to diagnose a patient as inoperable that can be the most difficult."

"You had a case like that today, too," Ruth guessed, aching with empathy.

"A child. Beautiful little preschool girl. Advanced glioma, or tumor in the inner brain. Her parents can't have more children. They begged me to operate even after I'd explained that there was nothing I could do surgically to extend her life beyond the six months she has remaining. It's never easy having to break that kind of news, but some cases make you feel more powerless than others."

Ruth wished she were with him so that she could touch and hold him. "Would you like to come over here and visit me or go out somewhere and talk?"

"I wouldn't be very good company tonight, I'm afraid. And I really am bushed. But maybe tomorrow night?"

She couldn't bear the thought of him alone and depressed. "Are you too tired to come over and get me? I could take a taxi."

"Don't worry about me. I'll be fine. It was selfish of me to call when I wasn't feeling very cheerful, but I'd said I would and I wanted to hear your voice. Just talking to you has given me a boost."

"It's even more selfish of you not to invite me over," Ruth accused him lightly. "Since I don't have a television or a marvelous stereo system here in my apartment." Her heart pounded during the pause before he answered.

"You have an open invitation, including a key," he said quietly.

"Then I'd like to be with you tonight."

"I'll come over and get you."

Lying in bed with him that night with the bedroom plunged into darkness, Ruth had never felt closer to him, although they hadn't made love. "Thank you for being with me tonight, darling," David murmured, his words muffled in her hair. "I needed you."

"I know," she whispered, deeply happy.

She never actually moved in with him as a stated living arrangement. He gave her a key and open access to his condominium but never pressured her. She kept her apartment but spent little time there and gradually transported most of her wardrobe to his place.

It was a matter of making the most of any time that they could spend together. David's work schedule was demanding, and it was sometimes seven or eight o'clock or even later when he got home. Ruth enrolled in a college course in business management and went to class directly after work three evenings a week. Sharing the same living quarters, they were assured of a few hours with each other in the evening, no matter how busy they were. Weekends they would have spent together anyway, either in Seattle or camping on the peninsula or taking an overnight trip.

Ruth had no domestic responsibilities other than those she took on herself. David didn't expect her to cook or do household chores. He doubled his cleaning service contract to twice weekly and even tried to convince Ruth to allow him to take her clothes to the laundry along with his rather than laundering them herself, using his washer and dryer. He wanted her purely and simply as a companion and never seemed to find any fault with her.

Ruth would have been blissfully happy if only she could have believed it all could last, but she knew it couldn't. It was only a matter of time before other people would have to be drawn into their relationship, and then the problems would begin. They couldn't continue forever going off to their separate worlds to work and then return to each other to spend every minute of their leisure time alone.

He was evidently declining all social invitations without making an issue of it. Several times he got phone calls during the evening, and Ruth could tell from his end of the conversation that he was refusing to be someone's guest at a party or dinner. In his personal mail he received at least two written party invitations that she happened to glimpse among discarded junk mail that he'd opened and tossed aside. One was a cheerful little summons to a cocktail party and the other a fancy custom-printed invitation to a black-tie reception.

She didn't mention the first one, but the second she just couldn't ignore. "I couldn't help noticing the invitation you received in the mail today," she told him, trying to sound merely interested but failing badly. "You left it in plain sight, so I read it. I gather you aren't planning to go."

David looked at her oddly. "That's the weekend we'd talked about going to Victoria and staying overnight at the Empress Hotel. We both have Saturday and Sunday off."

"I didn't notice the date on the invitation," Ruth admitted. She wanted with all her heart to stop right there, but she couldn't, now that the first step toward openness had been taken. "You've been turning down all the invitations you're getting to dinners and parties, haven't you?"

He frowned slightly. "Yes, I have. I've enjoyed being out of circulation. Besides which, the dinner invitations have been to fill in a place as an unattached male, and I don't regard myself as unattached. What exactly is the point here, Ruth? Are you feeling the need to socialize with other people?"

"No, that's not it at all," Ruth replied quickly, and sighed, wishing she had just left well enough alone for a while longer. "I just hated to think that you were cutting off all your social contacts because of me."

"You aren't trying to tell me indirectly that you're getting bored and restless being with just me, are you?" he pressed gravely.

"Don't be ridiculous!" Ruth scooted close to him on the sofa and kissed him. "I could never be bored with you."

He hugged her close to him, but he didn't look entirely reassured. "I've been happier these past weeks since we've been together than I've ever been before. I haven't wanted to share you with anyone else."

"I'm very happy with you, too," Ruth said softly, stroking his cheek with her palm. "I wish I hadn't brought it up."

"No, I'm glad you did, since it was bothering you," David said, his gravity still lingering.

Ruth didn't dare bring up the other matters bothering her. She felt as though she'd done damage more than cleared the air by trying to open up her insecurity to him. As the date grew nearer for his parents' arrival in Seattle, she was increasingly apprehensive but unable to voice her fears, since he seemed to treat the matter of her meeting them very casually. If she were more than just a girlfriend with whom he was momentarily infatuated, wouldn't his parents' approval of her be important to him? She couldn't ask him that tonight.

Nor could she admit that her feelings were hurt that he'd never expressed an interest in having her come by the hospital so he could introduce her to his colleagues and the hospital personnel he saw daily. She'd tried to show that she was interested in his work but never asked outright for an invitation, not wanting to put him in the position of having to agree unwillingly.

Was he ashamed of her? That was the real question she'd been asking him tonight when she'd broached the subject of the invitation. He hadn't answered that he would be proud to take her anywhere with him, the way she'd hoped he'd respond.

She could tell from his gravely reflective air throughout the rest of the evening that the conversation had disturbed him. He didn't share his thoughts, though, and Ruth felt shut off from him. She sat with a textbook, trying to read an assignment but having problems concentrating, while he thumbed through a stack of medical journals, turning the pages too fast for even him to be getting the gist of the articles, though he read incredibly fast, she'd learned. Music played in the background, but it didn't cast a spell of harmony, as it usually did.

When she went up to bed, he didn't go with her. "I'll be up in a little while," he said. "First I want to finish this article."

Ruth kissed him good-night and climbed the stairs, knowing that he really wanted some time alone. She remembered what he'd said about always being glad to have his place to himself again after he'd lived with someone briefly. Was he beginning to feel the need for space and privacy? she wondered miserably.

As soon as Ruth had gone upstairs David tossed aside the medical journal, dispensing with the pretense of reading. Folding his hands behind his head, he slumped down low into the cushions of the sofa and gazed at the photographs of her, thinking of her moving around and getting ready for bed.

He was perfectly happy spending all his free time with just her, but she was a more gregarious person than he was and was probably already feeling the need for a circle of friends. She liked people and could easily chat with total strangers in a way he never could. Others were drawn to her, as he was, because she was lovely and warm and natural. He was proud and yet jealous at the glances she invariably got from men but seemed not to notice.

Sharing her didn't appeal to him at all, but there was more than possessiveness behind his reluctance to take their relationship into a social arena and expose it to outside opinion. What they had together was so wonderful and yet fragile. Could it take the stress of skeptical reactions and cynical interpretations?

Not unless he and Ruth were deeply confident of each other's feelings. Therein lay the problem. David knew that

if he lost her, he could never fill the void, but he wasn't su
that he was essential to her in the same way.

When the telephone rang the next morning, Ruth looked
at it in indecision, hesitant about answering. David was in
the shower. She'd suggested an answering machine, but he
disliked them, and he carried a beeper so that he could be
reached for medical emergencies.

But the beeper was downstairs, and the call could be from
the hospital. With that reasoning, Ruth picked up the receiver and said as calmly and impersonally as she could
manage, "Dr. David Bradford's residence." Perhaps she
would be taken for a maid, on the job very early.

There was a pause at the other end. "Has David already
left for the hospital?" inquired a pleasant, assured female
voice with a faint note of curiosity. "This is Evelyn Bradford, his mother, calling from New York. I thought I might
catch him at home."

"No, he hasn't gone," Ruth replied in an agony of embarrassment. "Hold on, please. I'll get him."

The shower had stopped. She dropped the receiver onto
the bed and went to the bathroom door. David was towel-
ing off and looked at her with keen attention, noting her
appalled expression.

"Your mother is on the telephone." Ruth mouthed the
words more than she actually spoke them aloud. "I'm sorry.
I didn't know whether to answer. I thought it might be an
emergency."

"It's okay," David said unconcernedly, wrapping the
towel around his waist. "My mother knows I'm a grown
man." He gave Ruth a little hug on his way past her into the
bedroom to take the call.

Ruth went into the bathroom and closed the door, to give
him privacy, but she could hear his voice and his laughter.
He made no effort to lower it and sounded perfectly nor-

mal and at ease. Apparently it caused him no awkwardness for his mother to call and have Ruth answer at that hour, plainly having stayed overnight. It was a more sophisticated attitude than Ruth's, which she supposed was bound to be more provincial, since she came from a different background.

David tapped on the bathroom door after he'd concluded his call. "You didn't have to close yourself up in here," he chided her as he opened the door. "My mother was just calling to let me know their travel itinerary. They'll be staying downtown at the conference hotel. I told her we'd have dinner with them the evening after they arrive."

"Did you tell her that we were living together?" Ruth asked hesitantly, wondering exactly what he had told his mother about her.

"No," he replied. "She didn't ask, and I don't know if I could have told her that anyway."

"What do you mean?"

"Well, it was my impression that you've never really decided that you want to live with me. You're not thinking of giving up your apartment, are you?"

"No," Ruth admitted. "But I am living here with you. I hardly ever go there."

"You're just visiting," David said quietly. "But we've only been together a few weeks. I'm not trying to rush you into committing yourself before you're ready." He took her into his arms and held her very close, his cheek pressed against her head on his shoulder. "I love you very much," he told her softly. "Do you believe that?"

"Yes," Ruth murmured. "And I love you." But she was afraid love wasn't enough, and from the way he hugged her tight, with all his strength, she sensed he was trying to fight off the same deep-seated doubt.

"I have to get to the hospital," David said heavily, releasing her.

"I need to hurry and get ready for work, too," she replied, turning away quickly to go into the bedroom before he could see that she was threatened with tears.

He sent her flowers that day at work, and that evening took her out to dinner and gave her a present, beautiful sapphire earrings. Ruth basked in his complete admiring attention and took delight in his company. Afterward they returned to his condo and made tender, passionate love.

There was no mention of last night or that morning by either of them. Clearly David was making every effort to repair the slight rift in their closeness, and Ruth cooperated, grateful and willing to help him hold back the intrusion of the outside world for at least another two weeks. Then his parents would come to Seattle.

"How much have you told your parents about me?" she asked David the night before they were to arrive. He continued to act very casual about her meeting them, but just the thought tightened her stomach into a knot.

"I've told them just the obvious things, what kind of work you do, that you're divorced, the basic facts about your family background," David replied mildly. "My parents aren't going to interview you, sweetheart, I promise."

"You told them I was only a high school graduate?"

"I told them you were pretty and intelligent and highly personable," he evaded lightly. "All I ask is that you let them see that for themselves. Just be yourself, and they'll fall for you, as their son did."

"I still think I should stay at my own apartment while they're in town. It doesn't seem . . ."

"Proper?" he supplied teasingly. "You wouldn't want to spoil my pleasure in having my parents come to town, would you? They're fairly worldly people, Ruth."

He did everything possible to downplay her fears, but to no avail. Ruth agonized over what to wear and worried about how she could ever hold her own with conversation when both his parents were doctors. Getting dressed the next night, she was so nervous that she had problems applying her makeup, and not once during the whole evening was she able to relax.

She was thoroughly intimidated by his parents, just as she'd expected to be. Will Bradford was a trim man of average height, with a dignified bearing. David's mother was slight of build and wore a beautifully tailored suit. David had inherited her eyes and fair hair and coloring. Ruth felt much too voluptuous under the older woman's interested gaze.

Ruth knew it was obvious to anyone at a glance that both David's parents were self-assured, important people, thoroughly at home in the lobby of the expensive hotel and, later, in the fine restaurant where David had reservations. They were extremely articulate, just as David was, obviously cultivated and well-bred. They made every effort to be cordial to Ruth and include her in the conversation, but she felt hopelessly outclassed with parents and son, all three of whom were of above-average intelligence, highly educated and outstanding in their profession.

Every word out of her mouth sounded wrong to her, and she could almost see David wincing. She was keenly aware that her very presence restricted the range of talk and wished herself absent. Dinner seemed to last forever, and then they lingered over coffee. At long last, David was finally taking care of the bill, and dreaded relief seemed in sight.

"Mother, what are your plans for tomorrow while Dad's in his sessions?" he asked. "Would you like me to act as tour guide and drive you around? I've juggled my schedule to arrange some time."

"That's sweet of you, but I thought I'd do some shopping," Evelyn Bradford replied. "Your birthday's coming up, and it seems the perfect opportunity to go ahead and buy your present while I have someone to give me advice." She smiled at Ruth. "Would you mind if I came by the store where you work tomorrow, Ruth? Perhaps the two of us could have lunch together."

Ruth could feel herself turning pale. "Why, of course. I'd like that," she said, sounding utterly unconvincing to her own ears.

In the car driving back to David's condo, after they'd dropped off his parents at their hotel, Ruth spoke before he could say anything.

"I'm sorry," she apologized miserably. "I know I made a terrible impression and embarrassed you. Your parents are wondering what you could possibly see in me."

"You didn't embarrass me," David said in a faintly exasperated tone. "I do wish, though, that you could have been less tense. I'd wanted my parents to meet you, and they didn't really get to do that, since you weren't yourself." He reached over and squeezed her hands, which were tightly clasped in her lap. "I'm sorry it was such an ordeal for you."

Mild though the criticism was, it was the first time he'd ever found fault with her. Ruth tried to hide her hurt. She'd failed him, as she'd been bound to do. She hadn't measured up to his expectations of her.

The next day she was waiting on a customer and didn't notice Evelyn Bradford when she came into the store. It came as a shock to Ruth to finish a purchase transaction at the cash register and glance over to see David's mother observing her. When the older woman smiled, there was a hint of David's engaging quality, and Ruth smiled back automatically, feeling more natural than she had at any second the previous evening.

Surprisingly, Evelyn did want to get a present for David, before the two women went to lunch. That hadn't been an excuse. She didn't deliberate, though, but selected the first sweater Ruth recommended over in the men's department.

"I'm not what you'd call a maternal type," Evelyn confessed. "I'm sure David's told you that."

"He's never complained about being neglected or unloved," Ruth demurred. "He understands that you've had your own career. He talks as though he's very fond of both you and his father. And proud, too."

"I can certainly see why my son has such a mad crush on you," Evelyn mused with smiling approval. "You are lovely, and not just in looks."

The word *crush* with its juvenile overtones, struck Ruth with an odd unpleasantness that lingered, although she knew the other woman hadn't intended any affront.

Ruth had agonized over where to take David's mother for lunch, but Evelyn dispensed with that worry as they were leaving the store.

"Don't feel you have to take me somewhere elegant," she said. "If there's some quiet little restaurant nearby, it'll suit me fine. Lunch was only an excuse for me to have a chance to talk to you."

Seated across from Ruth several minutes later, Evelyn continued in the same casual, friendly vein. "Wasn't last night stiff and awful? Frankly, Will and I haven't had much practice at having David introduce us to a woman friend. He's never been engaged, to our knowledge, or even seriously involved for any length of time." She paused with a slight grimace of apology. "If you'll pardon my being perfectly candid, we were somewhat uneasy on the basis of what David has told us about you. We came to Seattle prepared to find him in the clutches of a designing woman."

"I'm not the sort of woman you'd expect David to become involved with." Ruth spoke the obvious with difficulty.

"No," Evelyn admitted, softening the truth with a smile. "But it's a great relief to meet you and see for myself that you're genuine and not an opportunistic divorcée pretending to be an ingenue and playing my son for a fool. I guess I've always worried that he didn't have a normal adolescence and might someday try to make up for what he missed. But then I suspect every mother has anxieties about her son's judgment where women are concerned." She shrugged, dismissing the subject, and brought up another topic.

Ruth managed to hold up her end of the conversation, but her heart felt like a lump of lead. Didn't Evelyn Bradford's vague fear explain perfectly why Ruth appealed to David so strongly? Wasn't she the high-school girlfriend he'd never had? It all fit together with painful neatness: the whole story of his infatuation with her, his hanging pictures of her in his condo, his romantic courtship with gifts and thoughtful gestures for every little occasion.

She managed to keep from pouring it all out to him until his parents had returned to New York. By then she'd built up such a strong case of despair that there seemed little possibility that he'd be able to make a truthful denial. He listened quietly and gradually became more and more withdrawn from her. When she'd stumbled to a halt, he replied with a mixture of hurt and anger.

"So my feelings for you are merely superficial and romantic, with no real basis. Which means you were right in following your basic instincts and never trusting me, never believing in what we had together."

"I wanted to believe in it!" Ruth cried. "But I knew it wasn't real! I knew what would happen as soon as other people were involved. That's why I dreaded meeting your parents." She bit her lip and summoned her dignity. "If you weren't ashamed of me, David, why didn't you ever ask me to come to the hospital? Why didn't you want to introduce me to the people you work with?"

"Maybe I was waiting until you had the confidence to meet them," he countered bitterly, and then wiped his hand across his forehead in a gesture of futility. "If you really think that I'm ashamed of you, Ruth, I have to agree with you that our situation is hopeless. But I think all of this is nothing but excuses. I was okay for an affair, but you're not willing to put yourself on the line again." He sighed. "Or maybe you can't because of your bad experience with another guy named Bradford."

"Do you want me to move out?" Ruth asked miserably.

"You mean do I want you to take your clothes back to your apartment," David replied bleakly. "Yes, I guess you might as well."

Chapter Fourteen

Ruth took off the skirt she'd put on and hung it back in the closet. She'd lost ten pounds in the past month since her breakup with David, and her clothes were getting loose. It wasn't the result of dieting but unhappiness.

She had little appetite, little enjoyment of anything, really. Her co-workers at the store were concerned about her. Her efforts at putting up a cheerful front weren't very success-ful. She threw herself into her work with a kind of desper-ation, trying to keep as busy as possible. She volunteered for Saturdays and worked extra hours.

But there was still time to think, time to regret, time to wonder over and over if she'd been wrong in not believing that her relationship with David could turn into something lasting. She hadn't heard from him or seen him, and she wouldn't.

"Don't worry. I won't come into the store again," he'd told her when they said goodbye. There had been disappointment and finality in his voice.

It was over between them, and yet Ruth couldn't seem to come to terms with the reality. She hadn't suffered the same despondency and sense of loss with the breakup of her marriage. She missed David terribly, missed waking up with him in the morning, missed the intimacy of their both getting ready for work, missed their evenings, missed talking to him about a thousand subjects, laughing with him, having fun with him, sharing serious moments, making love and lying close to him afterward in his arms.

How could she accept the thought of living without any of that ever again? Yet what choice did she have but to accept it?

Ruth put on another skirt that had fit snugly and took no pleasure in the sight of her slimmer figure in the mirror. What would be David's reaction to her weight loss? she wondered, and was struck with a deep yearning to see him.

It stayed with her all morning, like an ache from a wound. As her lunch hour approached, she tormented herself with fantasies about accidentally meeting him downtown somewhere. As soon as one look passed between them, she'd know if he missed her as desperately as she missed him.

Emerging from the store with an hour before her, she was swamped with a wave of desolation at the knowledge that she wouldn't encounter him and started walking aimlessly in the direction of the waterfront, taking no notice of other pedestrians or her surroundings. Pausing for red lights and crossing on green was automatic, the occasional squeal of brakes and acceleration of car engines all a background noise in a gray, torpid world.

The accident didn't seem real at first because of her detached state of mind. She saw it all clearly from less than a block away. A woman started across the street, moving parallel to Ruth's line of vision. A car burst through the intersection. There was a thud and the scream of brakes, and then the woman's body sailed through the air as though it were weightless. People rushed out of stores, and a crowd immediately gathered.

"Someone call an ambulance!" a man shouted. "This woman needs to get to a hospital!"

Ruth's legs buckled beneath her, but she managed to make it over to the side of a building, where she leaned, nauseated and trembling and horribly awakened to the tragedy that lurks just beyond every moment.

Her despondent daze was wiped away by the perception of life as precious and fleeting. Suddenly she felt clearheaded and resolved. It was only a matter of strength returning to her legs before she would go to David and do everything in her power to repair the break between them and revive his love, if it wasn't too late. There didn't seem to be a second to waste.

She almost lost her nerve when her taxi deposited her at the huge university hospital complex. By the time she'd managed to locate the wing and the floor where his office was, her lunch hour was almost over, and she felt as if she'd been through a maze.

The secretary Ruth approached in an outer office glanced at her and then looked again more interestedly.

"I need to see Dr. Bradford," Ruth explained, prepared to meet with inquiries about whether she had an appointment. "It's extremely important."

"Dr. Bradford is in radiology. I'll call and let him know that you are here. But first I'll show you to his private office. You can wait for him in there."

Ruth followed the secretary, taken aback by the almost personal treatment. The woman hadn't even asked Ruth her name. How was she going to tell David who was waiting for him?

Left alone, Ruth paced nervously, distracting herself with a curious inspection of David's office, where he came every day. After examining his framed certificates and diplomas, she walked behind his desk to caress the leather upholstered back of his chair and discovered the solution to the mystery of her easy entry into his office.

He had a picture of her on his desk. The secretary had recognized her.

For the second time that day, Ruth went weak in the knees. She sank into David's chair and closed her eyes against her own likeness, which mocked her with the unfairness of her accusation that he'd been ashamed of her.

The abrupt opening of the door startled her to attention, and David entered, stern and unfamiliar to her in a starched white physician's coat. He'd evidently come in a hurry, and the alarm on his face deepened at the sight of her.

"Ruth, what's wrong? Are you ill?"

"No, I'm not ill," Ruth assured him quickly, strength flooding into her limbs at his concern. She stood up and came around his desk to meet him, but she lost her momentum when he stopped several yards away. They faced each other. "I'm just shaky," she explained. "I saw a traffic accident about an hour ago, and it shook me up. A woman was hit by a car a few blocks from the store. I had just left on my lunch hour."

"You look so pale and thin," he said, frowning.

"I finally found the key to losing weight: being too unhappy to eat," Ruth replied with a wan smile.

"When you saw the accident you mentioned, you were on your way here to the hospital?"

"No, it was the accident that woke me up. I realized how foolish I was to give up a single day with you when there's never any counting on tomorrow or the next hour or the next minute." Ruth talked faster in her earnestness. "There's really only now. Time is so precious. As long as you wanted me, I should have stayed with you and not worried about when you no longer would need me. I've missed you so much, David. I've never been so unhappy." She searched his face, looking for some flicker of response in his somber expression, and added with open longing, "Haven't you missed me, too?"

He turned away from her abruptly and went over toward the door, where he was slow to face her again. Ruth took heart, aware that his retreat cost him some effort. "But I gather you still haven't basically changed your thinking about us," he said quietly, not answering her question. "You have in mind picking up where we left off and having an extended affair, for as long as it lasts."

"I want to be with you again," Ruth said simply. "We could just see each other or live together or whatever you decide."

"By 'live together,' you mean you'd give up your apartment and make my condo your residence? You wouldn't be a temporary guest, and I wouldn't have to wonder every night if you'd be there?"

"Oh, yes, I'd be willing to do that," Ruth answered eagerly.

"But is that the living arrangement you'd most prefer, Ruth?" he asked softly.

Ruth's eyes widened with his change of tone, and happiness surged through her as she realized what he'd been holding out for. "No," she replied, walking toward him, her smile taking over her face. "If I had my choice, I'd be your wife."

His arms opened for her and closed around her hard. He crushed her against the starched smoothness of his physician's coat and told her what she'd wanted to hear.

"God, I missed you. It's been so damned lonely."

"You weren't even a little glad to get your privacy back?" Ruth pressed happily, hugging him tight around the neck.

"I don't know what was worse, mornings or evenings," he replied with feeling. "And every piece of music I played on the stereo stirred up memories. Plus your pictures. I love you, Ruth, and I need you."

"I love you, too," Ruth told him in a voice choked with emotion.

He loosened his arms just enough so that she could lift her head, look into his face and see his vulnerability. "Would you really like to be my wife?" he asked.

"More than anything," she replied, giving him the answer to his question, which was all that he wanted, without any accompanying doubts or anxieties about her suitability.

"I'd like to be your husband. I would feel like a very fortunate man."

"I'd be awfully proud of you. I'd probably brag to total strangers," she warned him tenderly.

He smiled. "I can stand that thought. It'll make me a little less jealous, thinking of you out in the world without me. Get ready for a splashy, noticeable wedding ring, nothing discreetly tasteful."

"I'm the one who'll be glad to get a ring on *your* finger," Ruth declared. "I can imagine there's going to be a lot of very disappointed women around this hospital."

He glanced over toward his desk ruefully. "The word's pretty much out, I believe. You can bet that right this minute the news is making the rounds that you're here with me in my office."

"Do you mind?"

"I've never liked having my personal life a topic of conversation. It comes, I guess, from having been an object of curiosity, and I've always been basically shy and reserved."

Ruth remembered the encounter with the surgical nurse outside the store the day David had taken her to lunch at Ivar's, their first date, which seemed such a long time ago. He would have been uncomfortable, she realized now, no matter who his woman companion had been.

The thought of the incident served as an unwelcome reminder. "I should get back to the store," she told David regretfully. "I'm already late. And I know you need to get back to work, too."

David's arms tightened around her. "I wish I could take the rest of the afternoon off with you, but I have to meet with the family members of several patients and report on test results. They're waiting anxiously for some diagnosis. Plus I have appointments—"

"I understand," Ruth broke in. "You have people depending on you in matters of life and death."

"But I'll make early rounds," David promised softly, and kissed her with a tender, restrained hunger. "Tonight we'll have a very private engagement party." Reluctantly he eased his embrace, looking down at her figure possessively. "I want to take care of this weight-loss problem you've been having and fill out those luscious curves again."

"Don't worry! The pounds will come back," Ruth said happily. "Now I'd better call a taxi. I just hope I can find my way out again."

"I'll take you down myself and show you the easiest route to the staff parking lot," David replied. "You can drive my car and pick me up after you get off work."

He escorted her wearing his white physician's coat, introducing her to his secretary and several of his colleagues along the way, including his chief resident, a tall, muscular young man oozing with masculine confidence who eyed Ruth approvingly and remarked with joking friendliness, "So Bradford's finally bringing you out of wraps."

David's hand on Ruth's waist tightened. "Meet me in Radiology in ten minutes, Jinson," he said almost curtly. "We'll look at those angiograms together."

In the parking lot, he unlocked the door of his car for her, seated her solicitously behind the wheel, and then leaned in to kiss her lingeringly, in clear sight of any interested observer who cared to look.

* * * * *

TALES OF THE RISING MOON
A Desire trilogy by Joyce Thies

MOON OF THE RAVEN—June

Conlan Fox was part American Indian and as tough as the Montana land he rode, but it took fragile yet strong-willed Kerry Armstrong to make his dreams come true.

REACH FOR THE MOON—August

It would take a heart of stone for Steven Armstrong to evict the woman and children living on his land. But when Steven met Samantha, eviction was the last thing on his mind!

GYPSY MOON—October

Robert Armstrong met Serena when he returned to his ancestral estate in Connecticut. Their fiery temperaments clashed from the start, but despite himself, Rob was falling under the Gypsy's spell.

Don't miss any of Joyce Thies's enchanting
TALES OF THE RISING MOON,
coming to you from Silhouette Desire.

SD 432

Silhouette Romance

LONG, TALL TEXANS

A Trilogy by Diana Palmer

Bestselling Diana Palmer has rustled up three rugged heroes in a trilogy sure to lasso your heart! The titles of the books are your introduction to these unforgettable men:

CALHOUN

In June, meet Calhoun Ballenger. He wants to protect Abby Clark from the world, but can he protect her from himself?

JUSTIN

Calhoun's brother, Justin—the strong, silent type—has a second chance with the woman of his dreams, Shelby Jacobs, in August.

TYLER

October's long, tall Texan is Shelby's virile brother, Tyler, who teaches shy Nell Regan to trust her instincts—especially when they lead her into his arms!

Don't miss CALHOUN, JUSTIN and TYLER—three gripping new stories coming soon from Silhouette Romance!

SRLTT

Silhouette Intimate Moments

PARRIS AFTON BONDS
The Cowboy and The Lady

Marianna McKenna was used to bright lights, big cities and the glamorous life of a Hollywood star, so it came as quite a shock when she found herself living at the Mescalero Cattle Company, victim of a tragic mistake and a convict sentenced to work on the ranch for the next six months.

Tom Malcolm was a true cowboy, rugged and plainspoken, and he didn't have much use for hothouse flowers like Marianna McKenna. Or so he told himself, at least, though that didn't stop the yearning in his heart—or the fire in his blood.

Look for Tom and Marianna's story in *That McKenna Woman* IM#241, Book One of Parris Afton Bonds's Mescalero Trilogy, available this month only from Silhouette Intimate Moments. Then watch for Book Two, *That Malcolm Girl* (September 1988), and Book Three, *That Mescalero Man* (December 1988), to complete a trilogy as untamed and compelling as the American West itself.

IM241

COMING NEXT MONTH

#463 DANCE TO THE PIPER—Nora Roberts
When cheery Maddy O'Hurley (triplet number two of THE O'HURLEYS!)
scattered sunshine and color at cynic Reed Valentine, both were dizzied by the
kaleidoscope of emotions that began to swirl around them.

#464 AMARILLO BY MORNING—Bay Matthews
Chasing shiny city dreams, Amarillo Corbett tried to forget gritty Russ
Wheeler. But rodeo Russ kept bucking Amy's objections, refused to be thrown,
and vowed to hold on—forever.

#465 SILENCE THE SHADOWS—Christine Flynn
Pregnant, widowed and nearly bankrupt, Megan Reese had problems. Financial
wizard David Elliott offered assistance, but could he rightfully offer his heart to
his late best friend's wife?

#466 BORROWED TIME—Janice Kaiser
On the eve of Stephanie Burnham's wedding, tragedy struck, and the medical
profession abandoned hope for her fiancée. She found solace in compassionate
neurosurgeon Peter Canfield—until compassion evolved into something
more....

#467 HURRICANE FORCE—Lisa Jackson
Amid a hurricane and a storm of accusations, Cord Donahue had sailed away.
Heartbroken, Alison banning believed him dead. But now prodigal Cord was
back, accusing *her* of *his* crimes...and demanding sweet vengeance.

#468 WHERE ANGELS FEAR—Ginna Gray
When her twin tied the knot, Elise knew marriage was in *her* cards, too. But
could she accept intimidating Sam Lawford's chilly proposal? Find out in this
companion edition to *Fools Rush In* (#416).

AVAILABLE THIS MONTH:

#457 BEGUILING WAYS
Lynda Trent

#458 SUMMER SHADOWS
Pat Warren

#459 A DIFFERENT DRUMMER
Maggi Charles

#460 MOON AND SUN
Allyson Ryan

#461 INTENSIVE CARE
Carole Halston

#462 PROMISES
Mary Alice Kirk

MORE THAN A MIRACLE
by Kathleen Eagle

This month, let award-winning author Kathleen Eagle sweep you away
with a story that proves the truth of the old adage, "Love conquers all."

Elizabeth Donnelly loved her son so deeply that she was willing to sneak
back to De Colores, an island paradise to the eye, but a horror to the
soul. There, with the help of Sloan McQuade, she would find the child
who had been stolen from her and carry him to safety. She would also
find something else, something she never would have expected, because
the man who could work miracles had one more up his sleeve: love.

Enjoy Elizabeth and Sloan's story this month in *More Than A Mira-
cle*, Intimate Moments #242. And if you like this book, you might also
enjoy *Candles in the Night* (Special Edition #437), the first of Kathleen
Eagle's De Colores books.

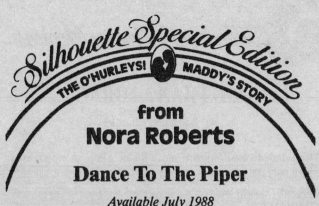